ILSA ROHE

Parsing Vengeance

Ilsa Rohe
Parsing Vengeance

Copyright 2014 Stephenson Ross
ISBN-13: 9780692275801 Bentley Avenue Books
printed in the USA

Requests for copy permission or any other queries
or commentary should be addressed to Stephenson Ross
% Bentley Avenue Books, P.O. Box 44040-0040,
Lemon Cove, CA 93244
email: thistles@ocsnet.net

ILSA ROHE

~-~-o<<<>>o-~-~

Parsing Vengeance

a novel

by

Stephenson Ross

2014
Bentley Avenue Books

This book is dedicated to
Velda Martin Stephenson of Grant's Pass, Oregon,
with gratitude for her kindness, friendship, and
excellent memory.

Research, completed by Velda and her husband Dale,
documented the crime that inspired this novel.

TABLE OF CONTENTS

I

II

III

IV

No stack of reasons behind an evil act,
no matter how toweringly high,
can serve as its excuse.

I

ILSA ROHE

Rohe Farm, Anderson Township, Ohio
1843, 1844

1~ Ilsa

A great confidence led the young widow to the fancy that if she were married to Mr. Ainslie Buchanan, he was a man who would willingly deny himself to please her.

The confidence came from her childhood, when she was the first, and by all considered to be the prettiest, daughter of Emil Mueller. Herr Mueller was a wealthy farmer and dairyman in Waynesboro, Pennsylvania. Though he had no sons, Emil had sired seven daughters. Ilsa had been Papa's darling, and neither her mother nor any of her younger sisters could challenge this favored position. None had eyelashes as long, lips so full, or eyes as bright a blue. None had as nice a form. Her sister Greta was also slim, but she was a boney girl, and all angles, whereas Ilsa was smooth and rounded, with small hands and feet.

She knew she was the person Papa Mueller loved best in the world. Even after she had married Franz, Papa wanted her to stand beside him in church on Sundays, and sit beside him in the evening, no one else. Her mother and sisters were never so favored.

Yet, when childhood ended, her life did not go on untroubled. She had seen much heartache and distress. Although she was still young, and knew herself to still be beautiful, she was far removed from those charmed and glorious days of her childhood. She now lived in Anderson Township, Ohio, four hundred miles from her father's farm, across mountains by road and trail and across rivers by ferryboat, from Waynesboro, Pennsylvania.

During the five years she had lived on Clark Road, Ilsa Rohe had occasionally turned from her children and her work to watch a particularly handsome and smartly groomed man ride past her window. If she had been one to feel embarrassed at her longings, she might have chided herself for her keen interest in a man not her husband, but the authority of her confidence overrode embarrassment. And she was a practical woman, intelligent enough to keep her interest in Mr. Buchanan to herself.

The man whose look she so admired would sometimes pause his horse and visit with her husband on the drive. He had never seemed to notice her even if she were on the porch with her children. Only rarely had Mr. Buchanan removed himself from his mount and stayed longer than a few minutes of neighborly conversation with Franz on a summer evening. On those random visits over the years, she would bring ale or cool water out to them, and feel a vague dissatisfaction that the man heeded her so little. His parents were the Rohe's neighbors, but it was obvious that he lived elsewhere. He, himself, wasn't their neighbor. She found the man so attractive, with his dark hair, rosy complexion and piercing eyes, his upright manner, look of success and lofty way of speaking, that long before Franz died, she'd known that Ainslie Buchanan was the kind of man she had always been destined to capture and call her own.

She regretted that during her girlhood there had been no men like him. Her life might have been very different if there had been. Nothing would have gone wrong. He would have been equal to her father all ways. She would have been the envy of every woman she knew in Waynesboro.

Her attraction to her deceased husband Franz had been true, but it had been girlish and soon outgrown, though she could make no complaint about his treatment of her. Ilsa was not fifteen anymore. She was a woman and a widow. She wasn't running to the barn to tease her father's workers. Franz had been the best of them, and he had been wild with love for her. But when she no longer thought like a silly girl, she saw Franz for what he was, a thickheaded dairyman. Her husband had been just four years older than she, but by thirty his hair was thinning, the blond curls she once liked to play with gone thin and lank. His neck and knees were scrawny, but his belly puffed out so big she didn't want to see him without his clothes or nightshirt.

She missed Franz. She could not tell herself otherwise. He had been a kind man, loyal to her, and devoted to all three of their children. He was strong and hardworking. But she knew her worth, and by the stars, the fates, even by Gott in his heaven, she knew Mr. Ainslie Buchanan to be a man she could truly love. He was a man courtly and worthy, a clever man, one who would appreciate her for her fine discernment as much as for her beauty. He would not be a man who only saw her face and form. He would be a man who could know her to her very soul.

After Franz' death, it seemed inevitable that she and Ainslie Buchanan should come together. No other woman in the county would be able to offer the widower Buchanan what Ilsa offered him. She had easily made an evaluation and arrived at a conclusion. Her mirror told her she was still beautiful. That she was a young widow and a mother would make her an appropriate wife and stepmother for Mr. Buchanan's children. She was some years younger than he but old enough to understand a woman's duties. A widower did not go long without finding a new wife in 1843, particularly in farming communities. Nor did a widow go long without finding a husband. Ilsa knew she was the best match Mr. Buchanan would find west of the city of Columbus, north of the river at Cincinnati, or east of the Indiana state line.

Rohe Farm's household was always in order and kept scrupulously clean. She knew her mother's training had made her a commendable *hausfrau*. She never failed to present herself with a soft smile and soft voice, melodic with compassion and kindness. She knew how to be the kind of woman a man wants in his home and keeps in his heart. Ilsa was well aware of her one handicap to remarriage. It had been with her night and day for ten years. She recognized other country wives might see Ilsa Rohe's time-consuming need to care for her firstborn child to be a pitiable burden, but the widow held a firm belief that Mr. Buchanan would see her devotion to her son Emil as a mark of good character. She held an equally firm expectation of him, that the man's nature would prove as tender as his form was beautifully *kräftig und schlank,* and his face was handsome. Soon fate and her good fortune would bring them together. She need only wait.

O<<>>O

—
3

~~~O<<>>O~~~

2 ~ A Neighborly Kindness

The handsome Ainslie Buchanan and Ilsa Rohe might not have come together so soon, if it had not been for Ainslie's mother, Elizabeth Buchanan. The older woman was not frail with age, but old enough that her ginger hair was fronted by grey. Her once bright blue eyes had muddied to the color of slow summer river. She was spirited and spry. Mrs. Buchanan lived a half-mile down Clark Road from Rohe Farm. She had seen much sadness in her own and other's lives. Although she did not know Franz Rohe's young widow, she worried about her as she would any young woman bereaved of a young husband.

The circumstances of Ilsa Rohe's life were such that she had never had much time or inclination to get to know her neighbors. The farms in the township were large. There was never an opportunity for a farmer's wife to have an over-the-back-fence conversation with a neighbor who might live an eighth, quarter or half section away. In 1843 and in rural western Ohio, a woman's social contacts would come through her church or her family. In the entire state Ilsa's only relation was her uncle, Adam Mueller, Esquire. He was a single man, busy in his law practice and he had no wife to befriend Ilsa. Franz attended a church in a distant town, but Ilsa could not attend. Their son Emil needed watchful care. She would not leave him.

Though solitary during most of her day, the mistress of Rohe Farm had led a busy, active, reasonably happy life. But it did not provide friendship or sociability with other women. But for the French girl, Vallerie Bernier, who worked for Ilsa, none of the farmwomen in the township had come to know her. They knew only that Franz Rohe was amiable, and he had a wife and that one of his children was sadly afflicted. Ilsa hadn't minded. She was busy caring for her husband and children and not the kind of woman who enjoyed idleness.

Ilsa faced difficult days after her husband died. His accident happened suddenly, in the late spring. She had not accustomed herself to thoughts of early widowhood. There was no war to call Franz to his grave. He was a young man, fit and energetic, never sickly, and he had been able to work long hours without any complaint. Franz was killed in a foolish accident one day. He fell while patching the house's roof.

On news of the sudden and tragic death of Franz Rohe, the pastor of The German Christian Church in Taylorsville, *Pfarrer* Gruber, had come to Ilsa's aid. With her uncle's help, he had seen to the details of Franz Rohe's burial. Two women from the German Church, whose husbands had been friendly with Franz, volunteered to travel by wagon the many miles to Anderson Township. They came out of the charity of Christian fellowship to help Ilsa through the early days and nights. When ten days went by, and they needed to return to their own families, Ilsa was through the initial shock of her husband's death. She was grateful for their help, but felt she could manage on her own. She assured the pastor and good women of the church that she was capable. From what they could see, the young woman was.

Although Franz's death had been sudden and running a dairy farm was complicated, Ilsa was not afraid of the work of running the household or raising their children alone.

She knew that Benjamin Wilson would stay on as foreman of Rohe Farm's dairy and cheese-making rooms. Franz had trained him well, and the farm had been good to him. The lesser dairy hands and farm workers would not want to go elsewhere. Benjamin would be as honest and fair a boss as Franz had been. She knew she could count on her uncle's help. Ilsa's uncle Adam Mueller had studied law in Pennsylvania, and he then came west to establish his practice in a place where professional men were in demand. He stepped forward immediately to help her in any way he was able. He was her father's youngest brother, and he was indebted to her father who had paid for Adam's education. Adam had helped Franz and Ilsa purchase their farm when they first arrived in Ohio.

Adam sat with Ilsa the afternoon of the funeral, and he outlined a plan for the farm. Benjamin could meet with him one afternoon each week in town in Adam's office. Together they would see that Rohe Farm's business continued as it had when Franz was alive. Adam assumed responsibility that the farm's income would continue uninterrupted. Ilsa had his assurance that she would have everything she needed. Adam would call on Rohe Farm monthly to make sure all was as it should be. He was in the habit of visiting Ilsa and Franz frequently, so Ilsa knew it would give him no additional burden. Her uncle did this kind of work, overseeing estates.

He presented people's cases in court and argued property contract disputes there. He was a good lawyer and a man who was held in great repute though he was a young man, only just thirty.

Adam complimented Ilsa as a woman of sound, good sense, one who was frugal and never frivolous or wasteful. Therefore she only needed to send a note to him if she needed money for the children or herself. Any other bills she incurred could be posted directly to his office. He would pay them. Adam told her that she was very fortunate that there was no mortgage on the farm. Franz had been thrifty. His family's income at Rohe Farm remained secure.

However, one unanticipated difficulty arose for the young widow. On a Sunday afternoon not long after Franz's funeral, Vallerie Bernier drove up in a shabby wagon from her parents' home on the Porter's Farm a mile down Clark Road. Vallerie had been Ilsa's domestic mainstay for the five years Ilsa had lived in Ohio. She came to announce that she was leaving her job at Rohe Farm. The girl had never given her any indication that she was unhappy working at Rohe Farm. She had never been warm with Ilsa, but she always worked hard and agreeably. She had been jolly with the children. Vallerie had been only fourteen when she began working at Rohe Farm, and the housemaid carried most of the household's heavier work on her broad and capable shoulders. Ilsa had trained her well.

As Vallerie told Ilsa she was quitting, the girl gave as reason that she was moving to live with her cousins in Taylorsville, ten miles north of Cossette, and fifteen miles north of Rohe Farm. Vallerie was promised a better job there. She reminded Ilsa that she had wages due. Ilsa was an honorable woman and did not like debt, but she customarily paid Vallerie on Fridays, and that had been the day Franz was buried. Ashamed of her oversight, Ilsa immediately went to the *kleiner schreibtisch*, where she kept her recipes, records and money and gave Vallerie all that the girl was owed.

Ilsa had taught her well. The girl was clever and only needed to learn discipline. She grew from doing simple scullery work to being most able to run a tidy household on her own. Ilsa offered to increase the girl's pay if she would stay, but to no avail. "I must leave you, Mrs. Rohe. Please give me leave to say goodbye." Vallerie said. She kissed a tearful Hetti and glum Jacob many times, over, then she embraced Ilsa lightly, and left.

With Vallerie's defection, the widow quickly grew desperate. The first woman she hired stayed only three days. A second woman came through recommendations from Adam Mueller, only to work one day and take her leave. The first had complained that the house was too large. Emil fell into a severe fit and that frightened the second woman away. A third woman came only on promise she could make a room for herself in a section of the attic, but didn't stay long enough to unpack her trunk. She gave no reason for leaving.

It was true that in spite of the small family, now only Ilsa and three children, there was much work for a maid to do at Rohe Farm. Ilsa insisted the house be kept in the Deutsche manner, with no dust in the corners, no stain left on a sheet or a shirt. The stove had to shine. Ilsa did not tolerate cobwebs in the attic, or dirt to accumulate behind shelves in the cellar. The older invalid child meant that there was more laundry than one would expect from a small family with only three children. She kept busy and expected that anyone who worked for her would keep equally busy. Rohe Farm's house was not easy for a maid. It had two unusually large main rooms, a storage room and a wash closet, a huge attic and an equally large cellar, plus the extra work demanded for a family that included an invalid child. Not even the German Church's pastor could find a woman in Taylorsville who was willing to come to work for Ilsa. The widow was desperate before her husband was in the ground three weeks.

Help finally arrived for Ilsa through the grace of a neighbor. Not long after Franz's death, Mrs. Elizabeth Buchanan came down the road, stopping her wagon to make a call of concern for the new widow. Mrs. Buchanan was on her way to Cossette to pick up three bolts of cloth that she had ordered. She offered to bring back any supplies Mrs. Rohe might need from the town but might be unable to fetch.

Ilsa had the use of Benjamin or one of the farm workers to do errands for her, and she politely turned down the woman's offer. She felt gratitude though, that the woman had the kindness to think of her need. In spite of her embarrassment that the slates of the farmhouse's floor had not been washed in three days, nor the chairs dusted, Ilsa invited the elder woman into the house to take a cup of tea. Mrs. Buchanan accepted, and Ilsa led her to a place at the long table of the farmhouse's uncommonly large main room. There her neighbor could sip in comfort and enjoy the strudel that Ilsa offered her.

Ilsa was pleased to observe that Mrs. Buchanan looked about examining the room very carefully, nodding at the painted decorations on the furniture and cupboard doors, cheerful curtains and cushions, colorful rag rugs in front of the fireplace. Ilsa was proud of her home and more proud to see that her neighbor admired its color and cheer. Ilsa had no friends here, and she missed the company of the hearty German women who had stayed through her grief, and were so like her own family in Pennsylvania.

—

The young woman's hospitality surprised Mrs. Buchanan. Rumor had it that Mrs. Rohe disdained any visitors, and preferred to keep to herself. No one, to the older woman's knowledge, had ever been invited inside the big, odd old house on Rohe Farm before. She had stopped once, when the German couple first moved into the big house on Clark Road and had felt rebuffed. Franz Rohe had accepted the willow basket with warm scones she had brought, but he had not called to Mrs. Rohe to welcome Elizabeth into the house. She had not been encouraged to return.

Ilsa was able to set the table for tea, and allow it a nice steep for her neighbor, but she was unable to sit and drink a cup with Mrs. Buchanan for longer than three or four minutes. Loaves had risen on the back of the stove and needed to be set into the oven. Certain that another farmer's wife would understand, Ilsa excused herself and went to the stove. She was hardly finished pushing the loaves into the oven when her daughter Hetti came into the room crying that she had a splinter in her hand. Scarcely noting the visitor, the child demanded her mother pull it out. Excusing herself, Ilsa went to her sewing basket sitting near the hearth and found a needle to pry the offending bit of wood from her daughter's hand.

While she was so occupied, Ilsa Rohe's infirm child began to slip down in the pillows of an odd cart where he laid near a window. The boy needed propping up. Since Mrs. Buchanan was nearer the boy, and Mrs. Rohe busy with her daughter, Elizabeth rose from her place at the table and went to reposition the boy.

The fair-haired child was some years older than the little girl. From his size, he looked to be about ten. His features were fine enough, but he had little control of his eyes. It seemed that he had no control of his body. Mrs. Buchanan had never seen a child like this. She had twice known change-o-life children. The ones she knew were sweet natured, able to walk, but odd looking and held forever as children. They did not live long. She had also known children so backward that they couldn't learn to button their own clothes. They often came to fatal accident on farms, or were taken with mild illnesses that other children survived, but she knew that their families grieved for them the same as a whole child. However, she had never seen a child so sadly afflicted as this one. Mrs. Buchanan felt great pity for the widow with her child. He might have been a pretty child, if he had not been so doomed.

Ilsa looked up from her daughter's hand. She was surprised that a look of caring crossed her neighbor's face as the woman bent to help the boy. Mrs. Buchanan showed no hesitation in touching Ilsa's son Emil, and no disgust at his condition. Ilsa sent her daughter away to wash the wound now freed of the splinter. Graciously, she thanked the older woman for her help and gave the names of her children, Emil and Hetti, and told her of her other

—
9

child, Jacob, who was in school.

The two women conversed for a short time longer over their teacups. The young widow felt overcome with feelings of gratitude. "I would appreciate that you call me Ilsa," she said to Mrs. Buchanan.

"I would be most happy to call you Ilsa," Mrs. Buchanan answered. "And you must call me Elizabeth. We have been neighbors over five years and should have known each other better and much sooner."

Ilsa smiled and Elizabeth couldn't but help ask, "How is it that you don't have a German accent? I remember the sound of Mr. Rohe's speech from one day when I spoke to him at the McFarland's barn raising."

Ilsa laughed. "My husband did not go to school as a boy, and held the old world sounds. But my sisters and I did. Our grandparents were Deutsche. But not all who come from Pennsylvania came across an ocean first. My parents were both born here in America. My father wanted that my sisters and I would be well spoken in English."

A further good result of that visit came about during the following week, when the handsome Ainslie Buchanan, Elizabeth's son, knocked at Ilsa's door. The man was so reserved and proper with the widow Rohe that he stood outdoors in clear sight of the road to speak to her. He would not enter her house. Courteously and firmly, he made it clear that he had stopped at his mother's request. Mrs. Buchanan had a suggestion she thought Ilsa would appreciate. It was that the Buchanan family knew Tansie Wilson, Benjamin's mother well. The Wilsons attended the Christian Church in Cossette as they did, and Mrs. Wilson had worked in Mrs. Buchanan's home for many years during times when extra help had been needed.

As foreman, Benjamin earned a good wage, enough for him to have savings, and enough that his mother no longer needed to sell her labor. The mother and son shared a small house on Rohe Farm's property as part of his wage. They lived at a distance of many acres from Ilsa's farmhouse, but it was an easy walk. The woman kept to herself, not wanting to be too familiar with her son's employer's family. Ilsa had scarcely ever seen her. Mrs. Buchanan recommended Tansie as honest and punctual, should no other help be found. Elizabeth Buchanan was the only woman in Anderson Township who had troubled to come to visit her. Mrs. Wilson wasn't her choice, but Ilsa felt she would have put herself in a bad light with Mrs. Buchanan if she ignored the offer.

The woman, Tansie Wilson, was in her fifties at least. Ilsa judged that she was still capable enough to do household work. The widow was canny enough to know that *honest* and *punctual* were faint praise, and they did not address the capabilities of the woman at doing laundry and the heavy household laboring tasks that Ilsa required. However Ilsa was in so much need of help. The house hadn't had a thorough into-the-corners washing since the funeral.

Ainslie Buchanan offered to use his persuasion to induce Mrs. Wilson to come to work and help Mrs. Rohe and her children. Ilsa was excited and pleased that Ainslie Buchanan had come to her home on any account. It was especially meaningful to her that he had come bringing a solution to her problem. Mrs. Wilson wasn't a perfect solution, but Ilsa was wise enough to accept that *bettler haben keine wahl.* Her grandmother's saying was true, and Ilsa was in the position of the beggar who has no choice. She asked that Mr. Buchanan to speak with Tansie Wilson on her behalf.

That very afternoon Ainslie took the path out to the house where Benjamin and his mother lived to the south of the dairy barn, and he exerted his skills of persuasion with Mrs. Wilson.

Tidy and ready to give Ilsa her best, Tansie Wilson began work the very next morning. Ilsa explained her requirements, and told the woman she expected her to come in work clothing, but fresh and washed. Ilsa also expected that a housemaid work hard. She allowed that Tansie would never have to feed or clean Emil. She didn't expect her to work as a nurse. Ilsa did expect the woman to work from eight in the morning until four in the afternoon as Vallerie had, Monday through Friday, and mornings on Saturday. Ilsa agreed that Tansie could go home for an hour at noon to fix her son's dinner, and promised that Tansie's employment would not include work such as tilling or weeding the kitchen garden, cleaning the privy, or picking and pruning in the family's small apple orchard.

Ilsa learned that Tansie was slow at work and tedious in conversation. The woman needed a burdensome amount of explanation then quickly forgot what it was she was expected to do. But the widow desperately needed her.

O<<>>O

~~~O<<>>O~~~

3 ~ Courtship

It was easy for Ilsa to keep her word to Tansie Wilson. Franz had sent workers to clean the privies, chop wood, and do heaviest work around the house. But Vallerie had done the smaller tasks, burning garbage, turning soil, caring for poultry and rabbits. Jacob wasn't old enough to do them as well as Vallerie had. Ilsa asked Benjamin to assign men to do those traditionally housewifely tasks. With those jobs taken away, by the time two weeks had gone by, Ilsa's house was once again in order and she and Tansie adjusted to a companionable routine in their work.

Tansie Wilson was unlike the strong, young housemaid that Vallerie had been. Ilsa felt the woman bustled about unproductively, doing what didn't need doing, while Ilsa had to point out work that should have been obvious. However, against her annoyance with the woman's limitations, Ilsa began to appreciate that Tansie provided some conversation and was not unsettled by Emil. The house ran better for an extra pair of hands. She could not complain that Tansie didn't try her best. The housemaid had even made friends with the arrogant tom cat who kept the big house free of mice. The Rohes brought him from Pennsylvania as a tiny kitten. He was good with her children, but suspicious with strangers and prone to using his claws when irritated.

Ilsa was broodish now, without the expectation of a husband coming in for his dinner at noon and supper in the evening. Though she was glad she had given Franz's clothes and boots to Benjamin to dispose among the needy and had felt little sentiment in so doing, she felt lonely to find herself with just the children for company.

A grief came from knowing that there was no man who would put his hand on her cheek and tell her that he loved her. Her husband had been coarse

---

13

in his passion, but constant, and she missed that part of him. Ilsa had wept hard when he died, not as much out of sorrow, but from the suddenness of it. She feared what would happen to her. Responsibility dried her tears. She had to take care of Emil, Jacob and Hetti, and she would endure. She knew herself capable and came to a firm and stoic restraint. She would not pity herself. When her husband's body was covered with earth, she shed no more tears.

Never in her bed did she miss Franz, for from the time when her son was born, Emil was the one who shared it, not her husband. But when the housework and her daily chores led her into the other places of the farmhouse, the wash closet or storage room, or the attic, places where she and Franz had found adequate privacy from the children, then a sense of what she had lost in the tenderness and the love of another adult would sweep over her.

After Tansie had been working for her for two weeks, Ilsa was not surprised when, glancing through a window at the front of the house, the young widow watched Mr. Ainslie Buchanan ride up the drive. It was a Sunday afternoon. Emil was still asleep, but Hetti and Jacob were playing outside. She couldn't but feel excitement as her children led him to the house. They were pleased by a visitor's arrival. Jacob knew Mr. Buchanan from his friendship with Mr. Buchanan's son Josiah. Hetti had been peeking around from the sleeping room door when he had come to give her the message from his mother. Ilsa opened the door in welcome, and invited Mr. Buchanan in. The two children raced back to their game.

Mr. Buchanan would not step far into the house. But he removed his hat and bowed to her. "I came on behalf of my mother, Mrs. Rohe. She wants assurance that Mrs. Wilson has worked out well for you."

Ilsa couldn't contain her happiness. She impulsively stepped toward the tall man, and threw her arms around him in an unlikely, unexpected display of affection. Mr. Buchanan was taken by surprise.

She held him for some seconds too long before she withdrew and stepped back. He was standing very straight and looked embarrassed. "Sir," Ilsa said, "you and your family have given me kindness. I am most grateful to you and to your mother." She hadn't expected that he would be shy. It endeared him to her. The widower was awkward with what she was aware some other man would take to be license to do with her what he would. She withdrew farther from him, to ease his discomfort. She began to chatter, enumerating many ways Mrs. Wilson was helping her satisfactorily.

———

14

He eased, and she offered him tea. "I thank you, Mrs. Rohe, but I mustn't tarry. There are other things I must attend this day. But I'm pleased my mother and I were able to be of assistance. "

"Mr. Buchanan, I am much in debt to your mother. Please tell her so."

"I shall do so. And, Mrs. Rohe, please remember that you may call on the Buchanans, should you have need. There are quite a few of us here in the township. Any of us would come to your aid. We were all saddened by Mr. Rohe's death."

He had hardly been in her house more than a full minute before he opened the door to take his leave. But in that time, she knew that he was hers, and her confidence was immediately confirmed. Her handsome neighbor stopped in the doorway where the day's light glowed in his eyes and made their brown color illumine to look like sweet, clear honey. He was some older than Franz, and the man's dark hair was beginning to grey. It was clean and bristled out from his temple. She had to hold her breath just at the look of him.

"I have business that will take me to Louisville this month," he said before he turned away and took the steps down from the porch. "I will call on you when I return, if that is permissible."

She didn't say anything, but she smiled, and that was the best answer she could give. He would return. She only need be patient.

Ainslie Buchanan returned from Louisville six weeks later as the sticky heat of an Ohio summer was ending. He found excuse to come by her house to ask about her family's well being. Again it was a Sunday afternoon. And again, he stood shyly at the door, and stayed in her company for but a very few minutes.

When school took up in September, Ilsa sent Hetti to ride the school wagon with Jacob. In a pinned note, attached to the little girl's pinafore and addressed to Schoolmaster Herbert, Ilsa requested that Hetti Rohe be enrolled as a first grade student. Hetti was not yet six, and Ohio children did not start school until the age of six or often age seven.

Hetti could read most words by tracking their sounds. She could print her name, and she was quick to add and subtract numbers of two digits. Ilsa was certain that her daughter would not be sent home. Hetti was very proud that she was accepted into Mr. Herbert's schoolroom, though still somewhat young for first grade.

In expectation of another visit from Mr. Buchanan, Ilsa made another change. Since Tansie conveniently went home at mid-day for an hour to serve her son's dinner, Ilsa asked the woman to take an *extra* hour's rest and not return to work until after two o'clock. Ilsa explained that she herself was often up in the night tending to Emil, and she liked to rest as he napped after his noon feeding.

Soon after that day, Mr. Buchanan stopped on a Wednesday afternoon to leave a book he had purchased on a trip to Dayton. It was identical to one of Josiah's books that her son told her he liked very much. "It is a small gift for Jacob. Our boys are good friends to one another," he said. "I saw this copy in a shop and thought Jacob might like a copy to keep. It is the same edition."

"Jacob shall thank you, sir. My son speaks of Josiah often. He speaks well of your daughter also. Anna? Is that her name?"

"Yes, Mrs. Rohe, Anna. I have an older daughter also. We call her Libby. Her name is Elizabeth, for my mother. Libby completed eighth grade a year ago. She manages our household well under my mother's nearby supervision and with our housemaid's help." He spoke with pride in his daughter.

The tall man looked intently at Ilsa, as though he had more to say. But then his eyes turned to the window, and she knew he was about to leave. She spoke to him hoping to hold him with her a little longer. "I must thank you again, sir, for arranging that Mrs. Wilson come here. It has been a blessing to me to have her help."

Mr. Buchanan nodded his acceptance of her thanks. Ilsa tilted her head and said brightly, "I don't want to tax Tansie overly much. She goes home mid-day to make Benjamin's dinner and rest. She does not return until two. My other children are in school, so it gives both of us a bit of mid-day leisure, or we'd work straight through the day." The words Ilsa said sounded like silly womanish prattle, but she knew as well as she had ever known anything that this attractive man, who had piqued her fancy for so long, would soon act on the information she had just given him.

Two days later, Tansie had scarcely walked away from the farmhouse before Ainslie rode into the yard. From the window, Ilsa watched him look back over his shoulder toward the road before he dismounted. Ilsa stepped out onto the porch. The tall man tossed the reins over a post, walked toward the house, and she called a greeting to him.

"Mr. Buchanan, it is still so warm. Don't you Ohio corn growers call this season Indian *Summer* as we did in Pennsylvania? Your horse might be more comfortable at the back of the house. It is shady and there is grass. Also a water bucket, and a hitching post."

"Mrs. Rohe, I had not thought to stay more than a short while."

He looked up at her, lifted an eyebrow and twisted his mouth into a crooked grin. It teased at her, though he was too handsome for it to be comic. He was ten feet away standing on the ground below her, and his smile drove a spiral of excitement to her belly. She reached back a hand to fix one of the pins that held her thick fair hair. She looked at him but said nothing.

He nodded, made a small bow and turned to lead his tall chestnut gelding around the house to the secluded spot she described. It was hidden from the street and the farm's outbuildings by a spinney of trees and bushes and also by the back walls of the poultry coops and rabbit hutches. No passerby on Clark Road or farmworker from the dairy barn would notice a horse tethered there. Ainslie Buchanan's wide shoulders and narrow hips moved easily with his stride, and all her body's parts from her mouth downward softened for him. Ilsa's breasts began to swell as though she had a babe to nurse. Her nipples hardened. The very hair on her arms rose, as from the doorway she watched the man walk in his easy way, leading his horse from the front of the house. She had waited so long for this day.

She made Emil comfortable in his cart as she did every day at this time. Familiar with mid-day routine, the boy settled into sleep. Ilsa Rohe came back into the main room to give a fine and bountiful welcome to Mr. Ainslie Buchanan. The ardor of her welcome might have surprised him, but to her it was not a surprise. She had been long in the waiting.

Later that September, on a particularly fine day, Ainslie came on foot from his farm. He was dragging a small, high walled wagon to Rohe Farm. Ilsa thought it was for a pony or goat cart. Ains padded it with blankets and quilts, and carried Emil outdoors. He led her to a small wood not too distant from the house. Ains played the pony and pulled the wagon.

It was the first time that Ilsa had ventured into the wood far enough to see the pretty little creek that cut across her property at the corner where Rohe Farm's land joined Josiah Buchanan's larger quarter section. She'd scarcely ever been beyond the post box at the front of Rohe Farm or the springhouse behind it. Ainslie Buchanan led them out to a picnic. It was high adventure for Ilsa. She had not been so far from the house since

---

she had lived here. Ainslie had a basket of bread, cheese, and fruit tucked in a corner of the wagon.

They made love in the rivers of dry grass streaming under and among the trees. The leaves above them were still green but soon would turn rosy and amber with autumn. In their passion, they forgot the basket of food, but loving made picnic enough. Emil woke, but appeared as happy as he ever had. The bird noises he made waking were more like cooing to her than squawking. He'd managed to move his head toward the west breeze, and it was moving soft wisps of his hair. He was comfortable here.

They returned to the house. It was so near two o'clock that Ainslie had to hurry to get Emil out of the wagon and back inside and in his cart before Tansie came back to work in the afternoon. "We must make certain Emil gets more time in the out-of-doors before the cold weather comes," Ainslie said. Ilsa agreed, smug with added pleasure as the look on his face showed how hard it was for him to leave her. He looked as though he wished that they could return to the wood right then to love each other again.

Ten minutes later, the housemaid noticed the wagon out the front window. It was something new to the yard. Ilsa made up a fiction that it was a gift from the Buchanan family, which was almost true. Tansie went to unpin the blankets that were airing outside on the work porch. As she went out the door to the work porch, she said, "The Buchanans are a fine family, ma'am, right down to the very last one of 'em. They wus pioneers here in the Miami Valley, you know."

By the first of November, before six weeks had past, it was common knowledge that Ainslie was courting Ilsa Rohe. No one seemed to be offended. Her Uncle Adam came to visit, and Ilsa told him she would marry Ainslie Buchanan at Christmas time.

"*Es ist Gute für Mann Frau zu finden*. I approve, and *Gott Zufrieden ist!*" Adam said, throwing his arms around his niece and kissing her. He knew the Buchanans as thrifty and solid in their business dealings. "Ainslie is a fine farmer and his colts and fillys bring top dollar. It is soon, but you have chosen well."

The widow delayed writing letters to her sisters in Waynesboro as long as she could. They might think it ill mannered and coarsely disrespectful to her husband Franz that she would want to remarry so soon after his death. Ilsa did not want their censure. Her sisters could not understand the difficulties of western life. But the time had come to tell them of her happiness. She wrote a separate letter to each of the six women, though

---

18

she usually only wrote to sister Hetti, the nearest her in age. She depended on Hetti to share any news of Ilsa sent with the others.

Before the month was over, Ainslie formally told his family what they already knew. He was to marry the Widow Rohe on Christmas Eve. By mid-month, the elder Buchanans formally paid her a visit to signify their welcome to her and her children into their family. Each of Ainslie's brothers and sisters-in-law came to call at her home and each couple brought a small gift to show their acceptance. The Buchanan men had known Franz in the way of farming men as hardworking and honest, but their wives hadn't known Ilsa. They were curious about the house at Rohe Farm and showed pleasant and honest admiration when they visited. They complemented Ilsa lavishly on the home she had created.

As soon as families were told of the wedding to come, Ainslie asked Ilsa if he might take Jacob and Hetti with his children to the Cossette Christian Church on Sunday mornings. His family had been in the congregation since the church was founded. The Rohe children had not attended the German Church in Taylorsville after their father died. Ilsa gladly gave her permission. Jacob was gentle in his nature and she knew he would grow up to be a good man, but Ilsa felt strongly that her daughter needed discipline and scriptural lessons. Too, her children had enjoyed the Sonntag Kinder Schola in Taylorsville. She expected that they would enjoy Sunday school with the Buchanan children in Cossette as well, and they did.

She sent a note to Adam to transfer her tithe for the children's church schooling from *Pfarrer* Gruber in Taylorsville to Reverend Johnson in Cossette. Jacob and Hetti Rohe were happy to be Sunday schooled with the Buchanan children, and they found most of the children that they knew from school attended the church in Cossette.

By December, everyone in two or three townships knew that Ilsa Rohe and Ainslie Buchanan were to marry. Ainslie was still reluctant to tie his horse in sight of passersby on Clark Road when he came to call on her. In the lavish joy Ilsa took in her coming marriage, she chose to find this covert behavior, performed to protect her reputation, an act of love. It was all the more proof that her fate had determined that Ainslie Buchanan, the man she had desired for so long, was her destiny.

O<<>>O

~~~O<<>>O~~~

4 ~ The Terms of Marriage

On the last Sunday of November, the banns of marriage were announced from the pulpit of the Christian Church in Cossette, between Ainslie Buchanan and Ilsa Rohe. So not to insult the pastor of the German Christian Church in Taylorsville, who had been so kind to her after Franz's death, Ilsa sent him a letter explaining that she was to be married to Mr. Ainslie Buchanan. The pastor of Mr. Buchanan's church in Cossette would officiate, but she would be very pleased if Pfarrer Gruber and his wife could attend. The wedding would be small, and it would be held at Rohe Farm on Christmas Eve.

Ilsa received a letter back from him, wishing her all good fortune and stating she had the pastor's blessing and the prayers of his congregation. He mentioned that he knew of the Buchanan family, and that they were a family of good reputation.

There was another matter that concerned Ilsa more than invitations to the wedding. She felt she must have Ainslie's agreement on a matter important to her before the ceremony when vows were said. She asked that he bring his family to live in her house on Rohe Farm, rather than move her family to his. She understood that it was an unusual request, but she was proud and stood very firm on this one thing. There was a practical good sense behind her demand.

Ainslie saw no good sense or intelligence in her demand. It would be difficult to uproot his five children again. They had already been moved once during the past year. In addition, the farmhouse on the property he had purchased from his father — only the past January — was an uncommonly fine house.

It was less than fifteen years old, had two full stories and was of brick, not logs. Ainslie's house had eight rooms, while hers had only two. Ilsa's attic was vast, but unfinished. Should he agree, he would be bringing the five children to crowd her home when they married. The log house at Rohe Farm was vast, but in essence it had only two main rooms.

Ilsa loved her house and Rohe Farm. It had been purchased with her father's money *for her*, and its eighty acres insured Ilsa's children's future. As much as she had hated leaving Pennsylvania for this raw prairie country, she had soon taken great pride in Rohe Farm. Within its over eighty acres were two ponds and the small wood at the front west corner of the holding. There a small creek meandered. The property held a small apple orchard with trees grown big, an old stable, a great, wide dairy barn, a foreman's cabin, and many useful outbuildings. Franz built the dairy barn and some milk processing buildings as soon as they had settled here. All else, including the house, came from its days at the turn of the century and just after as an army supplies station for General Wayne and his troops.

It was true that Ainslie had a fine large home. However Ilsa knew it was not a place to which he could hold great attachment. The year before, his wife had died when his youngest child was born. Shortly after her death, Ainslie sold his farm in an adjacent township and moved here with his children that they could be closer to their grandparents.

The Buchanan family had a number of farms in the township, but the *Ainslie* Buchanan family had only resided on Clark Road for a scant ten months, and therefore Ilsa had no bad conscience about holding fast to her demand.

"You are my love. I vow that is true," she said. "But we cannot be married until you promise that we will live here in my house with our families joined," she insisted. "I will not leave my home."

At first, Ainslie balked at her request. "No, lassie, your house is large, tidy, and prettily managed, but it's small in number of rooms. But, with eight children between us, we'd soon find sorry interference with each other. I canna agree to this whim of yours. It does not seem a sound idea to me."

He had reason on his side. She knew that, and she saw from his face that he could be stubborn.

But she was clever in turning his mind to what she determined would be best. "Just one year ago last summer, you told Franz *in my hearing* that Rohe Farm would make a better yearly profit if it were planted to corn," she'd answered back.

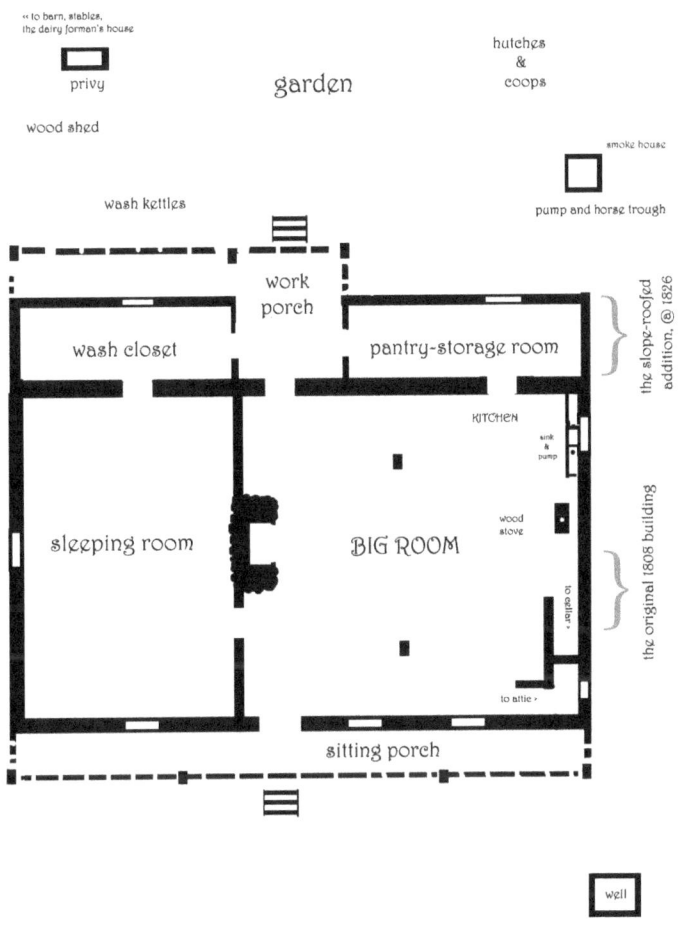

" to barn, stables,
the dairy forman's house

privy

wood shed

garden

hutches
&
coops

smoke house

wash kettles

pump and horse trough

work
porch

wash closet

pantry-storage room

the slope-roofed
addition, @ 1826

KITCHEN

sink
&
pump

wood
stove

the original 1808 building

sleeping room

BIG ROOM

to cellar »

to attic »

sitting porch

well

ILSA ROHE'S HOUSE
1844

"My dear and charming man, *you* are the one who advised Franz to set aside no more than twenty or thirty acres for pasture and that he should plant the rest to grain." She smiled sweetly as she carefully turned the argument in her favor. "You gave Franz very good neighborly advice, *meine liebst,* when you argued in favor of grain."

Ainslie was listening, not quite realizing how the direction of her request shifted. She had been talking about the house, but now she was talking about farming. He seemed puzzled at what she was saying.

She waited and watched as his face slowly opened in understanding. He'd remembered that he and his father Josiah thought Franz was thick in the head to pursue dairying when the land he owned was so fertile for corn. He remembered that he had once stopped at Rohe Farm to pass on that good advice to her husband. It was a Sunday afternoon when the weather was good. The family was enjoying the air outdoors. Franz was playing with their son and daughter while Ilsa sat on the porch by Emil's cart.

His eyes twinkled. "I am mightily impressed that you heard what I said so long ago. My little Dutch Ilsa has a business head on her pretty shoulders. What a surprise of a woman you are."

She continued, softly persuading. "You know that there would be a rich profit come next harvest season, if you live here on my farm, you will be able to insure that the first plowing and planting is done correctly. Nothing would be overlooked," she purred. "Your foreman is competent to plant on *your* farm. You have told me Thomas does well with crops. But the workers here know cows, not corn. You will be needed here to supervise and instruct." She reached to tenderly stroke Ains' shoulder, and added, "Then, my love, we will together have such a great profit, that we will be able to enlarge this house with the proceeds from our first grain crop." Her eyes were shining in excitement. "You are clever enough to see that my house can easily be partitioned into more rooms than just these two. They are so great, you see, they will lend themselves to interior walls and become parlors and a dining room.

"Upstairs, the chimney is tall enough that the roof can be raised, and what is now an attic might become ample sleeping rooms." She danced up from the table to twirl about. With grace and confident cheer, she serenely proclaimed, "My dearest, I know I can make you and the children quite comfortable until the dream of it is accomplished."

She hadn't given him a chance to make an objection. Her flattery won his attention. Her argument contained a logic which, combined with an appeal to his vanity, moved his mind into agreement. Benjamin, Rohe Farm's competent foreman, knew only dairying. Ainslie understood crops as well as husbandry. Too, Ainslie liked the idea of drawing working plans to expand Ilsa's odd house and make it more comfortable. He had always enjoyed drafting ideas onto paper and had enjoyed putting boards together to make something new, even as a boy on his father's farm. He could quickly set fences for two small pastures to the northwest of Rohe's dairy and build a good stable and foaling shed for his young mares before it was far into the winter season. The other horses could stay with Thomas, who might want to tenant the house on Ainslie's property and move his family into it. Better it have a tenant than let it sit empty giving invitation to mice.

The couple sat together companionably at the long table in the big room for many afternoons thereafter as fall deepened and winter came closer. They sketched out the ways they would like Ilsa's house adapted to suit their combined families while Emil, in his cart, watched the light change in the room.

"Do you think we'd have five bedrooms in the new attic?" Ainslie asked.

"It would fit six easily, with a hall wide enough for two to walk side by side and still have space for two wash closets," she answered. "I knew my house someday could be a grand home. It was so large and soundly built."

Ilsa drew rough plans as she talked, and Ainslie re-drew them into a more precise drafter's representation three times before she was satisfied.

It was suddenly December and the second of three banns was said in the Cossette Christian Church for the couple's marriage. And, a snag appeared in the smoothly flowing river of their plans.

Ainslie's older daughter, Libby, disapproved of her father's plans to marry and with the marriage move the family to Rohe Farm. She didn't want a stepmother, and the farm was a place that Libby thought was ancient, odd, and eccentric. It had frivolous looking painted birds and flowers on its post box and on its front door. It wasn't a bit as nice as the grand brick home that had once belonged to Uncle Francis. Besides, her mother had not been dead a year, her sister Harriet, gone only a half year longer. There had been changes enough for her younger sister and brothers. The girl worried at making a second move for the children in scarcely a year's time.

Libby was near sixteen. She felt the family was doing quite well without help from the Widow Rohe. Baby Johnnie, who had gotten off to such a poor start in life, was pulling himself up on the furniture and trying to stand without help. He'd be walking before he was a year old. Andrew enjoyed having his grandparents so near. He had stopped asking for his mother. Josiah was doing well and Anna, who had suffered greatly from the loss of her sister and mother, just beginning to recover. Ainslie's oldest child knew her own mind.

She voiced her protest, but to no avail. By the fifth day of December, Libby had been unable to dissuade her father from marrying Ilsa Rohe and was angry that her opinion had not been valued. She could not tolerate becoming merely a stepchild in the widow's house after having run her father's home, and run it well. Libby Buchanan took what she saw as the only option left to her. She ran off, eloping with the oldest Frazier boy. He was only a few years older than she, whom she had known from many summer-time visits to her grandparents. She liked his red hair and favored him over the other boys in either Anderson or Iwahata Townships. Billy Frazier worked on McKee's farm a half mile down Agatha Lane. He was a frugal young man and had saved his money. With his savings, and some household money that Libby's father had given her, the two of them found transportation to Dayton. They disappeared from their families, only to return in four days with a fancily printed and very legal marriage document. Libby, only a few days over sixteen, was married before her father.

After Libby's elopement, it was necessary that Mrs. Elizabeth Buchanan and her housemaid come across the street to Ainslie's farm daily to make sure the children didn't suffer from their sister's flight from the family home. It was a burden to Elizabeth, but Anna was just twelve and docile. The child could not insure that the woman working as cook-housemaid in the brick house didn't take advantage now that the stronger natured Libby was married and gone.

A family furor over Libby and Billy Frazier's rash decision blazed. Anna and the three young Buchanan boys felt that their sister had abandoned them. Grandfather Josiah Buchanan was anxious now for the marriage between Ilsa and Ainslie take place so his wife would once again be home the whole day, where she could tend to his needs. He demanded that his Elizabeth stay in her own house on the old Buchanan place and cleave unto him, as was his right and had been her vow. He had loved his daughter-in-law, the spunky Fiona, very much. But he thought it very inconvenient of her to up and die to create so much confusion in his life.

Ainslie was painfully distressed over his daughter's brash, foolish defection. He could not understand her sudden and seemingly senseless elopement. Saddened and depressed, he was tempted to put off his own nuptials. However, Ilsa consoled him sweetly and tenderly. She, who seldom talked about her own life, confessed that she had been but sixteen when she'd married Franz Rohe over ten years earlier. That caused him to remember that his lovely Fiona Reid had been only seventeen when they had wed. The man settled down to realize that a young marriage is not necessarily a bad marriage.

Good-hearted Waldo McKee, Billy Frazier's boss, gave the young couple use of a small cabin on his property as a Christmas and wedding present. He thought highly of Billy. Aunts and uncles and the grandparents on both sides found items to furnish the cabin for the young couple. Ilsa sent lovely linens that had never been used, that she had saved from the wedding gifts she received when she married Franz in Pennsylvania. And eventually Libby Buchanan Frazier stopped sulking and was reconciled to her father.

By Christmas Eve, the banns between the widower, Mr. Ainslie Buchanan, and the widow, Mrs. Ilsa Rohe, had been announced as customary in the Cossette Christian Church. Ilsa had spent the past weeks making matching dresses for her Hetti and Ainslie's Anna.

Ainslie took Josiah, Jacob, and Andrew to Cossette's mercantile store to be outfitted in new clothes as fine as his own for the wedding and brought home a gown of French lace and green velvet for Ilsa that he had ordered from Dayton. He ordered a similar dress, only slightly less elegant in a deep gold color for Libby and bought new britches and a vest for Billy Frazier. Mrs. Elizabeth Buchanan embroidered a pretty coverlet for Emil's cart with his name on it, so he would have a finery for the wedding as the other children did. This small gift touched Ilsa's heart deeply and brought tears to her eyes. Ainslie's sisters in law, nieces, and his daughter Anna came early on the day before Christmas, neglecting their own holiday preparations, to decorate Ilsa's house with mistletoe and wreaths of pine boughs.

That evening, the close family assembled at Rohe Farm, and Ainslie and Ilsa were married quietly in front of the fireplace in her home by the Reverend Johnson of the Cossette Christian Church. The pastor of the German Church sent his regrets but added the good wishes of his congregation that the marriage would be long and fruitful.

And so it happened that the next day, Christmas morning, 1843, nearly seven months after the death of her first husband, Ainslie Buchanan moved four children to Rohe Farm instead of the five he and Ilsa had expected he would bring.

The Rohe and Buchanan children saw it as an adventure. Little Johnnie Buchanan, the baby, finding his familiar crib and quilts in the sleeping room at Rohe Farm didn't seem to mind that they were in a very large and unfamiliar room. His sister and brothers were with him, and he was happy to see that more children were there too. If Emil didn't seem to notice the increase in noise and activity, neither did he appear to take objection to it.

Anna Buchanan suffered greatly from her older sister Libby's nearly ten days of absence from the family home. There had been too many changes in the girl's life.

She often resented Libby's demands and orders, but she found that life during the days after her older sister's elopement was far worse. She'd been thrust into a position of making decisions and carrying responsibility for the day and night care of her little brothers. It was lifted from her twelve-year-old shoulders by her father's remarriage. She was most happy to drop the burden down on the very willing back of her smiling and cheerful new stepmother.

O<<>>O

5 ~ Living at Rohe Farm

As Rohe Farm absorbed the large family, it didn't lose its charm. Ilsa was industrious and clever. By the time that Franz and Ilsa Rohe and their children had been living four full years in Anderson County, a visitor, on opening the farmhouse door, would enter a home adorned by colorful pillows and curtained windows. Its slate floor was shining clean. Its furniture was solid and well polished. Not a speck of dirt or dust on a windowsill or a shutter went undusted. No visiting neighbor, peddler, or parson entering the house at Rohe Farm would sniff out a tanging reminder of the farmhouse early years. There was no odor of army boots or gun oil. Nor was there the sharp reminder of whiskey and ale from its tavern days. Ilsa Rohe's home smelled of fennel, cloves and cinnamon, *quarkkuchen* or fresh yeast rolls. The building had become a showplace of a home, as neat and attractive a background for the pretty Ilsa as any farmstead could be for its mistress — for all that it had only two great spaces that would properly be called rooms.

With Ainslie and the addition of four more children, it took an adjustment, but the log house itself at Rohe Farm was to a great degree larger than the average frontier cabin. Back before the century was born when Ohio was not yet a state, General Anthony Wayne had been here with his army to drive the Miami Indians westward out of their river valley home. Buchanan men from Kentucky had been with him and came back to settle here.

Ilsa's house had originally been erected as an army stores building. It was well fortified, and designed to provide a place where officers could meet also. Some years later, it became a traveler's roadhouse. Although it was never a true inn, for decades it served meals and ale. The structure did not offer proper rooms to let, but allowed a weary messenger or lone traveler an attic cot, and provide a wagoning family a place to pasture the oxen and set a camp for respite in their journey.

In the space between the road and the house, where now stood a great oak tree, wagons once parked to allow peddlers and other travelers going west a safe night on their route. Over its years, many improvements had taken place. A massive stone fireplace stood slightly off-center, dividing the two main rooms. The mortared fieldstones stored warmth enough to provide comfort for both rooms. The building was high off the ground, allowing narrow, high windows to bring natural light into the cellar. The house's newest improvement was an efficient Franklin stove at the kitchen end of the bigger room. It augmented the huge, stone fireplace. Together they could provide warmth during the worst of winters.

Large, slope-roofed additions projected out beyond the house's rear wall. One room created thereby provided for pantry storage behind the big room, and the other functioned as a long wash closet behind the large sleeping room. A back door was centered between the two lean-to additions. Wood could be brought directly from the wood shed to the house. In the space between the fireplace and the rear door, there was a wood box, a short half-barrel suited to hold kindling, a hat shelf painted by Ilsa a cheery blue with *Deutsche* folk marks— swirls around hearts, little multicolored birds and flowers— on the trim piece that held hooks for coats. They were domestic decorations such as Ilsa had seen in the homes of her grandparents when she was a child. Franz had bought her the paints and brushes for her twenty-fourth birthday so that she could duplicate them in her scarce free time.

The cellar had a supplemental well in addition to the one in the pump house, behind the house, and there was another deep well in the front of the house. The one in the pump house was piped to the kitchen and washroom and was the one most used. The well in the cellar was seldom used. It was protected by the bulk of the house and kept tightly covered lest it contribute to damp as well as coolness. But its water did not freeze even in the harshest winter and though it had to be drawn by bucket, water could be had in the worst of blizzards. The cellar had rows of shelving that provided ample room for crocks of sauerkraut, pickled meats and bins of vegetables. The space between the floor and the cellar was well insulated. Ilsa did not allow the children to play in the cellar, attic, or sleeping room, though she allowed *Prince Streifen* freedom to chase mice wherever he wanted.

Ilsa had not liked the oddity of the house at first, but she had grown comfortable in its wide spaces. It had a singular way of holding the splashing light from the windows. If they were not shuttered, the rooms were bright to their corners most of the day. There were few places dirt could hide, and Ilsa could watch her children play and roll Emil's cart near her as she worked. From any place in the big room she had supervision of the children's indoor activities. Yet it was large enough that the noise of their play was not disturbing, and she didn't have to stifle their giggles or childish bickering.

The one sleeping room was smaller than the main room, but easily spacious enough for the addition of the cots of the Buchanan children, Anna, Josiah, and Andrew, and hold a crib for their baby brother, Johnnie. There was easy room still to move about. Her children had gone from cradle to cot, but Ilsa was glad Johnnie's father had a solid crib for him. It would keep the baby from wandering in the night. He had proved to be a child who was early to walk. There was still ample space in the room for Ainslie's sturdy, high bed that he had carted from Iwahata Township to the home and farm he had purchased on the vacant property across from his father's place, and now once again moved into Ilsa's home.

Rohe Farm had a cherry wood table. It was old, possibly from the house's army days. With some chairs and beds, it had come with the house when Franz bought the property. Ains added tall, well-made chairs to the table, superior in craftsmanship to the old tavern chairs that Ilsa had at each end of the table, and more comfortable. When he found that Ilsa did not object to the addition of better furnishings, Ains then brought his familiar reading chair, a second rocking chair to be companion to the single one Ilsa had, a Chinese rug, lathe-spindled stools to replace rude benches, and a chest of drawers for each of the children to keep by his or her cot. Hetti and Jacob were delighted with theirs. Many decorative lanterns and framings for the walls, and a filled book cabinet also came with the Buchanan family's move to Ilsa's house.

Between them, the couple had furnishings to spare, and were glad for the all the space the house provided. Rather than store all the extra pieces in the attic, with Ilsa's concord, Ainslie offered Libby and Billy what they might use of the items that were surplus. Libby was a practical young woman. She looked to the future and took more than she had space for in the tiny cabin where she and Billy lived. She commandeered storage space in McKee's barn loft and took possession of all that she could get Billy to tote.

With her marriage to Ainslie Buchanan, Ilsa delighted in finding ways to accommodate the larger sized family that the handsome widower brought to her. Her children, Jacob and Hetti were glad for the companionship, and made little or slight complaint at the crowding. Emil continued to show no difference by his manner that he had any awareness of the change. Ainslie's children made no complaint at all, for their new stepmother doted on them, and her farmhouse was brighter and as nice than any they had known.   Their own mother and their grandmother grew herb gardens outdoors, and had grown pots of flowers, but Mutti Ilsa brought the flowers indoors with pots of paint.

 It had been more than a year since their mother died, and recently the children had been under the rather shrill full-time care of their older sister Libby and the intermittent care of their grandmother. This care had been supplemented by the indifference of hired help. The family had been kept healthy in spite of the still fresh grief over the loss of their mother and sister, not yet faded from memory. But it had not been a happy or good time for them. Though their grandmother visited daily, and the children were welcome in her house just across the road, the change to living at Rohe Farm provided a constancy that was calming and beneficial for them. The Buchanan children felt at home and made a rapid adjustment.

Ilsa proved herself to be a kindly stepmother. The sentiment that showed in her bright and decorative paintings, also showed in her treatment of the children. Where the Buchanans' sister and grandmother might scold them, Ilsa showed her dimples and let her eyes twinkle, while she petted and coaxed what she wanted from them. The young woman had great sympathy for the difficulties of the children's past year, and sympathy for Elizabeth Buchanan. When his wife died, Ainslie's mother was put under great strain. She had a large house of her own in Anderson Township to manage. She was no longer young, and she had to care for an aging, gentle-souled, but sometimes petulant husband. She had daughters-in-law who would have helped, but they were so busy with their own families, already including grandchildren, that they could not be asked to do more than take a single child of Ainslie's to raise in their own homes.

Ainslie would never allow the separation of his children from himself or from each other. Nor did his mother encourage that the family be torn apart after suffering so much loss.

But poor, dead Fiona Buchanan had no relatives nearby to give Ainslie help with the new baby and other children but an elderly uncle, Johnnie Reid, who was scarcely able to care for himself.

It remained to Elizabeth Buchanan the choice to travel the fourteen miles from Anderson Township back and forth daily to help her son's bereaved family through their grief, or to stay over in their home. As his only grandmother, she felt she needed be in the house at night through the crisis to tend the newborn baby, Johnnie and solve any other problems that might arise. She didn't trust to housemaids to care for her son and his family.

However, old Josiah Buchanan missed his wife. He grew so crotchety in her absence that their longtime housemaid threatened to quit her job, and even his farm foreman spoke up to tell Josiah that he was behaving unusually rudely to everyone. So, giving in to his father's need and acknowledging his own, Ainslie Buchanan sold his farm and stables in Iwahata Township, and purchased the eighty-acre parcel across from his parents' quarter section. The parcel had once belonged to his deceased brother Francis. It had lain fallow for over ten years. The houses on the two farms faced each other, their post boxes aligned but separated by the road. The McFarland place was next to it on the south side Clark Road. Josiah Buchanan's larger property to the north shared a fence line with Rohe Farm. The town of Cossette, which serviced four townships, was a little over five miles away, down Clark Road.

Ilsa learned more of Ainslie's past life than he did of hers. She was reticent, and did not want to revisit her past troubles, while he was a talkative man who came from a talkative family. When they found uninterrupted time together when the children were in school or asleep, Ainslie told Ilsa of these difficulties and how he came to make the move to Anderson Township. She listened to better understand him. His difficulties after losing a spouse seemed greater than hers had been. After his wife's death, he told her, his mother urged her son to allow her to take all the children, or at least the baby, into her own home so that she could care for them with less strain. Ainslie resisted. He did not want to lose his family as well as his wife. He told her tearfully that he could not part with baby Johnnie any more than his other children.

She enjoyed listening and learning more about the handsome man she had loved for so long. Her first husband had been a good man, but he was quiet. He seldom spoke, and then only to complain of the weather or politics. In contrast Ainslie told her of the history of his family in the long ago, and of his sorrows over the loss of his brother Francis. He told her of his two older sisters who had gone to their graves as young married women.

Yet, Ilsa shared little of her own life. She told him the names of her sisters, and said that she had named her daughter for a sister she dearly loved, but Ilsa was not one to talk or share confidences. She showed him her love in other ways. Ainslie and Ilsa suited each other. Their union was undeniably happy, and it was apparent that the children were doing well.

In spite of the upset that Anna had felt when her father announced to his children that he was to be married, the child settled into her life at Rohe Farm and found an honorable niche with her new family as its oldest daughter. If she grew lonely for her grandparents, she and Josiah were old enough to walk to visit them on a weekend afternoon. On a Sunday, Libby and Billy would often visit, for Libby missed her family.

———

As the months went by, Ains' younger daughter developed a loving friendship with Ilsa. The child, at twelve, was of an age to have resented a stepmother, but she seemed happy to have any kind of mother again and was often singing and smiling. She was as helpful and affectionate with Ilsa as she had been with the mother who bore her. The two older boys, Ilsa's Jacob and Ainslie's Josiah, had been chums at school for the past year. They were glad to be able to be chums at home also. The two of them were mischievous but had been raised to keep their mischief out of doors.

The younger boys, Baby Johnnie and four-year-old Andrew, were quiet natured, gentle boys who gave Ilsa little trial or trouble. Andrew was responsive to her demands for orderliness and soon learned to put his toys away and be careful and thoughtful when using the commode. He already took it as his task to shepherd his infant brother away from any possible harm. Though he didn't like taking naps, he understood that was what allowed him to stay up with the older children late into the evening. He dutifully went to mid-day rest with Emil and Johnnie. The baby was thriving in Ilsa's care, and he began to walk and talk, happy in the predictable routines of his new family.

Ilsa's own cheeks grew rosier too. She liked having so many children about her. She had grown up in a large family. The Muellers had been busy, noisy and active. It was only through some difficult and unusual circumstances in her adulthood that her life had become so constrained and solitary. Now it was again filled with laughter and the family sounds that she remembered.

Ilsa's days in Ohio had been lonely. Occasionally she passed a greeting with a dairy worker sent to do some farmhouse chore that Franz had no time to do. But farm women had little time for visiting each other, and Ilsa had none.

The housemaid Vallerie was poor company, interested in the children more than in Ilsa. Rarely, people Franz knew from the church in Taylorsville stopped by Rohe Farm to buy holiday cheeses, but not often. They seldom brought their wives, and she sent them on the path to talk with Franz at the dairy. The German community was not near enough for sociability with a family living as far away as Anderson Township. She had never been able to attend the seasonal events and socials there that Franz, Jacob and Hetti sometimes attended. Emil's need for constant care kept her home. She never left the boy. She had never left him with Vallerie for longer than the time it took her to use the privy or bathe. She trusted no one but herself to keep her son clean, fed, and comfortable. Travel was too difficult with him, and from her experience in Pennsylvania when he was a baby Ilsa doubted that Emil would find honest welcome in the German Church.

But now, with a new life started, Ilsa was almost giddy with the happiness she found in her new marriage.

She saw that Ainslie was kind and companionable as a father to her children. It was her husband's habit to read aloud to his children in the evenings. Franz had not done that. Franz enjoyed playing checkers, but she was a disinterested opponent, and the children not competition for him.

She felt reading was a great improvement and much to her children's benefit. She enjoyed it also. The reading provided entertainment and educated the children. She watched as Hetti and Andrew, still too young to understand all that he read to them, enjoyed the sound of his voice during the reading. In the past, when she had time, she painted or sketched, or wrote letters to her sister Hetti, but her evenings were rarely so enjoyable. Ains often had stories to tell the children and her of interesting happenings on the surrounding farms or in the town of Cossette, or from his horse raiser's meetings in Ohio and in Kentucky. He was happy to listen to their stories too. He expected Anna and Josiah to read aloud too, now and again. And not long after the Buchanans had come to live at Rohe Farm, Ainslie invited Jacob to read. She saw the pride on her son's face when he took the book offered him and read a poem with few mistakes.

Ilsa found a great joy in the addition of Ainslie's daughter, Anna, to her home. Anna was a thin, dark-haired girl with sharp features that were more attractive on her father than on her. But she would someday be a handsome, if not pretty, woman. The girl's ways reminded Ilsa of her sister Hetti. They were opposite in their physical appearance. Ilsa's sister Hetti was fair, and heavy like most of the Muellers. They were different in that Anna was quick and agile while Ilsa's sister was slow to move. But in some intangible way, they seemed similar. They both assessed situations quickly, but acted thoughtfully.

When Anna proved herself tender and caring with Emil, she surprised Ilsa in the same way the girl's grandmother Elizabeth had when first they met. Never once had Anna looked at Emil with disgust or seemed to find his spasms or fits to be frightening and unpleasant. Ilsa observed that her stepdaughter tended to Emil in the same way the girl looked after her own little brothers. She had never shown any trace of revulsion.

The seasons of 1844 passed in regular progression, and Ilsa was more and more aware that she finally had the idyllic life she had always wanted. She had beloved children around her and a superb and worthy husband. She worked hard and felt blissfully happy. Each day that passed was good at Rohe Farm, and as a bonus, her husband attended to her ideas.

—

35

Under Ilsa's advisement, and with Adam Mueller's approval, Ainslie sold two-thirds of Franz's dairy cows to finance planting sixty acres of grain on Rohe Farm. There was still good pasture for the remaining third so that the profitable cheese-making operations could continue. The farm's dairy workers who would have been laid off for having fewer cows to tend, were absorbed into the work of building a new stable for Ainslie's mares and constructing stout fences and arenas for training.

When the threat of frost had passed in spring, plowing would begin on both farms and then the crop would be planted. Ilsa dreamed of rows of corn covering her property, tall and green with fat husks filled with golden kernels showing between the leaves on each stalk. Cows were her Papa and Franz's venture. Corn was hers. She knew it would bring profit to Rohe Farm. Franz brought home the weekly newspaper and she was the one who read it. She knew where the money was in Ohio. Ilsa's farm would go to corn and be worth far more than her father's had been.

She had the life she wanted. She had the handsome husband she deserved. She had as many children as her mother did, and her farm had greater potential on this rich and rock-free soil than her father's land ever had. Life was already as good as she had dreamed it could be. She savored each moment of her every day.

O<<>>O

6 ~ The Value of a Gift Declined

Ainslie Buchanan was a good, thrifty and weather-watching farmer, but he took more pride in his horses than he did with his grain crops. His income came as much from one venture as the other, but his mares came from lines that had come with the Buchanans brought with them to America when they came from Ulster over a hundred years earlier. He wanted Ilsa to share his pride in what he did best. So, in early spring, when the small bulb plants were popping up from the black winter soil, he surprised Ilsa with a magnificent gift. In his estimate, it was the finest gift he could give. He chose a time when the older children were in school and when Emil and the younger ones were napping. Ainslie led his wife out to the drive and introduced her to a lively black filly from his stable, saying, "She is for you, Ilsa, my lass. It is my great hope that you will one day come riding with me."

Ilsa knew from Anna and Josiah's chatter that their mother had been fond of horses and of riding. Therefore, she was annoyed by the idea. She didn't want to slide into his memory of his first wife. Ilsa gave Ainslie an obvious and practical reason for refusing the gift. She told him that she could never trust anyone else to watch Emil with her away and added, "With a houseful of children to care for, I don't have time to go out riding."

"Perhaps someday, love, if not now," he answered. He raised his hand to pat the neck of the slim and glossy young filly as though consoling her for his wife's rejection.

Worrying, lest he feel his gift had been spurned and his feelings wounded, Ilsa stood on tiptoes and whispered in his ear to bring him back to his usually cheerful self.

"What are you whispering, wife?" he asked tersely. "You know well I canna ken the kraut speech."

Using the teasing voice she knew could jolly him, and aware that Tansie was gone and there was no one but him to hear her, Ilsa repeated her words louder — and this time in English. "I don't want to mount your horse, my dearest. I want you to mount me."

Her words brought the twisted smile that she loved back to his face. "What a wicked little woman I've married," Ainslie said.

He left the filly tied and followed Ilsa back into the house, where the matter of wickedness was finished to the complete satisfaction of both husband and wife.

Ainslie, had already set his mind that the high-stepping and valuable young filly, the pride of his stable, should be a gift. Since his wife didn't want her, he offered the horse, with tack which included a fine, costly English saddle that had once been his wife Fiona's, to his older daughter, Libby.

"Now, girl," he told her, "this gift will make it very easy for you to come and visit us whenever you'd like, yet be back home in time to fix your Billy boy his supper. My only condition is that you give the filly good care and never sell her. When you want her bred, I will arrange the right stud that her foal be as worthy as she is."

Libby recognized that in the long view the gift could be the start of a comfortable life for her and Billy, and she was quick to accept the conditions of the gift, both stated and implied. She didn't regret her hasty elopement, and she found Billy Frazier to be a fond husband. However, the girl was young and missed her sister and young brothers, her father, and her grandparents very much. It was over three miles walk, nearly four, from the small cabin where she and Billy Frazier lived to her relatives' homes. She was comfortable with horses and would make good use of the black filly. She was sweetly touched by the gift of her mother's saddle.

Ains and Ilsa were very busy. Together they planned the future of the farm. Soon, the pastures were cleared, and with spring, land that had been fallow or in wood, was plowed and a good corn crop seeded. Summer came. Jacob and Josie raced each other down the rows of corn and waded in the creek with the family's three dogs, two with German names, *Flecken* and *Flöhchen*, and one named Blackie who came to Rohe Farm with Josie and Andrew. Anna and Hetti helped Ilsa in the kitchen and with tasks around

—

38

the house without complaint. Anna learning a different style of pastry baking than she had known before, and Hetti was happy to follow Anna around and do whatever the older girl did, even if it was helping Tansie with the laundry. Johnnie was walking and was a healthy, playful toddler.

However, at the end of summer, in spite of the joy Ilsa shared with Ainslie and the company that his children brought into her life, a problem arose for her. The household, now enlarged to seven children where there had been three, had gained so many members that if Ains had hired three women no better than Tansie, it wouldn't have been enough to do all that needed doing, particularly at the time of the garden's peak at the end of summer.

Ilsa loved her new husband as much as she'd ever imagined she could love a man. He was affectionate with her, generous and kind. Ainslie satisfied her in every way she had wanted in a husband. Yet before the end of that first summer married, Ilsa was feeling burdened. The strain of keeping a home running as smoothly as her conscience demanded, with everything in its place and a place for everything, became more and more difficult. The garden harvest peaked at the time the school term started, when an enormous amount of work was filling Ilsa's kitchen. With only Tansie to assist her, she couldn't manage. *Dummkopf* Tansie couldn't make a decision. She'd sit looking at a cabbage and not know which leaves to discard and which to keep. Ilsa needed the help of Hetti and Anna, the daughters of the household. They were good little workers and wiser than the housemaid who was at least forty years older than the children. In the vegetable and fruit clutter of the season peaked, Ilsa badly needed the girls' help.

When September arrived, and the new school term began, Ilsa begged Ainslie to allow her to keep Anna away from school to help. Anna had already been to school for six years. It was three years longer than Ilsa had gone to school, and well past time for Anna to learn the duties of a farmer's house. The good rains that grew the fine corn in its sixty acres of rows on Rohe Farm also caused a burgeoning, abundant volume of garden harvest. Foods to store in a twice-bigger amount were needed for a more than twice bigger family's coming winter, spring, and early summer meals. The garden produce had to be dried or salt-packed and stored.

Ilsa was shocked when Ainslie refused the request she presented with his mid-day meal. It was their first disagreement. She tossed the dishtowel she was holding down on the sink edge in annoyance. It was a small thing she asked.

"Anna is to keep to school. I'll listen to no argument," he sharply replied. The tone of his voice sounded as though he were offended by what she needed from him.   In place of argument, Ilsa gave him good, sound reasons. She insisted her need until he put his hand up, fingers spread widely apart, listening to her voice, but he was blocking her from reaching to touch him.

When she stopped talking, he used the strong, resonant voice that she loved to hear when he read to the family in the evenings. But he perverted its sound as he refused to consider her request. "I promised their mother I'd ne'er neglect our daughters' education. And, lass, I keep my promises, Anna will not keep from school to help in the kitchen." he responded.

He was firm, and he didn't show any trace of concern for her needs. He just kept spooning soup into his mouth.

"Your graveyard vows give me no help," she'd snapped back at him. "And they tell me the true denial of your love for me."

"No, my sweet girl, they only prove I am true to my word once it's been given."

He paid her no more attention on the issue. Worse, he made light of her need by grinning as he stepped away from the table, as though he were proud of his rejection of what she needed. He said lightly, "I'll not break my promise." Maddeningly, the man blew her a kiss as he left the house to return to his horses in the stable.

Yet the garden and orchard produce needed to be preserved before winter's chill. Come butchering time, hams would need to be smoked and put to hanging, sausages made. Her larder was more important than his precious horses. She needed the girls' help from August until mid-October.

Anna could already read and cipher well. She needed nothing more from a schoolmaster. Ilsa and her sisters left the schoolhouse when they turned nine. Anna would be thirteen in October.

Girls had so much to learn at home: how to preserve and store, which woods when put in the stove burnt fast and which burnt slow, how to tend a garden, raise poultry and keep it healthy, how to keep eggs fresh to last through the molt, how to make compotes and custards, and the room temperatures for hard and soft cheeses, which plants from a kitchen garden would cure and which would poison, how to remove stains from laundry, how to keep infants from dying in their first year. The list was endless and more important than school poems or the whys of ancient historic battles far off in other lands.

Ilsa had more to teach Anna than any schoolmaster did. She was very annoyed with Ainslie's unreasonable refusal. She was especially annoyed, since Ilsa's request had not gone against the girl's desire. Anna had been willing to stay out of school to help.

This was not to be the only episode in Ilsa's harvest-time troubles. A worse event came the following morning when Ainslie dared to insert his taking command of Hetti over Ilsa. That he would come between her and her *own* child in such a way brought her a misery that would last longer than she could now imagine— or he would ever know.

The children were gathering their things together to leave for school when Ains came back to the house. He needed his money belt and to change into his town boots before he went to Taylorsville to examine another breeder's new purchase. He noticed that Hetti was doing kitchen work and looking glum while the other children were picking up their books and lunch buckets. "Are you not ready for school, dear Hetti?" he asked the little girl.

Hetti glanced at her mother. The child let a smirk linger on her mouth for just an instant before she looked at Ainslie and simpered, "Papa Ains, Mutti says I have to stay home to work in the kitchen."

Hetti Rohe was *Ilsa's* child, not his. Her name was not Buchanan, but ignoring Ilsa's complaints and cries, Ainslie picked Hetti up in his arms, told the boys to pick up her schoolbooks and slate. Taking long strides, Ains carried the little girl out to the schoolhouse wagon. The boys followed along, looking perplexed, but they wisely realized it was not a time to either talk or question. As the school wagon had pulled away, Ilsa's daughter snuggled down on one of its benches next to her stepsister. Hetti flounced her dark curls and stared back at Ilsa, her haughty face glowing with the insolent candor of a child when she has outsmarted her mother.

Ainslie's usurping of Ilsa's control of her child was an event that would cause Ilsa's mind great unrest. He had no right to decide what was best for her child. She turned away from him in all the ways a wife can turn away.

Following that day, Ainslie worked to win Ilsa back to him. He tried tempering the coldness she showed him with his own warmth. He stayed pleasant when he spoke to her, but she did not answer. Two days went by. Finally, thinking at last on the issue between them that had displeased her, rather than the issue that had made him stubborn, he determined to win Ilsa's favor back. Ainslie addressed the seriousness of her problem. He hadn't realized how important the neatness and order of her home was to her, since a little domestic untidiness bothered him so slightly. But to correct the situation, he rode out to McKee's farm and had a conversation with his daughter Libby. They arranged that Libby would come to Rohe Farm to work for Ilsa every day but Sunday, from September through mid-October.

Ilsa looked from the window when the dogs began barking early the next morning. Libby Buchanan Frazier arrived on the filly, sitting astride like a wild girl, her stockings showing high to her thighs further aggravating Ilsa. However, when the girl entered the house Ilsa could see that she was wearing worn work clothing and she'd brought an apron and a headscarf suitable for household labor.

"Da says you need help, and I am here," the girl said. Libby nearly pushed Tansie aside at the cherry wood table where she and Ilsa had been coring apples in her eagerness to begin work. A burgeoning abundance of the garden was displacing the household's everyday work. Ilsa was not pleased with the girl's commanding presence, but was in no position to refuse her help. With Libby to help her, she could release Tansie to scrubbing and laundry labors. She could take time to do what she needed for Emil without concern for kettles bubbling over.

The silly Frazier boy Libby had married made little as a laborer over at McKee's. The two of them were living in a tiny hovel down on Dry Creek. Anna had said that the place had but one small window and walls too thin for an Ohio winter.

Libby was more than happy to take a share of the harvest as her wages. That arrangement suited Ilsa well. Soon again, she and Ainslie were at odds. She found that he was giving Libby coin. When they were in the storage room and the door was closed, Ilsa frowned at Ains. "You needn't pay her in money," Ilsa asserted. "I'll see that she takes home a share of our stores to feed the two of them well this winter."

"Libby's my daughter, Ilsa, just as Anna is—just as Hetti is," he answered. Ilsa was infuriated, and he had more to say to anger her. "We can afford to pay her the same as we pay Tansie."

Ilsa frowned at Ains. "You needn't pay her in *money*." Ilsa said again, with more emphasis. "I'll make sure that she takes home an ample share. It is payment enough."

"Now that we are married, Ilsa, Libby is your daughter too. We can afford to pay her the same as we pay Tansie. Soon enough, she will have young ones. She won't be free to work for a bit o' money to spend freely. She can use what little we give her."

"She and that boy will waste it. They will go off to Dayton for the fair and throw away every penny you give her," Ilsa angrily retorted.

"Likely they will. But I remember taking a girl to a fair when I was young. Surely they had fairs in Pennsylvania when you and Franz were young. You ought remember those gladsome days, as I do."

However, Ilsa couldn't complain of the girl's work. Libby was tall and strong, and like her father, she was quick and smart about seeing what work needed doing. But she was a surly girl, not so easily agreeable as her sister Anna. While the older girl worked hard and accomplished much, she also annoyed Ilsa greatly. Libby made no pleasant conversation. Her speech was full of snippy questions and near-rude suggestions. By the end of September, when the work had been caught up, Ilsa was happy to glibly thank Ainslie and firmly tell him that she no longer needed his older daughter's help. She thought, but did not say, how lucky it had been for her that he had given the horse she declined to his daughter.

O<<>>O

~~~O<<>>O~~~

7 ~ Binding the Child

At the first of October, the corn on Ainslie's farm, as well as on Ilsa's Rohe farm, had been harvested and gone to auction. The couple sat together and took account of their success. Rohe Farm made as great a profit in corn as any of the other county farms per acre, and it claimed a better yield than most. Ainslie counted more money on his farm's crop, but Ilsa knew it was only because his farm had more acres planted. Ainslie had also sold four foals in Cincinnati at high dollar. Benjamin's cheeses from the dairy found another good market bringing profit from as far away as Dayton. And Ilsa was overjoyed with the couple's combined success. With the profits earned from both farms, Ainslie convinced Ilsa that they should hold a grand harvest feast. "We'll have a grand party, my girl!" he said. "An *Oktoberfest* as they do on the continent. We'll begin with a horse race and end with dancing on the front drive just as I've read that they do there. My family will help with the food and I'll hire a band."

"I think not, my husband."

"And why not? It is a turn for us to repay those who have been kind to us. You can invite the Taylorsville church people who helped you when Franz died. Invite their families and their good pastor too. And too, my love, recall that we had no party for our wedding."

"I think *Pfarrer* Gruber would look critically on drink and betting on horses. And it would be costly, Ainslie. We are rich with the harvest, but not so rich we can waste our profits on foolishness."

"My brothers and sisters would help. Cameron has horses to parade. You would need to do nothing, my love. There are plenty of young Buchanan cousins to do all the work.

She could not deny him, when he had conceded so much. He lived in her house. He planted Rohe Farm to corn. It was all for her. She would allow a celebration for him.

Ainslie decided that the festivities would be held on the third Sunday of October and should begin with races. He didn't expect to hold serious horse racing, but just a pleasurable out-of-season morning race for other breeders and owners to show off the best of their stables. Even in Ohio people knew of the popularity of the German harvest festivals and that they traditionally began with horse racing. Journals published in the big eastern cities came by post and had features about wealthy Americans traveling to Munich in the fall for a frolic. As the day drew near, Ains had his farm workers plot a track through the corn stubble and mark it by ribbons. A gala affair was coming and this would start it off.

From the colonial days when they crossed the Cumberland Gap with the Boones, Gays, Porters and McCrearys, The Scots-Irish Buchanan family had been known for their great talent in two areas, raising fine horses and making equally fine whiskey.

"The truth was," Ainslie told Ilsa, "that my father, Josiah Buchanan was born to a grand family of drinkers and gamblers, rowdy men who lived high and well." He went on to tell her that before his mother Elizabeth would agree to marry his father, she made him promise to hold to *her* family's high Presbyterian standards. "Then," he said, "after my brother Jimmie was born, but before Ma and Da crossed the river to claim this Ohio land, Da himself converted to the God's straight road. He kept his horses after for his joy in raising the beasts," Ainslie explained, "but me Da never again put money on a race, and neither do my brothers or I."

"But some might."

"Then 'tis their consciences and their wives that will scold, not mine. It is to each man to do as he chooses."

"I don't want fighting or drunkenness at Rohe Farm."

"There will not be. There will be gaiety and laughter, and I'll dance you a reel! You don't know yet what a fine stepping man I am. Have we yet before had music, lassie? We've not, and it is time."

"I have Emil to consider."

"You didn't know Emil would like the breeze in the small wood last year at just this time of year, but you trusted me. Trust me again."

46

The grand day came and Rohe Farm's celebration was the finest in Anderson Township memory. The business of breeding fine thoroughbreds, called *English horses* though they had come from Ireland, had given old Josiah Buchanan the capital that enabled him to do well in Ohio. A more scrupulous conscience might have felt that the racing sport was edging too close to sin to be a worthy enterprise, but Josiah continued to raise racing horses.

When their father gave up keeping his stable, Ainslie and Cameron Buchanan followed their father's lead and kept their own filled with highly sought after English thoroughbreds developed from old Josiah's lines. Ains' brother Andrew was a farmer with little interest in other ventures, but one who had done well working the soil. Like their father, the Buchanan sons were careful, temperate men. The oldest son, Jimmie Buchanan, who had been born in Kentucky before the family's crossover into Ohio, edged a little closer to the sin line. He practiced the distiller's arts with great talent. But Jimmie kept his whiskey making as an art, not a craft. He only used it for gifting and never for selling. Not even he had a dark mark on his reputation in Anderson Township.

All the Buchanans came together to assist in the making of Ainslie and Ilsa's Oktoberfest a success. But as much as Ilsa wanted her sisters in Waynesboro with her this day, it might be two months past the event before her sisters received their invitations in the post.

On the day, the weather was fine, cool and crisp, and sunny as autumn can be. Family and friends all arrived early. Ainslie's fellow horsemen brought their wives with them and took lodging at Cossette's two inns.

Many came with horses to be shown off as stock for sale, if not for the entertainment of the races. Ainslie's brother Cameron had purchased gaudy ribbons for the winners. The formal racing season was half a year away but ribbons added to the excitement — though times would not be recorded. Word was posted that there was to be no betting on the heats.

Ilsa was freed to enjoy herself. Ainslie had hired women with nursing skills to sit by Emil, and Anna, Elizabeth and Tansie promised to stay with him whenever Ilsa was out in the crowd. She had never been to a horse race and was curious. She noticed that after each of the runs' winners were told, Ainslie and Cameron Buchanan turned aside and watched the track or the horses being led way. They appeared not to notice men clustering and taking moneybags from their pockets. It seemed that while her husband might be too righteous to enter into the betting, like his father, he did not interfere with what sins others chose to commit. But he was true to his

---

word. There was no fighting or argument that she could hear, only guffaws and jousting about in jovial camaraderie.

She had not attended any grand festivity in eleven years, and she noted all that happened with wonder. The people seemed too finely dressed for an outdoor event. Ainslie looked like a royal prince as he walked his horses out Though he was wearing a plaid vest under his green coat, he seemed more as her grandmother described princes from Prussia, than he matched any notion she had of Scotsmen in their kiltie skirts. Ilsa watched him walking the horse, warm with pride and then warmer yet with tickles of passion. She grew so excited by the look of him, as he strolled the improvised track, she thought that if he had asked her to go walk in the woods with him, she would leave their guests and all propriety and go with him.

But as she glanced around at the people lining the edge of the track, she also noted many females of different ages but with the same smiles and flirtatious eyes that morning that she might have shown. They were watching him as she had been, and too many were waving kerchiefs, vying for her husband's attentions.

Ilsa felt unpleasantly anxious. The horsemen's wives were stylish, many of them in the tall, plumed bonnets of city women. She almost wished her husband were less an attraction to them. It was the first time she had seen him in the company of females who were not his relations. Her discomfort did not please her. She left the track and went around to the back door of the house to enter. Anna was sitting near Emil's cart as the young girl had promised she would. Hetti was beside her. They were playing a string game. Ains' sister Mattie, the wife of his brother Cameron, was governing the kitchen. The guests were at the track or at leisure in the yard. Tansie told her that no one had wandered into the house yet.

"Mutti Ilsa, may I take Emil outside? It is a pretty day and he would like it so," Anna asked when Ilsa went to Emil's side.

She was about to answer when two of the women from the races came into the house. They were older than Ilsa, and finely dressed. One woman wearing a jaunty brown hat with a blue plumed feather came up to Emil's cart. Ilsa knew they were certainly horse breeder's wives, perhaps even from Lexington.

The woman wearing the brown hat bent down to smile at the boy and touch his hair. "Is the child yours?" the woman asked Ilsa.

"Yes, my son's name is Emil," Ilsa answered as the second woman came near. All worries of flirtatious women left her. She was tense under the scrutiny of the two women.

48

"I once had a child like him," the woman wearing the hat said. "A sweet little girl. She lived but a year. I lost her to a cruel seizure of all her muscles. I have never forgotten her and know she lives in heaven."

The woman took Ilsa's hand and squeezed it gently. "Does your child seize?" Ilsa nodded. Tears had come to her eyes from the elegant woman's compassion. Seeing them, the woman in the brown hat grew teary too.

"Do you mind that we came in to see your house?" the second woman asked, taking the other hand of the first woman in her own. Ilsa thought that they might be sisters.

"No, not at all. If you tire and want rest later, come here away from the noise. You are welcome to my home. Mrs. Wilson will assist you however you need." Tansie, in crisp apron and white cap, stood to curtsey at the mention of her name.

"Thank you, Mrs. Rohe. You have a most unusual and very lovely home. You were generous to allow Ainslie to hold this fete. My husband likes to show his horses, and to let them run. He has purchased three mares from your husband's lines and favors them over his others." The women shared some pleasantries with their hostess, then nodded to Ilsa and to Anna, and went back outdoors.

Ilsa sent Hetti to ask her Papa Ains to prepare the wagon and carry Emil outside, and gave instruction to Anna. "You girls must stay with him until I prepare his noon meal. Call me should he have troubles before then. The servers will set out food from the tent at noon and you two can then help them."

"We will, Mutti Ilsa," Anna promised.

While she washed and dressed Emil to go out and spend some time in the air, she thought about the women who had visited the house. They were well intentioned and charming. One of the women had called Ilsa's husband his proper name, Ainslie, with intimacy. She should have asked their names. She was affected by the short conversation, the moment of affinity with the woman in the brown hat. She forgot her manners. Perhaps the women were wives of horse breeders Ainslie knew from travel.

Ilsa realized how often her husband was in the company of horsemen and their wives and daughters. She felt her earlier anxiety return and surround her. Could she lose him? She took a deep breath. *"Binding the child binds the parent,"* a proverb she had once heard, came to her mind. She was confident that she had bound the Buchanan children tightly to her. There was only one child of Ainslie's whom she had not already bound, Libby.

—

49

After Ains moved Emil and he was situated under a tree, but in sight of the porch where Elizabeth sat with Josiah, Jacob and many of her grandchildren, Ilsa went to find her older stepdaughter. She was in the midst of her cousins, all laughing and working.

Libby resisted. Her tone bordered on rudeness. "I'm very busy here. My aunts need all of our help setting out the platters and tableware."

But Ilsa persisted against the taller girl's resistance, and drew her away from her work and the others around her. Libby was a handsome girl, but in the muted way of Ohio women. The women's clothing was drab and their faces seemed content to look dull and plain.

Any woman could be made prettier, Ilsa knew. And she knew how to make Libby into a beauty. It was not only furniture and cabinets that could be enhanced with paint, and there were many ways to be an artist. Ilsa led the curious girl through the guests, across the yard, and into the house. In the wash closet at the back of the big sleeping room Ilsa pointed Libby to a stool. The girl was puzzled, but intrigued into compliance. Ilsa opened *un kleine gegenstande,* a gift she'd been given at her marriage to Franz. It was a small box made of cedar, carefully crafted. Libby was watching everything Ilsa did.

Inside the small chest were tins and jars. One of which held a concoction of carmine powder and lard. The smooth paste smelled of lilies. Ilsa used it to redden Libby's lips and then dabbed them down with a flannel to look natural. Then Ilsa took a dab from a tin of black ash to enhance the girl's eyelids. The box held a compound, pale in color, which hid freckles and blemishes. Another held dry powder that pinked the cheeks.

Ilsa pulled the girl's dark hair up and bound it high with a jeweled tortoise shell comb she had carefully chosen from among others in the box. Its amber and lapis flowers were set in enameled blue leaves that matched the blue in the girl's gown. When Ilsa was done, she led the girl to the mirror.

Libby examined every thing Ilsa had done to her. The changes were subtle. She didn't look like a tavern girl, but like a great lady in a painting. She drew back to see the whole of herself in the mirror.

Libby was gleeful. "I'm beautiful!" she exclaimed.

"Yes you are."

"I wasn't before."

"Yes, you were. But you didn't know how to make people notice."

Anna and Hetti had followed them into the house and were watching with shiny-eyed envy from the doorway. "It will be your turn one day, my girls!" Ilsa said. The two giggled and ran from the doorway and out of the house.

Ilsa looked at her stepdaughter and was satisfied. She had won the girl over. Kindness wove the tightest bindings, and it was so easy to give and cost so little.

O<<>>O

~~~0<<>>0~~~

8 ~ *Oktoberfest*

As Ilsa left the house to go to her guests, she passed by Elizabeth surrounded by a cluster of children. Ilsa had a quick concern that her mother-in-law might be telling them the stories Ilsa didn't like, tales of banshee women screaming death's arrival, or headless ghosts riding the byways through the night. She had spoken to Ainslie of his mother's stories. She didn't want Jacob and Hetti frightened. He had given his assurance that his mother would refrain when Ilsa's children were in hearing, but his tone let her know that he thought his children unharmed by what they heard. Her children were not among the ones sitting with Elizabeth, her alarm unnecessary. She didn't like silly folk tales. The books Ainslie read gave them instruction and entertainment at a higher level.

All was well in the yard. The racing appeared over. People were strolling to the food tables. Horses were being led to pasturing areas on the other side of Clark Road that Mr. McFarland had offered, with Ainslie's bribery, to the use of the horse owners. Groups of people were nodding and chatting. The Buchanan cousins were offering water and punch to anyone thirsty. A cluster of young men Ilsa didn't know set up a horseshoe toss game, and before she crossed the yard to find Ainslie, the bands began to play.

Her anxiety was growing. She began to worry that she had been too intense in her earlier demands and complaints to Ainslie. She didn't want her husband to see her as a petty, shrewish woman. In a very few years, she would be thirty. Her beauty would wane. Niggling, distressing thoughts drove her to find her husband across the yard, tuck her hand in his and cling to Ainslie for some moments. It had taken her so long to become truly happy, she didn't want anything to take this life away from her. She was tortured with the knowledge that other women found him attractive, and he might reciprocate. It was something she hadn't considered before today.

53

It was past mid-day when Ilsa returned to the house. Ainslie carried Emil in for her and she fed the boy and put him down to nap. Elizabeth gathered Andrew and Johnnie inside the house, gave them an ample meal, and put them down to rest, keeping them to their routine. The women left Tansie to sit by the sleeping room door with instructions to keep guests from entering and disturbing the boys.

Ainslie's brothers, Billy Frazier and Ain's nephews had been working as the day's roustabouts and jesters. Billy had smiles for everyone and a special one for Ilsa, for he had seen his wife transformed. The Buchanan brothers' wives, Elizabeth, Ilsa, and Tansie, prepared food in abundance — enough for a whole town. A famed German beer had been purchased and brought in kegs on a wagon. Jugs of cider and a cool tea of mint leaves spiced with ginger were on each table, and frequently replenished. Early that morning, Ainslie's oldest brother brought a small oak barrel of fine distilled and aged corn as a gift just for Ilsa and rolled it into the storage room. "Lassie," he said. "You might not want to taste it yourself, and Ains is not fond of its strength. It is a hearty drink. But heed this. If the mayor of Cossette comes to call, you must serve it."

Jimmie was a hearty man, more jovial than the other men in the family and less subtle. He reminded her of the men she had known as a child in Pennsylvania, and they had an easier rapport than she felt with Cameron or Andrew Buchanan. Jimmie told her that both the mayor and his imperious wife were known to prefer *Buchanan Corn* to any other liquor. But he advised her not to allow the barrel opened on this day, even for them. He explained that if she did, there would be none left at some important time, when it would be better appreciated than on a fête day like this. Ilsa followed Brother Jimmie's advice, and placed a thick draping cloth across the barrel lest some guest inadvertently wend his thirsty way into the storage room. But the guests were all gracious, men and women both. Few went into the house at all. The party kept to the grounds of Rohe Farm, happy with beer and cider.

It was all as Ainslie had promised, and not at all as rowdy as the Deutsche fetes Ilsa remembered from Pennsylvania. She and her sisters had been frightened when men had too much to drink and began to shout and brawl. But there was the music Ilsa remembered fondly. Ainslie had hired a German band to come and play at his Ohio Oktoberfest to suit the German beer he had purchased and the German lass he had married. There was a second band made of musical Buchanan nephews playing pipe, fiddle and mandolin. They were set to play alternately until the day turned dark and the last guest's wagon pulled away. Ilsa had glimpsed Hetti dancing with the other children at the edge of the yard near the bands. She saw a gleeful joy in her daughter that she had never seen before. Ilsa met Mrs. McFarland and Mrs. McKee and their daughters. Ilsa was happy to know her Clark Road neighbors at last. She also met Mrs. Tyler, and saw quickly why her son Jacob had troubles with the Tyler boys. Mr. Tyler had a scowl and they stayed at the party a very short time, just long enough to fill their plates and stuff their pockets with bread and yeast rolls.

Old grandfather Buchanan's log cabin had been the scene of the county's first Christian assembly, back in 1819. For that reason, Ilsa had asked him to step forward and pray the words of grace after the come-to-dinner bell had been rung. Both the German Church's *Pfarrer* Gruber and Reverend Johnson were present with their families. She knew it pleased Josiah to be given preference over the ordained ministers of the gospel. Ilsa's father-in-law had touched her arm as she walked by his chair. She stopped to ask what he needed. "Nothing but you, dear child. I'm proud that Ainslie had the sense to marry such a good woman." She knew then that she'd wrapped bindings around Ainslie's father as well as around his children.

When the guests had eaten, the tables cleared away and the band well warmed up, Ainslie pulled Ilsa to the clearing by the trees. They danced two reels and Ains called for a polka. Then Ains swung Ilsa out and around to loud applause and for a few minutes, before they needed to return to being Rohe Farm's host and hostess, Ilsa was the center of the dance circle, in Ainslie's arms, holding everyone's attention and feeling nothing but bliss.

All the afternoon, Ilsa and Ainslie had been so busy making sure that their guests had everything that they could desire, that neither stopped to eat. The only time Ilsa was away from her hostess duties was when she needed to care for Emil and Johnnie. Elizabeth had been a great help to her. Anna too. Daylight was going. Soon, the older people would go out to their wagons, and then the younger people would drift away also. Most of the guests had a long way to travel. It had been too grand a day for fatigue. The family women had been careful to clean the tables promptly, so there was little mess for her to attend to. Ainslie and his brothers were still outdoors packing the tables and benches into wagons and clearing barrels by torchlight.

In the quiet, dim house, Ilsa reflected on the day. For the first time as a mother, she had the opportunity to observe her two healthy children at a social gathering. Hetti was a particular favorite. More than one person had commented to Ilsa that her daughter was a beauty and a delight. She remembered that one of the horse owners said that Hetti was "the image of her mother in all but her dark hair and eyes." He meant it as a great compliment to both daughter and mother.

But for their difference in coloring, Hetti did look like Ilsa. They had the same heart-shaped face, the same nose and dimples. Her daughter was a child who gave Ilsa pride.

Ilsa could see that the little girl was a great beauty. Her rosy cheeks and dark curls captivated people. If children came to her and Ainslie as she hoped, they could have the Buchanans' dark hair and eyes. With Ilsa's softness, added to the Buchanan coloring, the children that she and Ains had together might all look like Hetti.

It had been a day of triumph for Ilsa. She knew that she had been perceived as that sad little Rohe woman down on Clark Road who had the infirm child. Franz's death had made her even more dismal in the township's eyes. She hated pity. Ilsa was the mistress of Rohe Farm and she was the much-envied wife of the dashingly handsome Mr. Ainslie Buchanan.

She liked arousing envy. She wished her parents had lived long enough to see her on this day. If her parents had been here today, Papa Mueller would have gotten down on his knees begging to dance with her, and Mutti would have felt people's pity.

O<<>>O

II

ILSA ROHE
~~~1845~~~

Josiah Buchanan's Farm

9 ~ Anna Finds A Voice

5 March 1845, Wednesday afternoon

Mr. Laughton, sir, my grandmother wishes that I should speak with you. I shall, but only because she asks that I do. And I have agreed— if you will allow that I may talk with you here, in my gran's parlor.

No, sir. I cannot endure to go anywhere else.

No, I have not been in school. Mr. Herbert comes here each Saturday morning to examine my week's work and set more for me that I not fall behind. He is determined that I not fall back, and that I will be ready for eighth grade come next September.

Oh, yes. He is very kind. But he is persistent too. Gran told me you went to college with our schoolmaster in Boston, and that you will be staying at Mr. Herbert's house while you visit in Ohio. He recommends you as an

—

honest man so she trusts you over other journalists who have wanted to talk to me.

Oh, no. Not since November, but I have promised Mr. Herbert that I will return to school soon. I couldn't speak for a very long time. I was ill.

No. I can't answer questions about what happened.

Yes, I understand. I will talk to you about what happened *if* I might be allowed to do it in my own way. In November, the constable and other men asked so many questions. I couldn't answer, but they wouldn't stop asking. They were angry with me as though I had done something wrong. My gran da and uncles made them stop and sent them from the house. And then for a long time I could not talk at all to anyone.

Reverend Johnson and Mr. Herbert have been good to me. Pastor told my family that I would talk when I was ready, and he told me that I should just talk to God until my voice came back.

Yes, it was good advice.

No. Mr. Herbert is my teacher and I like him. But I am not talking to you for him, but for my grandmother. Gran told me that you worked for *The North American Review* in Boston, and that journal has a fine reputation. She said you would write what was the truth. You're not a *newspaper* journalist, but a 'man of letters.'

No. I don't appreciate them at all. The newspapers told what happened, but they made mistakes.

Yes. I want what happened to be told correctly.

Gran says you will come visit every other weekday to talk to me, and that you are not in a hurry so you won't rush me. She says that you will show her everything you write down before you take it from the house. That is a good idea, in case I remember something wrongly.

No. It was difficult when I first began to talk again, but it no longer causes me much pain, though I tire soon when I talk. I will stop then.

Yes. I do know what the newspapers said.

I know because My Aunt Mattie brought them to my grandmother when my uncles wouldn't. Gran cut the columns out and put them between pages in my da's Bible. After I began to get better, I found them there.

I know that papers must report news, but their mistakes made me angry. The Dayton Transcript said Josiah was fifteen, but last November he was only nine. His birthday is August ninth. He was born in 1835. The Cincinnati newspaper said that I was fifteen. I am thirteen, Mr. Laughton. I was born in October of 1832 in Iwahata Township, Ohio, where my family used to live before my mother died. I was only a month thirteen in November.

Then we are agreed. I will tell you no lies, and you will write none.

I would like to begin by telling you about my mother, my first mother, and about my first family. I know that for your magazine you would rather hear about my second family, but I would like to tell you what happened from the beginning. Is this all right? May I tell it as I like, and in my own words?

Thank you. Then this is where I will begin. My mother's name was Fiona. She was born in Ireland near a town called Belfast in a place called Ulster. She told us that the land where she was born was foggy and damp, but never so cold in the winter as Ohio is. She didn't know that people had wells in their cellars, until she came here and found that in especially cold years, yard wells could freeze four inches thick in January and one must keep water for stock in shelter against freezing. My mother Fiona came across the Atlantic on a boat, then by stage across the mountains from Philadelphia on the National Road. It took her six months to go from Belfast to Dayton. She came to live with her uncle Johnnie Reid and his wife after her parents and brothers died. I never met his wife. She died before I was born.

In Ulster, Johnnie Reid was called Ian, but here he is called Johnnie. He came to Ohio when the road was just a trail through the mountains long ago when crossing a river meant you had to walk days out of your way to find a ferry. It was very hard. My mother was eighteen when she came across the ocean some years later. She traveled with groups of other people, strange to her, who were also coming to America. It was easier then.

Mr. Laughton, sir. It may take me days to tell you the whole of it this way that I want. Are you sure it is all right and that you have the time?

Then I'll be happy to tell you the all of it.

Everyone we knew called my mother Fee. Gran Da and my uncles and aunts, and even her uncle Johnnie, all of them called her Fee. She told us that in Ireland she had been called Ona. Neither name is as pretty to say as Fiona. Only my da and my gran called her by that, her real first name.

My mother Fiona was never timid. She wasn't afraid of catching the little green grass snakes in summer, or of subduing a mean rooster, or of racing my da down the lane, her sleek bay horse against his chestnut. My mother Fiona would ride her English mare fast as a bird can fly through the sky. Often as not, Mama won. Sir, it wasn't because Da made it easy for her. She was a fine rider.

My mother wasn't afraid of sickness either. She never made us bundle up if we didn't feel cold. My mother Fiona said that in Ireland when the contagions came, it hadn't mattered whether people took good care of themselves or not, some died and some didn't. So she said, "We should eat well and take reasonable care, and not worry." She said typhus and cholera, measles, and scarlet fever carried off the careful as well as the careless.

None of us worried about sicknesses until my sister Harriet took sick and died. We would have done anything to protect ourselves from the consumption, if we'd known what it was we should do. That coughing sickness killed my sister Harriet. It wasn't a contagion my mother knew about from Ireland.

Consumption is something that comes into people slyly. They don't even feel sick. But it wears on and on until they die, no matter what good care they get. That is what happened to my sister and then to my mother. Da and Mama took Harriet to Dayton when a famous doctor visited that city, but he couldn't cure Harriet. He had an elixir that he prescribed for her. He told my parents to keep her well fed and make sure she had fresh air every day. But that was the way we had lived, and my sister still had taken sick. When my parents were in Dayton with Harriet, the doctor asked to examine Mama because she looked pale and feverish to him, though she had no cough.

He told Da and Mama that it was likely that my mother had the consumption too. He advised that she take the elixir every day also and he arranged to have bottles of it sent to us every month.

It didn't help. Harriet died in June of 1841, and my mother died just after the year turned, on the fifth of January 1842. It had been not quite six months.

Harriet was just two years older than me, and we were fond sisters to each other. She loved me better than my sister Libby did. Harriet never nagged or teased, and she would keep my secrets forever if I asked. I miss her badly, almost as much as I miss my mother. I was ten when Harriet died. I turned eleven in October, just midway between their two deaths. I had missed my sister, and often cried for her when I was in bed at night, but it was the saddest day of my life when my mother died.

I think what it was that killed my mother was not just consumption, but that she couldn't endure my youngest brother and the other little baby being born. She hadn't coughed for a long time and had seemed well until those babies were born. Then just after, my mother began coughing hard. She took high fever and was spitting out blood. Gran was still staying with us because Johnnie was a wee infant, and because Da had been so pitiful worried about my mother.

Excuse me, Mr. Laughton. This may not seem to be part of what happened. But it is how we came to move to Anderson Township and how my da came to marry Ilsa Rohe and make my second family. It is important to me that you hear it right. I have thought about how I would tell you, so you would know how it was. If you have time for the telling.

Oh, then, I'm glad your magazine has given you so much time to stay here in the west and write about Ohio.

The everyday of our life was a happy time for me before our sister Harriet took sick. She was the sweetest sister anyone ever had. If she were alive now, she'd be fifteen and old enough to go to the county dances and dance with the boys. She wasn't so beautiful as my sister Libby. Our Harriet was pretty, though. She was the only one of us with blue eyes. All the rest of us have dark eyes like our mother and Da.

Harriet was very fair in her coloring. Her hair was a pale ginger red like Gran's is in behind the grey, and in summer my sister would get ginger colored freckles to match. My brother Andrew's hair is a bit toward the

---

61

ginger, but he has dark Buchanan eyes, not the blue that Harriet's were and Gran's are. Mama's hair was plain dark brown as is common among all the Reids and Buchanans. Libby calls plain brown hair all other names like chestnut and sable and brunette.

She would rather I be more particular in telling you what kind of brown hair each of us has, but that isn't what I find important in what I should tell you.

I see you are smiling.

I think for Mama and Da, Harriet and I were easy to overlook. Not because they didn't love us, but our sister Libby took most of the attention in the family. Libby is sometimes charming, but not all the time. She has what our mother Fiona called 'the Reid's prickly nature.' Mama was never what I would call prickly, but she said it came from her side of the family, her having been born Reid. Truly, Uncle Johnnie Reid is often crabby about what can't be changed. Our mother said that she was determined that she would eradicate the Reid fault out of Libby so that other people would find my oldest sister more tolerable.

If Mama and Da didn't have so much time for Harriet or me because of our sister's prickly ways, we knew that they loved us as much. Maybe they even loved us more because Libby was such a handful.

When Josiah came along, we were excited because he was a boy, and Da naturally was happy to have one of his own sort in the house at last and not be outnumbered by women.

I was young but I remember what Libby did at Josie's welcoming ceremony so well. The day Josie was taken to church for the first time, we three girls were so proud. Gran Da and Gran, and my uncles, aunts and cousins were sure to all be in church service that day. We didn't yet live here, but the church in Cossette serves five townships and is near to the County's line. The farm where we lived is four miles from town on the other side of the line. Not too far, unless there is a bad snow or the creeks rise too high. So we have always gone to the same church as our relations who live here in Anderson Township.

Reverend Johnson said a prayer to welcome Josiah in front of the whole congregation and we weren't downstairs in Sunday school, but in the church and in front of the whole congregation. Pastor said, "We are not our own, but God's." He was quoting John Calvin, but I didn't know that then. It is what Reverend Johnson says when any new child is introduced to our congregation and blessed with his name.

I would never forget that day. And if my sister Harriet were here, she would tell it to you just like I do. We talked often to each other of that day when our brother Josiah was welcomed into the congregation of our church. Mama told us the story too, so it will *never* leave my mind. Mama let Libby hold our new babe at the front of the church, because she was already in school and nine years old. Libby thought Josiah was hers, not Mama's or God's. Da used to say that Libby had an "audacious" nature. He wasn't as annoyed by Libby as Mama was. He was easier about our failings.

When Reverend Johnson had finished his prayers and blessings, it was time for our family to leave the front of the church, and retire to our family pew. Mama went to take our baby Josiah from Libby's arms.

"No, Mama," Libby spoke up, "*I'm* holding the baby."

She said it right there in front of everyone. Her voice wasn't at all quiet or respectful. Mama turned red, and tucked her bonnet down.

The Reverend looked very stern, but he nodded to Mama and Libby. My audacious sister Libby proudly carried Josie back to the pew in line with us. Da stood there at the aisle to seat us as a family, and he was frowning when Libby passed him to go back into the pew. It was only then that she let Mama take our baby back.

"Libby is going to be in trouble with Da," Harriet whispered to me as we slid into the pew. I didn't whisper back because I didn't want to be in trouble.

Our grandparents were never so upset with Libby as our mother was. Gran Da favored her, in spite of her acting so like the Reids. Gran often defended her, but then Gran tolerates most people once she knows them.

Gran told Harriet and me that Libby had done very hateful things when she was a wee girl before we were born. Once, she deliberately turned over the butter churn sending sour milk leaking all over the floor of the farmhouse kitchen. Gran said my sister couldn't talk yet, but she was all that angry because Mama wouldn't give her another sugar biscuit.

The way Gran told us that story it seemed like she was telling us that she knew Libby would outgrow teasing Harriet and me, just like she outgrew turning over butter churns. She didn't intervene on our behalf when Libby tormented us with her criticisms the way our mother did. Gran wished us to be more tolerant of Libby bothering and picking at us and not complain so much about our sister. She told us to be grateful to the Lord that Libby didn't slap or hit us as some older children did to the younger.

Mr. Laughton? I have to say that Gran was right. Libby is very dear to me now. She rides here twice a week from the McKee place. She helps me with anything in my schoolwork that I find difficult, and she is teaching me to knit a vest for Andrew. She bought the yarn for me from the McFarlands who keep sheep and spin yarn. Libby and Billy have little money to spend. It was a great kindness. I am working hard to learn. One must be very particular and precise in counting to become such a fine knitter as my sister Libby is. Perhaps particular, precise, and prickly go together in people?

Oh, see now. I've made you smile. If you please, sir, I'd like to stop talking now. I think I've talked more today than I've ever done.

O<<>>O

10~ Coming to Clark Road

7 March 1845, Friday Afternoon

Mr. Laughton, if you remember, on Friday I told you about Libby and about the Reid family's prickliness. It has made me worry that you might think my brothers also were sometimes contrary. They were never. Not even Josiah, who was Papa and Mama's first son after three girls, and likely to be spoiled.

Please believe me on this. Mr. Herbert will tell you that Josie was a good boy in school. Mr. Herbert doesn't know my littlest brother yet, but Johnnie seldom cries or makes a fuss— unless perhaps he has hurt himself, and then he usually just gets big tears in his eyes. He is three now and I see him often. He is not in school yet and will come for a day here with Gran and me. Andrew started school after Christmas, He was old enough then, and Aunt Mattie thinks it best that he be there with other children. Mr. Herbert will tell you what a good boy he is.

Our mother Fiona never said where a pleasant nature came from in the family, but that she admired the Buchanans more than she did her own people. I think the pleasantness came through our Da's family. Josiah was always wise and kind, and Buchanan through and through.

He looked like Da, but he looked even more like Gran Da. His nose was thinner than Da's and his eyes darker. He was taller than most boys his age, and that comes from the Buchanans.

Gran Da can look harsh, but he isn't. Josiah had that same look from the time he was a baby. He was well named for Gran Da. He certainly didn't go looking for faults in others. He was laughing all the time and never took offense when it wasn't intended. Even if it were, like on the playground at school, he wasn't a boy quick to argue or fight.

Josiah learned to sit a gentle horse before he was three, and by four he could ride along the road beside Da without being tied in, or ever slipping out of the saddle. He was good with all kinds of beasts. When we started to Dry Creek School after we moved to the house on Clark Road, Josie was seven. Our brother Josiah didn't want to ride in the schoolhouse wagon with the rest of us. He thought it went too slow. He asked our Da to let him ride to school. Da refused, and told him he could fly if the school wagon was too slow for him. It made all of us laugh. It made Andrew buzz around the big room with his arms flapping like a bird flying.

Da did let Josie ride alone, but never for so far, only over to help Gran Da or to see our cousins whose farm is behind Gran Da's by way of Agatha Lane. He couldn't allow him ride so far as the school. Da asked Josie, "And what's the sense in us paying a tax so there is a school house wagon for the township children if our own don't ride it? You'll go with your sister, and be grateful you don't have to walk the three miles." But our father promised Josie that on his tenth birthday he would get a fine horse, all his own, to ride to school if his grades stayed high in every subject. Josiah always did his schoolwork, and never made excuses or begged off school as I sometimes did. By the time school ended last June, he was ahead in every subject and working in the sixth grade arithmetic book, though he was not yet quite nine. Da was very proud of him. I'm nearly five years older but I had to work hard that my brother Josie not overtake me.

Our next brother is Andrew. He was born when I was eight. He was a jolly, laughing baby, but quiet and not so noisy as our baby brother Johnnie is. Mama let Harriet hold Andrew in front of the congregation for his church welcome, just as she had let Libby hold Josiah.

Harriet was nine and she was proud to be Mama's pick. I felt some envy, but I was glad it wasn't Libby who got to hold Andrew. When Andrew was welcomed, Reverend Johnson said the exact same thing he had at Josiah's christening, "We are not our own, but God's." He said it in his strong and Godly voice and Baby Andrew almost jumped from Harriet's arms. He then read a long sermon that was written by John Calvin.

On the drive home from church that Sunday, Da entertained us by telling us about John Calvin who lived centuries ago. I learned that he had been a great Christian reformer. It was more interesting to hear of the man, than to hear the sermons he preached. He had to flee to Switzerland because the Catlicks didn't like what he thought. I remember wondering how far away Switzerland was from our country.

The older students in my school in Iwahata Township had to learn the continents, the countries of the world and all the states in our own country, but I was only in second grade then and didn't get tested. I liked to listen to the older student's lessons. I knew Switzerland was very far, beyond the ocean, beyond Ireland.

As we drove home that day from church, Da said that though John Calvin was a fine man, Reverend Johnson might be a better parson if he quoted less from preachers and more from King James. Mama and Libby laughed as though it were a great joke. Harriet, Josie and I didn't see the humor. Americans didn't hold with kings. We looked at each other but didn't say anything. After dinner that afternoon, Da read to us from the Bible, just like he did every Sunday. When he finished the reading, he held up the book. He told us our church in Cossette honors The Oxford Edition of the *King James* Bible.

Harriet and I were embarrassed because we had seen that book so many times, and we had never made mind of its full title. Then Da told us King James was a Scot king before he was an English king, and that made his Bible even more valuable to our family. Da spent more time explaining things to us than our mother did. Our mother Fiona, was tart and sparse with her words, but she was not so quick to correct others as our sister is. She was only quick to correct Libby.

Mr. Laughton, We were rich in that we had a lively mother who loved us, and a Da who read to us and wanted us to know things. I knew early from my friends at Elderwood School, that most children have fathers who scarce read at all and never talked to them. They have to depend on school to learn. I worry for my brothers because of what happened. I know Gran and my uncles do too. Andrew was not yet four when our mother Fiona died. I fear he has forgotten her already. So much has happened since then. Baby Johnnie knew our mother only but a few days. The boys won't remember the family we were, or how it was before Harriet and Mama took sick. I might forget to tell them all the things that I remember, and then they won't ever know.

Libby won't think to tell them. She is a person who does things, more than one who remembers things. I suppose she is like our mother Fiona in that. I'm more Buchanan, like Da. We like to read and we don't forget anything to do with the family. Libby says we have an unfortunate tendency to ignore disorder, but I don't agree. We are orderly with what we like to do. Andrew is like us. I don't know about Johnnie yet. He might be more Reid.

When my family lived in Iwahata Township, our farm was near Mama's uncle Johnnie Reid's farm. Johnnie Reid had been a famous jockey in Ireland, but he hurt his head in a fall at a jump, and then he came to America. My mother Fiona told me his wife was a kind older American woman who he married late in life. She encouraged Johnnie to send money to Ireland for my mother to come here and be a daughter to them. They had no children of their own what had lived.

Mr. Laughton, my da grew up here in Anderson Township. It was when he was courting Mama that he bought a farm near Uncle Johnnie Reid's. He moved farther away from his family so his bride could stay nearer hers. I think that was a sacrifice and a romantic thing for him to do. It tells you what he was like. My da always found it satisfying to do grand things for others when he could.

I don't want you to think he was foolish, he wasn't. My da and my mother Fiona were thrifty and careful and taught us not to be greedy. The farm we owned in Iwahata Township was a smaller farm in size than the one Da bought here, though it was well large enough for a good corn crop and Da's horses. He built a post and beam house and good barn and stable. Our home there was near to our school.

I loved that house and did not want to move here to Clark Road. But after my mother died, my dad was doing very poorly and there was trouble with the baby's feeding and his bowels. Gran had to stay with us to work out the right milk for Johnnie. None of the women in our family or among our friends could take him to nurse, as none had an infant of her own as was still a nursling. We were very troubled and didn't know what we'd do for him without a mother. Sometimes milk from cows doesn't suit a baby. Our tiny wee boy was sick so much with the diarrhea. Gran took it on herself to buy a nanny goat from a French family who lived in her township. We brought it back to Anderson Township just weeks later when we moved. Gran made a concoction of goat's milk, syrup, and a few grains of salt. It suited him. His cry grew stronger and he grew fat.

Gran is good with babies. None of hers died as infants or as children, not one. And that is very unusual and a source of pride for my grandmother. But three of her children have died since they were grown. I could list them, but I don't think it is what your magazine would find interesting.

My gran was still afraid to leave us with just the housemaid after the baby began to thrive, because my da would sit in his chair in the parlor and drink corn whiskey from afternoon through the evening every day. He went out to tend the farm and his horses for just a few hours in the morning and came home to look sorrowful and drink.

He wouldn't eat but porridge, and not enough of that. He just wanted his drink. I ought not to have said that, but it is true, and I want this story to be right. My gran may choose to take it out of your journal, and I know you should respect that, if it is her choice. But I will tell you what was.

Gran turned harsh with Da and said, "Fiona's darlin' children deserve better than you're givin' them, Ainslie. Get up out of your chair. Fee's gone and buried, but these young ones aren't." Gran nagged Da that he was strong and well, and should get back up working, and that he needed to find some cheer in life to bring to us children after all we had lost.

Gran Da didn't like that Gran stayed with us so much, but I heard my gran tell him that she had been all the mother poor Fiona had in the world. And that now she was all the mother that we had in the world. During this time, Gran Da missed our gran terrible. He'd ride the nine miles to and fro every day to see her, and complain that she was forgetting where she lived. Finally, when our mother had been buried nearly a month, Gran Da had the idea to offer my da the farm and house that had once belonged to our Uncle Francis.

That way Gran Da cleverly got his wife back.

Our uncle Francis Buchanan owned the farm across the road before we did. He was the oldest of my grandparents' children but he was a bachelor, so his farm went to Gran Da when he died. It has a fine brick house, but was empty. Gran Da had shut it up when our uncle died. He grieved too much to allow tenants to move there. But he allowed us the house. A horseman my da knew wanted our property in Iwahata, for it had good stables. On Gran Da's advice, Da sold it to him.

Soon after, when our farm's sale gave Da the money, Gran Da sold Uncle Francis's farm with all its house, many acres and good equipment to my da. But we moved only so that our baby Johnnie and the rest of us could be nearer our grandparents.

After we moved across the road, we were closer to all our Buchanan relations, but Da felt we'd abandoned my mother Fiona's uncle Johnnie Reid. Our mother's uncle Johnnie is old and feeble, and he had no family but us. He was going to sell his farm and move into a boarding house in Cossette. But Gran says family by marriage or by blood makes no difference. She said that Johnnie Reid deserved better than a boarding house. She has made him welcome here. He refused to live with Da and us because we had too many children and therefore too much confusion. He proclaims loudly that he dislikes noise and rushes frantically around to protest confusion.

Oh, Mr. Laughton. I do like it when you smile.

I help Gran take care of Gran Da and Uncle Johnnie Reid now and the two of them make a lot of work for her. She needs me, but she is ever after me to go back to school. I know I should. It is a good school and Mr. Herbert is a good teacher. It was not too hard for us to change to Dry Creek School when we left our home in Iwahata Township to move here.

We missed friends, but it had already been so sorrowful for us to lose Mama and Harriet, it didn't seem to matter where we lived. It took seven wagons to move our furnishings from Iwahata Township, and more wagons to move the farm's working equipment. And it was a terrible month to move. February is so cold and bleak. My uncle Cameron took us in his carriage.

Da and a drover moved the stock, but not the chickens, geese, rabbits, dogs or cats, or our precious milk goat. My uncles and older cousins did the crating and carting. All the Buchanans helped us. Our aunts supervised the cleaning of the new house so it would be nice for us to move into. And it was shiningly clean and there wasn't a cobweb anywhere.

Libby said that being near Gran Da would help our father right himself. It did, because Da began eating and going to church with us again. He soon again read to us in the evening as he used to do, and he wanted to see Baby Johnnie and hold him for a while in the evenings before supper. He swore off the drink and came back to his old self, reading to us and listening to us tell him of what we were doing.

Our family began to feel we were back together, even though we still missed our mother and Harriet most painfully and of course it wasn't like it had been when they were with us.

I might not want to say Libby was right, but she was. I must admit that. Da hired women to come in and help, and Gran gave them their duties so that they wouldn't take advantage of Libby being so young. Libby was happy to have the job of running our new home and taking care of us. She was out of school. Da had pleaded with her to go to board at the young women's seminary in Dayton. When our mother died, she had good reason to refuse. I think she felt responsible for us all.

Sir, I have talked a very long time. May I be excused now?

O<<>>O

~~~O<<>>O~~~

11 ~ Ghosts

10 March 1845, Monday afternoon

Da insisted we start at Dry Creek School as soon as we moved here. I try to keep things in order when I tell you how everything happened, but I don't always remember the order. I apologize for that, Mr. Laughton. It was February of 1842 and it was very cold when we started school here. Our Mother Fiona had been dead just over a month. I was eleven and Josiah was six. Andrew was nearly three. Libby had graduated from eighth grade the June before.

When Josie and I went to school here, Andrew cried. He was still a little boy and it was hard for him to see us leave him behind. He had Libby and the baby, and our new housemaid, for company. Gran was across the street and coming in and out all the time, but it wasn't the same and he missed us. With our mother's death and then the move, we had missed school often, and he'd grown used to our company. We knew he was confused by so much as had happened. Gran assured Josie and me that Andrew would adjust to our being away, and not to mind his tears. He would get to go to school in his turn.

We first met Mr. Herbert at Dry Creek School. He was very kind and welcoming. Mr. Higgins drove the wagon team that picked us up for school and brought us back home. Perhaps you have met Mr. Higgins? Mr. Higgins is the custodian of the school property. Mr. Higgins is very old, almost as old as Johnnie Reid and older than Gran Da. But he is ever busy, never cranky, and always working for our school.

You haven't yet? Well now, if you are staying with Mr. Herbert while you are in Ohio, you will surely meet him. Dry Creek School was built on land he donated, and it is only a short walk from Mr. Herbert's house. That house where you stay was Mr. Higgins farmhouse once, but he gives its use free to the schoolmaster of Dry Creek School. We wouldn't have a school if he hadn't given the land. He built a small house behind his farmhouse and moved into it, so that the farmhouse proper would be an enticement for a teacher to come to Anderson Township. That was a very good idea, for Mr. Herbert makes extra money over what the township pays him for teaching by renting the extra rooms.

I'm sure you know that Mr. Herbert rents out rooms in the house. Constable Davies is one of the men who live there so you may have seen him. I'm not eager to see him if I go back to school. I hope if I go back to school that he will always be away working in town, and I will never see him. I never want him to ask me any questions again.

Please don't write this down, but Constable Davies is a rough and impatient man. I would be so harsh as to say he is cruel and rude. You should watch out for him. You probably don't have such men in Boston. I'm happy to talk about Mr. Higgins who is good and kind to everyone. If Mr. Herbert didn't tell you, you might think that Mr. Higgins is merely our janitor and driver, and not take notice of him. But you should know he is a very important man in Anderson Township for all that he looks humble.

Mr. Higgins' little house is only the size of a worker's cabin, but he told Josie, Jacob, and me that he liked it better than his old house. He said his old house was filled with the ghosts of those who had passed on. Somehow, that idea of Mr. Higgins' ghosts made me miss my old house more. I think I'd like the ghosts of my mother and Harriet around me, but Gran tells me that the living must stay with the living. She says that ghosts are never good. I disbelieve her. I think ghosts can be good dead if they were good alive.

Oh, Mr. Laughton, I can see from your face that you agree with Gran. It is no matter. Our old house in Iwahata Township belongs to other people now. I can never go back there to visit my mother and Harriet. Though I want to, and I would if I could.

Mr. Higgins does not get pay to drive the four-horse schoolhouse wagon team to pick up those of us who live far down Clark Road. He does it because he likes us and wants us to be educated. Gran says he never had proper schooling and always felt poorer for its lack, though he was a very successful farmer and is not at all poor now. Mr. Herbert drives the smaller wagon to pick up the children far down Dry Creek Road. Our old schoolmaster in Iwahata never cared how we might get to and from school. I think he was happier when we students stayed home because of bad weather and glad when the distance was too great for small children to attend on their own. He wouldn't have to bother with little ones then.

In Iwahata, Da would ride us to school on his horse or he'd drive our carriage, if the weather was poor. But not all families were able to do that. He told us to appreciate that Mr. Herbert and Mr. Higgins are very good to us and treat them with not only respect, but gratitude.

Excuse me, Mr. Laughton. I know this isn't what you'd hoped I'd be telling you. The school has nothing to do with what happened at all. But I'm supposed to go back to school before the first of April. It frightens me a little to think of leaving here. Some of the students may ask me questions and stare or look at me oddly. If you don't mind, I think talking about school will help me become accustomed to the idea of it. That's all right, isn't it?

Thank you. I think this is enough for today. I'll see you on Wednesday.

I don't want to be disagreeable, but to be truthful, I think you and Gran are wrong about ghosts.

O<<>>O

~~~O<<>>O~~~

12 ~ Meeting Mr. Rohe

12 March, 1845 - Wednesday afternoon

My little brother Andrew is six now and this year he goes to Dry Creek School himself. I saw him Sunday and he told me that there are five other new children in school. That means there are now 20 students since I dropped away in November when there were only eighteen. Andrew is fond of Mr. Herbert. And my brother is bright and good with arithmetic, especially for someone so young. I hope I haven't fallen far behind. It was important to my mother that we girls, Libby, Harriet, and I complete eighth grade. She told us many times that she would be happy to see us go to the seminary in Dayton. She'd be sorry that Libby refused to go. Our mother Fiona said that if we had adequate enough educations, we could become teachers. Or if we married, we could present ourselves in any kind of society. Our mother said that these were modern times and we should not allow ourselves to be backward women.

Mr. Herbert said that when he went to school in Boston, he was in a school building that was bigger than any building in Cossette or Taylorsville. He told us that every class in his school had its own classroom and its own teacher. Mr. Herbert said that a school in Boston might have eighty or even a hundred children attending all at once. Our school in Iwahata Township had only eight students the year we moved away. Our teacher there was a parson when he wasn't being the schoolmaster. My da didn't think kindly on the Reverend Elderwood's kind of preaching. I didn't think kindly of Master Elderwood's teaching, but I never said so.

My da said that Master Elderwood preached Hell but forgot Heaven.

Master Elderwood did his preaching in country church. We never went there. We are in Reverend Johnson's congregation at the Christian Church in Cossette where all of our family has attended since it was built.

Da had to go see Master Elderwood once because he had twice mistakenly marked a paper of Libby's with a poor grade when all her answers were correct. If Libby had had a teacher like Mr. Herbert, she might have wanted to go to the seminary in Dayton. But she didn't. Dad also spoke to Master Elderwood once because when I was little, he used the ruler on my hands if I forgot and used my left hand to make my letters. I think our teacher there only approved of Harriet.

Master Elderwood didn't like Libby, and he told Da she would not go far in the world unless she learned to curb her sassiness. It made Da laugh. Da said he'd be happy if Libby stayed right here in Ohio and didn't go far in the world. Mr. Elderwood and Da didn't see things the same way at all. Da was glad that our move gave us a new teacher.

Oh, but Dry Creek School *is* important to what I'm telling you because it is how Josiah and I first became friends with Jacob Rohe, the first member of that family we knew, and school is the reason we met Mr. Rohe.

This is how it happened we came to know them.

When the weather is terribly cold or there is a blizzard, Dry Creek School's basement is used for games at recess periods. And once we slept there all night when there was such a sudden storm come up that no one could get home. Constable Davies had to get word to our families that we'd stay in the school building until the storm lessened and that they shouldn't worry.

Mr. Herbert and one of the eighth grade boys went up in the school attic to get quilts and pads so we'd all be warm and comfortable. They did help make the floor seem softer. We girls were given the warmest corner of the basement. I was glad we girls had our own sleeping place away from the big boys' antics. Some of the older boys were mean and rude. But my da said every child needed an education even the mean and rude ones, and that we needed to learn that there were mean and rude people in the world as part of our education. He liked that Mr. Herbert didn't want us to call him Master. Da said that it was because Mr. Herbert didn't approve of slavery any more than we Buchanans did.

Mr. Herbert watched out for us. He tried to make a party of staying at school over night so we wouldn't feel afraid and miss our families.

Mr. Herbert found a tin of biscuits in his desk and we shared them, and some of us had things left in our lunch buckets. We shared them too. Then Mr. Herbert had us sing. We sang rounds, and hymns, and school songs, and pretty soon the little ones were soothed. But that night, little Jacob Rohe had a nightmare. I didn't wake up, but the next morning when Mr. Herbert left us to go and see if the snow had stopped, the Tyler boys began teasing Jacob and calling him a baby because he'd cried out in the night. They are extra big because they were held back more than once, and they like to pick on younger kids. My brother Josiah stood up for Jacob. Josie was going to fight both Abe and John Tyler if they didn't stop pestering Jacob. They were yelling at each other the way boys do. I ran over to stand by my brother to defend him if they tried to hurt him or Jacob. I would have fought to protect them.

Mr. Herbert came back and when he found out what was happening he said that neither Abe nor John Tyler was as brave as Jacob Rohe when they were in first grade. He made us sit together on the floor and he told Abe and John that he had seen tears flow on both of them when they were younger. He said that anyone, even grown men could have a nightmare. Mr. Herbert said that even President John *Tyler*, who is so brave and honorable that he once gave up his seat in the Senate rather than cast a vote against his principles, could cry out from a nightmare.

After that, Jacob and Josiah were fast friends, and sat together in the schoolhouse wagon and on the lunch bench.

I'd missed my own friends from the time when we lived in our old home and went to Madison School, but I met Suzanna Marie Molesworth, Lucretia Brown, and Jane Bradshaw who were near my age and they befriended me. Whenever they can, they come to visit me here at Gran's. I think I will be all right when I go back to school. But I don't wish to have the other children stare at me.

Two days after the night we spent in the school basement, Mr. Rohe came to see Da. Mr. Rohe had come to thank us. Jacob told his father that Josie had stood up for him against bigger boys. Da called us to come downstairs and meet Mr. Rohe. He took Josie's hand and said that he was "happy his son had made as good a friend as young Josiah Buchanan." He took my hand too and said we were well-raised children and he was proud to know us.

When I told Gran about Mr. Rohe's visit to thank Josie, she made a face. I have never forgotten that, though it was two years ago or more. I think this is what she said. If it isn't exactly word-by-word right, it is almost right. I hadn't met Jacob and Hetti' s mother yet and I can't ever forget it.

"That German woman doesn't have any sense," Gran said. "She doesn't allow herself to encourage friendliness with other women along Clark Road, and instead spends her time painting the post box or haulin' that sad child around the yard. And the husband, poor man, raises cows when every farm for miles around has its milk cow, and there is no big city nor proper city at all, nearby to buy the milk shy of Dayton."

You might not want to write that down either, Mr. Laughton. Gran will surely cross it out if you do. I love my gran and I didn't sass her back. She is rarely hard on people in her talk, and never in what she does. She didn't know the Rohe family then.

I thought Mr. Rohe was a very polite and nice man. I know now that he had sent Rohe Farm's cheeses all the way to Dayton to sell in stores. He did make a lot of money on his cows, but Da told me that Mr. Rohe was a humble man and he wasn't one to show off or talk about his business, so Gran didn't know.

The paintings on Rohe Farm's post box and window shutters were a whimsy and helped me not mind so much that we had to leave the home we knew in Iwahata after our mother died and come to live near Gran. I saw them twice a day from the school wagon. What happened wasn't the fault of the paintings, or of Emil.

Mr. Laughton, I'd watched for Rohe Farm since I was very small when we would drive Clark Road to come visit our grandparents. I watched for it all fourteen miles, not because it signaled we were close to Gran and Gran Da's, but because it was the only place I had ever seen that had been made so pretty. It did have paintings on the porch and post box. I wish you could have seen it. Most houses are wood or log and not painted at all. If I had a farm, I'd paint the house white with a red door and I'd paint leaves and white flowers all along the top planks of the fences. My farm would be circled in a daisy chain no matter the season.

The house at Rohe Farm was just down the road hardly more than a quarter mile. You must go past there to come here or go back to Mr. Herbert's house. The house is gone now, though. After what happened, my uncles and our neighbors burned the house down. My uncles had the right to burn it because it is our property now. They burned it to the ground. I didn't see the fire because I was still in bed most of the day and no one told me about what was happening. For a long time, no one told me very much. And it grieved Gran too much when I asked. My aunt Mattie is the only one who tells me serious things without crying. My uncles run tears as much as Gran does.

Yes, it did. It had decorations inside the house as well as out. There were birds and flowers painted on the cabinet doors and on some of the furniture. My baby brother Johnnie first began talking because he liked a blue bird with a yellow beak. It was painted on the lowest door of the shoe cabinet. Bird was his first word, though he said "ber". He couldn't get the last of it quite right in the beginning. He said the cabinet painting was *his* bird, and at bedtime he'd want to kiss it goodnight after he had kissed Papa.

My brother Johnnie was so little when it all happened. I hope he doesn't remember it. I hope he only remembers the bird on the cabinet door.

I wish you could have seen the house. But I'm glad that my family burned it down. If I go back to school, I'd have to go past it. I don't think I could stand seeing it, and no other family would ever want to live there now. I wish I could have watched it burn down.

O<<>>O

81

~~~O<<>>O~~~

III

ILSA ROHE

Rohe Farm, Anderson Township, Ohio
1844

13 ~ An Early Winter

After the grand harvest celebration, autumn moved closer to winter. Winds came with a sharp drop in temperature. There had been some rain in the first week or two, but now it was dry and freezing hard at night. Ainslie had been busy insuring that the pumps and wells were protected from icing through, the latches on the barn, stable and tack building's windows and doors were oiled and tight in preparation for Ohio's winter. He had two farms to consider, and he and his brother Cameron were also double-checking their father's property. It was becoming more difficult for old Josiah to supervise all that needed supervision on a farm. The old man's bones ached. The cold weather made it hard for him to do all he wanted.

Josiah had stubbornly refused to hire a foreman. His sons didn't want workers on their father's property to take advantage of the old man and slack off doing what was necessary.

For Ilsa, winter was a time of rest. She was already well prepared for the quiet, indoor season and looking forward to it. The storage room was full of barrels and tins, lines of dried tomatoes, apricots, peaches and other fruits hung from the attic rafters.

She felt she went into hibernation like the wild animals. The days shorter, the nights longer gave her more quiet time. The children spent more of their time indoors. There was less dirt in the house or on their clothes. While there were also many inconveniences to the season, she had planned for them. Ilsa insisted that Benjamin's men clear the kitchen gardens and do a good cleaning of the coops and privies, then dose them with lime. Those things needed to be done before hard freezes came. Ilsa strung lines from the hooks high in the mortar of the chimney to the hooks in the logs at the back entrance to the great room for hanging wash indoors, but still out of the way, to dry when it was so cold she or Tansie's fingers would freeze to the line if they tried to do the task outdoors. It seemed to her that the children, acting like little bear cubs, sensed the seasonal change and took to quiet games, reading by the fire, and earlier bedtimes.

She enjoyed that time more now for the companionship of Ainslie and Anna. Particularly in the evenings after the children went to bed. Ainslie went to bed at nine, like her father and Franz had. Men were so physical in their duties their bodies tired. They took no time to sit for a moment and take a cup of tea as women liked to do. Men worked a harder day, but women worked a longer day. She and Anna often sat past ten in front of the fire doing the mending. Ilsa liked the company.

One November morning, Ainslie was planning to ride into Cossette early and tend to farm business and go to the bank. He'd dressed in finer clothes than his usual work togs. The man loitered until the children were off to school and Tansie had arrived. Ilsa fed Emil, always a slow process, and Johnnie and Andrew were playing on the floor near her son's cart. After that, she had a moment, and she sat with Johnnie to try to get him to count to ten with her. He would be two just before Christmas. But she had started young with Jacob and Hetti too, and they loved arithmetic when they went to school. Andrew was helping by counting along with them. Ainslie teased her for being overly zealous with her mothering, but she knew he was happy that his children were so fond of her.

He came to kiss her goodbye. She put down the small kindling sticks that she and the boys were using and got to her feet, fussing that Ainslie hadn't eaten enough at breakfast and ought to at least put some of the little sugar creams she had made the day before into his saddle pack.

He took what she offered and promised that he would be home for dinner by noon, and he asked that she or Tansie prepare a dessert for the orchard workers. It should be a special treat, that after his dinner, he could carry down to the migrant crew in the farm's family orchard. They were doing post-harvest work, stripping the trees and pruning them back. They had been on Rohe Farm for a day and a half and would be in their wagons by nightfall to camp at the next farm on their schedule. They worked hard and he'd pay them this afternoon, but he wanted to leave them with good feelings and a desire to come back the next year to harvest and strip for him. He planned that he would tote whatever Ilsa and Tansie could prepare down to the crew, after he'd returned from his business in town and had his meal. He was affectionate with her, and she followed him out on the porch to wave him away.

The morning was easier than usual. There had been no spills, no spats, no forgotten mittens or lunch buckets. The older children had gone off to school, clean and laughing, with their schoolwork finished. Emil settled easily to sleep after his mid-day meal of gruel and mashed vegetables, and Johnnie and Andrew, who had been fed before Emil, would soon be ready to go to nap.

Tansie had worked hard all morning, She seemed full of energy, but now Ilsa could see she was tired. She released Tansie to go home and fix her son's dinner before the clock struck noon. Knowing that the woman often would fall asleep after eating and return later than the expected one o'clock, Ilsa had begun allowing her two hours at mid-day. They had built a good understanding over the past year. She kept Tansie at the same pay, though she was working a shorter day. It was to Ilsa's benefit. She knew she could call on Tansie to help her in time of need, as when a child took sick, or on a Sunday should guests make her necessary in the kitchen.

Ilsa deliberated on what kind of a treat she should bake for Ainslie's orchard workers. She did not choose his favorite, *apfelstrudel,* for the crew, expecting that they may have had enough of apples, having worked in the orchards from the first of spring thinning jobs on township farms until stripping at the end of fall. Instead she'd made a *stollen.* It was more bread-like and could be cut with ease. She made three that morning, and sent one home with Tansie as she left. *Stollen* was a Christmas-time treat. She looked at her calendar and saw it was November 20. She was early by nearly five weeks, but she thought that the men in the crew would like it.

The fragrance of baking still filled the room. She would cut a piece for Ainslie's dessert and save the rest for the children after school. Ilsa picked up Johnnie who had been playing lazily with his wooden animals on the slates and hugged him. It was nearly time to put the boys down for a nap. Andrew knew what was coming and put the toys up on their shelf and trudged into the sleeping room. After Johnnie used the *töpfchen*, Ilsa pleased with him, lifted him into the crib. Both boys' eyes soon closed.

Just after the clock struck noon, Ainslie rode into the yard, his town business completed. He'd dressed finely that morning. In the furor of doing all she had to do before the school wagon picked up the children, Ilsa had scarcely noticed. He was wearing his white vest and red cravat with his good, tall boots. The sun was lower, and from the window it seemed that winter was waving a greeting to him. Most of the leaves had fallen. Only a few clung to each branch. More sun came into the small wood near the road, but the sun was weaker.

She watched as he tied the mare to the post and crossed the short yard to mount the steps to the house. She could feel an excitement grow and begin to bubble in her chest, and since she loved the feeling that the man induced in her, she was smiling when she opened the door. He came in looking so dapper, she reached to brush his jacket. As he stepped into the house, she thought no other woman in Ohio or Pennsylvania —or anywhere else in the world —not even in France or Germany or far India could claim such a fine man. She could smell the crisp, cold morning on him, and a faint odor of his horse's sweat. It was good, but better was Ainslie's own smell, like bark and crushed plane tree leaves. It pulled her toward him. For a few moments she could claim him away from his thoughts of the stables or the farms or horses or his children to touch his hair and his ears and his neck. She took ownership of his particular fragrance through her fingertips.

He washed and changed his clothes and boots as she set the table. At supper they sat at each end, but at noon with just the two, she moved her service to where Jacob usually sat to Ainslie's right. They ate together. He was quiet, after riding to town and back that morning. It was close to ten miles round trip, and she didn't expect that he would be interested in talking. She carried the conversation. Ilsa told Ainslie of the housework she and Tansie had done that morning and how nicely his baby Johnnie used the boys' night pee pot just as big brother Andrew did. It was too cold for them to go out to the privy.

She'd prepared a good Deutsche dinner for him. He quickly finished the bowl of rabbit stew she'd prepared. She'd used juniper berries, and the smell and his greed told her she'd used just enough. She got up and sliced a thick piece of the *stollen* and served it to him. Ilsa didn't return to her chair, but stood by his, very close to him. Ainslie fondled her with one hand

—

as he bit into the sweet bread he held in his other. Then when she moved away to prepare the orchard crew's basket, he followed her to stand behind her and nibble the back of her neck. Goose bumps raced down one side of her body from the place where his lips touched her neck, straight down to her toes. He pulled her around to kiss her breasts, biting at them lightly through the twice fabric of her apron and gown.

His elbow would have knocked a jug partially filled with milk from the kitchen sink-board, but that she twisted back to steady it. Ilsa, laughing merrily, pushed him away to finish her work, putting a large flask of tea in the basket. It would be cold before the seasonal workers received it, but they could heat it again over the fire where they burned the orchard debris.

"Be gone, you oaf. Leave me to my work, or your men will not get their treat."

But Ainslie continued to play with her. She acted as though she were indifferent to him, but she was only acting. She had grown very eager for his busy day to pass and it to become night. His hands gave her such loving expectations. Tonight, when the children would be abed, she and Ainslie would take a lantern and steal away to their private nest in the storage room as they so often did.

He kept teasing at her skirts until she knew he was more impatient than she was. She knew she would not need to wait until the clock struck ten and all the children asleep. Therefore, with a touch but without words between them, Ilsa had moved away from him. She'd left Emil to nap in his cart as she often did. The sun was mid-day high, but her child was now in shadow, and the boy liked sunlight. She dragged the cart to a place where the late fall's weak sunshine filled a window. She made sure his pillows were placed best to clear his breathing and his spine propped straight and elevated, the better to help for his lungs to fill. Ilsa bent down to kiss his forehead. He turned his eyes to look at her. She thought Emil smiled. He would sleep. She glanced over her shoulder at Ains, and he was leaning against the sink waiting for her. She could feel her cunny snapping for him already.

When she came into the kitchen, Ainslie reached for her. He kissed her until she was clawing at the buttons of his vest and her thighs were getting slippery. He pulled away, sauntered away from her toward the door to the storage room.

Waiting was almost agony, and he knew that about her. And so he moved slower, stopped to pinch a bit of stollen from the table. She was enjoying the agony and refused to rush after him or even follow, until he opened the door and beckoned to her. It wasn't necessary that they hide away. The

---

boys would sleep. They could have come to each other on the rag rug or even the cherry wood table. Ainslie ran the bolts on both doors. The older children would be in school hours more before the school wagon rumbled down Clark Road. Tansie would be gone for at least another hour and a half. But, no matter, Ainslie was as cautious now that they were nearly a year married as he had been when they were courting. It was something she liked.

When they stepped into the storage room, he wedged a block under its door and let the cold curtain slide down across it. "We are very alone now, lassie," he murmured. "Take the concealing apron off."

His voice was low and rumbling. "The dress too, wife. And the petticoats. I want to see the pink garden of your flesh. I think it might need a watering."

He twisted her heart with the very look of him. He didn't need to say anything. But she loved the rowdy man and his choice of words. She loved him most when private words came to her, bawdy and rough sounding, in the same voice as the low, poetic declamations she heard during the family's evenings, when the proper and cautious Ainslie read from the Bible, famed plays, or lyric poets.

"Then too, untwist your hair, Lassie," he said. "You release it for naught but me, and it is my pleasure to look at it," he said.

That voice showed the welding of the two Ainslies she loved, the scholarly bookish man and the man who knew the value of turning a plow to spring soil. The man's voice and its rumbling cadences set her body to burning.

O<<>>O

14 ~ In The Storage Room

Stepping slowly, not to disrupt the careful clutter of the pantry's wealth of stores, she moved backward away from him. Unrushed, she took the ribbon and pins out of her hair. Ilsa felt its thickness fall down her back. She shook her head so he'd notice how full the strands of her hair were, and how long it was. She resented the little room for being so shadowed and dark that Ainslie could scarcely see how it shone.

Her hair was still fair, though more golden than the white winter-sun color it had been before her children were born. In spite of having borne the three, she had lost no teeth. Hers were even and strong. Her waist was still slim, her breasts full.

Ilsa was proud of what she presented to him and loved to have him watch her undress. He liked to look at her and she liked to please him. But the room was too cold. It lay to the north of the big room but had thin walls of poor man's planking, unlike the massive, well-chinked logs that walled the house proper. The shed roof was poorly shingled over this part of the house. The storage pantry was good for keeping food, but too chilly for trysting in cold November day. She'd hung a curtain, and nailed a strip of padding made from old, worn blankets to the inside of the door frame to keep the storage room's drafts from sneaking through the cracks of the frame into the kitchen.

Her curtain and padding worked both ways. It kept the warmth of the stove and fireplace from penetrating the room and hastening spoilage of fruits and fresh foods barreled to last the winter.

"Take your clothes off," Ainslie asked, softly purring his words. "Don't keep me waiting or I'll give up on you and find some lass more eager."

She played coy with him, imitating a young virgin girl by throwing an arm up to her forehead in mock horror. Dancing back farther from him, she almost bumped the pickle barrel. She giggled and played haughty. "No, Ains. Get yourself a tavern girl. It's cold in here for me to go naked. I'll not freeze myself for you."

"Sit on the bench and lift your skirts, then girl. If you refuse me the look of all of you, I'd be agreeable to look at the softness of your thighs and to admire the lily between them."

She twirled around so her back was toward him. Ilsa swung her skirts up behind her and bent forward. Knowing, but not saying, that it had been Franz's favorite way to take her, she gave Ains a barnyard invitation. But Ainslie wasn't Franz, and he took his pleasure in slower and more varied ways. He came toward her and she straightened up. He put his arms around her, turned her to face him, and lifted her up off the floor to hold her tightly against him. His big hand under her buttocks was pressing her to him and she felt how much his body wanted her. He was enough taller than she that she felt like a child in his arms.

She had a flashingly vivid memory of herself wearing a striped petticoat under a soft green gown. She must have been four or five. Her Papa had held her like this. She remembered how it tickled so nicely when her father held her tight with one hand and fondled her through her green gown with his other. She liked it so much when Papa stroked her face and touched her lips then tickled her on her bottom and up between her legs. On the day she remembered, Mutti came into Papa's room and was cross and shouted at her. Papa dropped her down on the floor roughly. Mutti yanked her arm and pulled Ilsa out of his office. Mutti never allowed her to go in the dairy office again, and it had been Ilsa's favorite place. It smelled of tobacco and her father. Mutti's face turned angry if Ilsa even kissed Papa goodnight, and she hovered if Ilsa even wanted to sit on his lap. "*Verführerische*," her mother had called her. "Have shame," she scolded. Ilsa felt no shame. But after that day with her father, Ilsa's mother never liked her again. Mutti whipped her if she ever caught Ilsa with her Papa when no one else was around. Her mother was always telling Papa how pretty and good her sisters were and she pushed them forward to him as she pulled Ilsa back. Now Ilsa was an adult, she knew how jealous Mutti had been of her.

"I don't want your backside, Ilsa. I like to see your face," Ains whispered, bringing her back to him and away from what was long past. "I like to watch your passion grow as mine does." He made her laugh. Papa and Mutti left her thoughts as Ainslie put Ilsa's small hand on his growing passion.

—

There were racks of jarred preserves all around them, barrels of pink and white beans, tins of meat and brined fish, crocks of sauerkraut weighed down with bricks. She had made curtains for the storage room's single window. They were made from the dress she had worn when she married Franz. The dress's seams had been turned twice. A favorite, she wore it until its bright colors had faded and its elbows wore too thin to patch. When she was sixteen, and she and Hetti were leaning on a fence watching a cow brought to a bull, curly haired young Franz had come up from behind her and rubbed the front of his britches against her back side. Papa looked up from the yard and Franz jumped away. She'd liked that his new dairy worker couldn't resist her. Franz liked the dress that made the curtains. Ains would never know their history.

The window was just above a wide hinged bench top. Beneath the top was a coffin-like space lined with tin to keep flour and corn meal safe from mice. She and Ainslie kept a blanket there to soften the bench. She was wet and swollen by the time they lay down, before even he had pulled open his britches wide, or she had unbuttoned her dress to push the neck of her shift down below her breasts releasing their fullness to his desire. So much did his need trigger hers, she convulsed to his hands and his mouth twice before he'd ever set his pole to enter her. Then again.

She laid on the bench with him afterward, loose in all her joints, his heft a warm and pleasurable weight on her. When he'd pulled out of her, she recognized a vinegary smell that was her own, not his. Observant, the woman knew from her memory of the day she had gotten Hetti that the sharp smell meant that on this day, her body was ready to make a child.

Ainslie straightened up on his hands and knees and came up higher on her until he was looming over on her and prodding his sex between her breasts. He'd reached for something with one hand while his penis was prodding faster in her soft flesh. He held his own convulsion until hers came again. Then he pulled quickly back and his spew exploded into his kerchief.

She grew dreamy and whispered, "I want you to put your spunk into me and fill me up so that we should have us a child together."

He made no response. Instead, he rose and went to the box where she kept a flask of water and some flannel rags and began cleaning himself.

She watched him. She was exposed to the chill air of the storage room but still felt warm. The cool air touched all the parts of her body that lay open and naked. Her own moisture was drying between her legs still sprawled apart and she waited for the sense of cold to come back before she moved.

91

If she watched him longer, she would begin to want him back in her again. She let one of her hands smooth the soft hairs that decorated her cunt as she called to him. "Ainslie, we are married. You don't have to be careful of scandal. We are married months long. You can love me fully. We *can* have us a child together."

"I'll not do that, love. Don't expect it."

"Why?" she'd asked. "I want a baby from you. Come back here and give me one." She was happy and smiling at him, teasing him but meaning what she said.

He pulled up his britches and fastened his belt. Then he came and sat on the bench beside her. He leaned down and said, "Wife, I love you enough to give you my seed a thousand times more before we grow old and die."

He bent down and kissed her forehead, her eyes and her mouth, ran his finger down the dishevelment of her gown to find a breast and slowly trace circles on it. Then he sat straight again. He looked at her and shook his head. He put his face next to hers so his mouth was at her ear, his hand moving up to caress her head and wrap around a strand of her hair. "But no, my lovely girl. No, dear Ilsa." He was kissing her sweetly with tiny dry puckers of his lips.

"I can't do that," he said softly. "You mustn't ask me. I could not bear that this selfish prick of mine should kill another woman."

Ilsa moved a little to look at him. He had tears in his eyes. She understood. She wanted his child, but she loved him all the more that he didn't want a childbirth death to take her away. His refusal proved how much he loved her. "I'll not ask again, Ains. But if you change your mind, know that I would be happy to bear your child and I am a healthy, strong woman. It would not kill me."

He slid off the bench and stood. Slowly as in a dance, he reached down to help her to her feet. She stood unmoving. He pulled her shift up and the dress back up on her shoulders and pulled its bodice together.

He kissed her on her forehead and eyes and mouth. His hands were at her waist and he began buttoning her dress closed. When his hands finished his thumbs were at the sump where her collarbones met. He let them scrape smooth small circles up her throat until his thumbs crossed the line of her jaw and chin. They still circled tiny rounds until they came to her lips. She opened her mouth and he stretched it wide, bent down and put his tongue into it, then moving his fingers from her face to kiss her long and hard and forever. He made her go liquid again with his tongue. Then bent sideways, reached a long arm to the floor and recovered her apron. Straightening up, he slipped its loop over her head. "We've had enough pleasure for one day," he said.

By then every joint in her body was loose. She felt she was made of air or clouds or dandelion fluff and had no body at all. He turned her around as though she were a ragdoll and tied the loops of the apron at her waist in back. He stooped to whisper to her, though no one else would hear if he chose to speak loudly. "You have brought a happiness back into my life where I thought it was gone. When Fiona left me I thought I'd never love again. My daughter's death was terrible enough, but when Fiona died I thought I'd gone mad. I could take no pleasure in anything, not my horses, not my farm. Not even my children could bring me back. I love you, Ilsa for yourself and also for what you have given me. I will love you until I die."

She leaned back against him. She was safe from harm, safe from shame, safe from everything bad that had ever happened, and she had just spent an hour of perfect happiness.

Then she stood straight, reached up to give him a quick sisterly kiss on the cheek. She followed it with a not so sisterly tug at his britches. It was just enough of a tug to be a tease, and let him know she was well primed for more of his love tonight when the moon was out and the children fast asleep. She went to check on Emil, though it would yet be a while before the little boys awoke. Ainslie had to carry the basket down to the orchard crew before mid-day was too far past. They had time for no more dallying.

O<<>>O

~~~O<<>>O~~~

15 ~ A Letter to Write

Ains did not stay in the house long. His young horse needed to be taken back to the stable, watered and groomed, and he needed to get to the orchard to supervise the end of the stripping. With her hair still down and bunching softly around her face, she followed him to the door and watched him cross the yard, swing the basket she had prepared, and lead the animal away. She felt proud of her life as it was now. God had been good to her.

Just over a year ago, she'd been puffed with vanity when she and Ainslie planned their marriage. She compared him with her sister's Hetti's thick faced, stumpy husband, and the solemn little town tailor Greta had chosen. She didn't know the husbands her younger sisters found. They were still in her father's house, unmarried, when she and Franz had come to Ohio. Hetti had sent news of each marriage. Trudi married the man who had taken Franz's place on her father's farm, Hans Kraus. Liesl married Constable Braun. Maria and Lena married farming men. How jealous they would be to see this western frontier land, nearly stone free and wanting to kiss the plow with its fertility. Her father didn't know what he bought for her. Ilsa felt a rude and smug pride over her sisters. Last winter, she had made a pencil rendering of Ainslie and mailed it to her sister Hetti. She wanted Hetti's envy. She regretted that rash action today. Her sister had always been so good to her and didn't deserve that Ilse show her off her own good fortune in a way that pointed out Hetti's misfortune. Hetti's husband was a good man. But Otto was ungainly and ill favored.

Otto had not allowed Hetti to come to the Mueller farm to say goodbye to her and the children when the wagon was ready and Ilsa and Franz left Waynesboro. He did show the kindness later to allow Hetti to keep writing to her. Ilsa had the bitter realization that she was too far to be a threat, but she was happy enough now to forgive poor Otto that time-past sin.

She also regretted sending the drawing she made because though she had tried her best, it was poorly done. If Hetti showed it to her sisters, they would laugh at her scribbling. The portrait was coarse. The little stencils she'd designed and used to paint decorations around the house did not make her the equal of a great artist. But in spite of her unskilled handling of light and shadow, she had captured his likeness. The crude portrait drawing did look like Ainslie.

This afternoon, she thought of her sisters. Hetti, Greta, Trudi, Lena, Liesl, and Maria, she loved them all. She felt conscience stricken at her own vanities. Now that she had so much happiness in her life, she truly hoped that they had happiness in their lives. She'd given up the bitterness she felt toward them for having each other —while she had lived six years here with no sister anywhere in this place to share confidences with or to love. If her sisters' husbands gave them the kind of happiness that she felt this afternoon, she was glad for them. Ainslie had left her lighthearted and feeling like she was floating through the house.

She owed Hetti so much. She had named her little daughter for the sister who was the dearest to her of anyone in her family but Papa. But that alone was not enough repayment for all that Hetti had done for her. She had to do something more for Hetti, something that would show the depth, width and height of her love for her plump, ungraceful, but very loyal sister. Hetti had stood up for her twice when it was a hard thing to do. She couldn't remember a time when she had done anything for her sister. She'd knit her sister a pretty shawl, but that wasn't equal to what Hetti had done for her. Ilsa felt ashamed too as she remembered what a boastful letter she sent to Pennsylvania with her drawing. Although she had a grievance against her parents, her sisters were not part of it.

She decided to write a letter to her sisters this evening, not put it off another day. It would be a kind letter, telling them how she missed them and wished them well. She would ask about their children. She had kept a list of her nieces and nephews in Waynesboro, the cousins Emil, Jacob and Hetti would probably never know.

She retreated to the wash closet, quietly going through the large sleep room. She washed, brushed her hair and repinned it. Tansie would be back soon. They had much to do before Emil and the boys woke up and the older children came home. It had been a warm, balmy fall, but winter had his big foot on Ohio. Winter's breath was cold and he was shaking the trees in his big hand. She thought of winter's breath and it gave her the thought of Ainslie's sweet warm breath. She wished him back to do again what they had just, within two full circles of the minute hand on the clock, done.

The season demanded that she go to the attic and get blankets from the trunks, Ainslie's dull tartans and her Pennsylvania blues. The colorful crocheted quilts and lap robes needed to be brought down for the big room. They'd been packed with laurel leaves and lavender sprigs to keep moths away. Half a year had gone by, and they would still smell good.

Thoughts of her sisters wouldn't leave her. As she worked, she decided to write a letter to Hetti that evening. She had something to tell her sister. It was of an incident with the children. Hetti would understand the story's importance. She wanted to be able to tell it, exactly as it had happened and went over it in her mind.

Anna, Josiah, Jacob and little Hetti were at the table doing their schoolwork. Ilsa was far across the room with Andrew, Johnnie as the little boys played near Emil's cart.

Jacob said, "Abe Tyler is a hard boy and he will never be my friend."

"I agree he is not the best friend to have, but what did he do today to make you angry?" Josiah responded.

Josiah sounded exactly like his father and that made Ilsa smile.

"On the school wagon, after you went up to sit with Mr. Higgins, I called to Hetti to come sit by me. She and Anna were crowded because the new girl pushed in by them. When Hetti got up to move, Abe elbowed me and he said, 'She's not your real sister.' "

"I said, yes she is. Then he said, 'She's not. She has dark eyes and hair, and all you Rohes else are fair. My mother says you can't be true brother and sister to each other.' I said we were, and he laughed at me. "

Ilsa glanced up, worried about how this affected Hetti. It didn't seem to bother her daughter at all, but Anna was sitting straight and looking prim. Ilsa held her breath, not knowing what the girl was about to say, but afraid to interfere.

Anna rolled her eyes and spoke to Jacob. "He is a silly boy and his mother doesn't know anything," the girl said.

Ilsa sat still and didn't look toward the children, but from where she sat measuring Andrew's feet for new stockings she was listening closely and watching the expressions on the older children's faces. The little ones weren't even listening, but Josiah and Anna were paying close attention.

97

Anna spoke up. "Just because you and Emil and your family are fair, it doesn't mean Hetti isn't your sister. Josiah and I are dark and we had a sister who was fair. Our Harriet had ginger gold hair and blue eyes."

"But maybe she wasn't your true sister either," Jacob said glumly.

"Now you are being silly. Harriet's face looked like us. She had one crooked tooth just like I do. It was just that her hair and eyes were different. You know Gran Buchanan. You see her all the time. She's grey around her face, but her hair in the back is as fair as your mother's. It just has more red. Our gran's eyes are blue as the sky."

"Yes," Josiah said, supporting his sister's argument, "Study this, Jacob. Two brown horses can have a pure white foal, and we can look like any of our ancestors. One of our new litter of rabbits is speckled though its parents are gray."

Andrew interrupted to call out, "Gran's not an ancestor. She's not dead."

Ilsa could not refrain from smiling, and Tansie was at the sink and could no longer eavesdrop silently. "Oh, Lord above, leave us hope that good woman has many, many more years!"

The children began laughing, and the housemaid said, "Lis'n to Anna, Jacob. She got more sense in her brain than those Tylers have in thur fambly together. If I get a single minute with Miz Tyler Sunday after church, I'm going to proper edjacate her wit' young Anna's less'n."

Ilsa was watching her daughter carefully, observing the little girl's reaction to this conversation. Hetti was sitting up straighter, looking toward the window and had a satisfied smirk on her face. Ilsa understood her daughter well. Hetti was envisioning a line of beautiful dark haired women as her own personal Mueller ancestral line.

Ilsa's eyes filled when she remembered that tender conversation and what it meant to her. She had all the more reason to love Ainslie and his dear family, and good reason to write the story of the children's talk and send it by post tomorrow to her sister. Sister Hetti would like the story and share it with the others. Anna was but twelve years old and she had the wisdom to give Jacob a sound explanation. Ainslie's daughter found a place in the family for Hetti that Papa Mueller couldn't find. Ohio welcomed what Pennsylvania had discarded.

O<<>>O

16 ~ A Visit from Adam

After school that day, Jacob begged to fly a kite Ainslie had made for the children from heavy paper. She had given them some of her paints and let them color it in vivid reds and blues. Today she had given the children permission to go out while it was still light, although the older four had not yet done their schoolwork. The days were becoming short and they had less time to romp after school. It would soon be the dark of winter and too cold for kite flying. Already the days had grown shorter.

Ilsa found bits of worn shirting she used to make patches in her sewing basket and gave it to the boys for the kite's tail. Soon, Jacob had the kite up and was running across the front drive trying to keep it in the air and out of the small woods. Josiah, Andrew and Hetti cheered him on. It excited *Bärli*, the new puppy. He had replaced old *Flecken* who had died early in the summer. The young pup jumped after the kite's tail. *Flöhchen* and Blackie, the older dogs, who were not sedate or lazy, but not frantic with youth either, raced in circles and loops about the children.

Tansie and Anna were shelling nuts at the table when the children's shouts made them look out the window. They saw Adam's trim one-horse Tilbury turn into their drive. A small wood had grown in the space between the curving drive and the road, but it was kept trimmed and the road visible from the house.

Ilsa had gone to work, washing, drying, and stacking the baking bowls and pans that Tansie had washed and were dry. She still felt warm and loose, joyful from her time earlier in the day with Ainslie when he came in for his dinner at noon, and afterward she had spent the early afternoon making pies and biscuits. She might be dancing as well as stacking bowls. She felt as light in her body as in her heart.

It was an unusual visit. It was not a Sunday, and if Adam had wanted Ainslie, he would have taken the side drive and gone directly to the barn. She felt a slight alarm that Adam was coming to the house. The last time he had come to visit on a weekday, he came to tell Ilsa that her father had died.

Ilsa had the concern that perhaps he had received a letter or other family news from Waynesboro important enough to bring straight to her. She hoped all was well with her sisters and their families. It worried her that she had been thinking of them this day. Perhaps she felt a premonition that something had gone wrong in one of their families.

Jacob dropped the kite, and Hetti rushed ahead to open the door for her great-uncle as Adam came across the yard. The Buchanan children held back. They were not yet familiar enough with him to expect Uncle Adam's candy, trinkets, or the man's affection as Jacob and Hetti did, but they shared the Rohe children's excitement at having a guest come to the house. Adam brought treats enough for all the children but Emil. Solid foods gave a danger that the boy would choke. Anna, Josiah and Andrew understood that quickly, but Ilsa had to be firm with Johnnie who wanted to share whatever he was given with Emil. Ainslie's baby was still so young he didn't realize danger yet.

Ilsa noted that her uncle did not even glance toward the boy in the cart. Adam was, after all, a Mueller. The Muellers were uncomfortable with the imperfect. It helped her, during her lonely days following Emil's birth, to count and make long lists of the Mueller family's many imperfections. Adam was a Mueller. It was Adam who had helped them settle in Ohio. He had found this property for them so that Franz could start a dairy like her father's. And Adam Mueller was the only relative either she or Franz had in the west. He was the reason Papa had sent them here. Adam had been good to them. He was still good to Ilsa, and had become a friend to Ainslie. She couldn't fault him when he had been so good to them, and he was a bachelor who knew nothing of children. She thought sometimes that he was afraid of them all, and not just Emil.

During her years in Anderson Township, she had grown to count on her uncle's visits. She greeted him with a warm embrace, telling him that Ains and the tree workers would be working late, stripping the remaindered fruit in the apple orchard. He was never interested in farm events. She teased him by giving him details he didn't want.

Today, she told him that the team gave but a day and a half to any farm with trees planted. "We will only have a good apple harvest next year if no fruits are left on the trees."

"Are you going to tire me with how much milk was pulled from the cows' teats today too? How many eggs your chickens laid?"

She smirked at him. "You tire me telling me how many wealthy clients you see, and how much they pay you for your advice."

Tansie had the kettle heating for tea as soon as the children had called out "Uncle Adam!" The woman was setting out the china cups. Hospitality was her single efficiency. Ilsa advised the children to put the kite away and see to their schoolwork. As they did so, she invited Adam to take tea with her.

"I came to only to see you, *liebst*, and daughter of my favorite brother. How are you this afternoon, beautiful girl?"

She *was* the daughter of his favorite uncle. Emil Mueller had paid to send his promising youngest brother to an academy and study law. Ilsa was observant. She noted that Adam was speaking rather more smoothly than with his usual jolly gruffness. He seldom flattered her. She suspected there was some coming unpleasantness and wondered again if it was bad news about her sisters or their families in Waynesboro. She had been thinking of them. Perhaps her thoughts were a premonition that bad news was coming from Pennsylvania.

"Leave the *kinder* to their books and come out and sit in my new Tilbury," Adam said softly, pulling her away from the children's notice. "I have some things I want to discuss with you."

Ilsa told the children to stay inside. With a nod to Tansie, Ilsa put a knobby shawl around her shoulders against November's cold, kite-loving breezes, and she followed Adam outdoors. She held the hope that he had some tidbit of town gossip, since he wanted to talk to her away from the children's ears. Adam usually knew everything that was going on in Cossette. She didn't want it to be bad news.

Her uncle helped her to climb up onto the carriage's padded leather seat, and then climbed in himself. Adam wove his lawyer's words into *un vertrag*, an embroidered coverlet. It was obvious that he thought to distract her with long words and fancy talk as though she was a child. But everything he said, no matter how lulling, tore into her. There was no trouble in Pennsylvania affecting the Mueller sisters. The trouble was here. His eloquent, lawyer's language proved her husband had acted against her. Words proved Ainslie's evil doing. Adam and her husband conspired a vile plot against her, and told her nothing of it until it was accomplished.

Out in the drive in front of her house, this man who had always been her friend, a man whom she had depended upon, her only relative in all of Ohio, and the man who had helped her most in the time of her greatest troubles, became a man spewing out words as cruel and bloody as knives. They sliced and stabbed her.

Adam Mueller, Esquire took his time explaining the mechanics of a devious court filing he'd made that morning. Ainslie had told her nothing to prepare her. Together, they had come to agreement, and worked out its details. It became court-approved that very day. Ainslie had dressed so well that morning to celebrate a conspiracy against her. Adam's speech to her at this moment was a corrupt and patronizing attempt to soothe her into an easy accord. Ilsa felt her life had come to its end.

She was not so stupid that she didn't recognize what they had done to her. It was Ainslie, her husband who had pulled her uncle into this vicious plot. With Adam's help, never once asking her permission, or gaining her consent, Ainslie had taken Rohe Farm away from her.

It was hers. It was her children's inheritance. Ilsa rocked on the soft leather seat of the carriage as her mind processed what she had been told. Bile rose in her throat. She felt ill, and was afraid she would vomit. She did not want Adam to see her distress. He would pose at giving her warm, loving consolation. There could be no consolation. She had been the victim of a conspiracy between Ainslie and Adam. *Sie verraten wurde.* Ainslie had betrayed her and used her uncle, the lawyer, to help him. All that Adam said was true. She had no doubt that it was as he said. Adam Mueller, Esquire did not make mistakes or tell lies.

The only way she had to secure her children's future was gone. There was no way for her to protect Jacob or Hetti's future, or to insure that whatever might happen to her, Emil would always have good care. Ainslie had legally stolen Rohe Farm from her.

Mutti had taught her daughters "*tränen zeigen schwächen*— weeping showed a woman's weakness. Showing it to men only made *das manner* behave a worse way. Ilsa and her sisters had learned well. They knew that they should be strong, cheerful and uncomplaining and a husband would never treat them badly. Never had she wanted to show herself weak or glum to either Ainslie or Franz. Never would she tire a husband by bringing him petty household grievances. She did not want to cry before her uncle, but angry tears flooded her eyes.

Trembling with what Adam had said relaying the horror of what he and

Ainslie had done to her, Ilsa slid from the carriage to the ground. She stepped away a few feet away, caught her breath and forced her tears back. As she turned back to face her uncle, she paused for a scant second, but her mind was racing. Adam's one horse-carriage was the finest in the county. She took careful measure of his smart young gelding and expensive tack.

The man himself was wearing a maroon velvet jacket and striped cravat beneath his overcoat. His shoes had a city man's polish though he only practiced in country townships. He posed as a rich man. But he was not. How much of this fertile Ohio land did Adam Mueller own? None. How the man must have envied Rohe Farm's rich acres to use his legal expertise to help Ainslie to rob it from her. How much envy brought him to help Ains hurt her. Did he expect Papa to educate him and buy him a farm as he had for her?

She held Adam's eyes and shouted up at him with her voice turning shrill. "Leave my property. I don't want you here."

He looked patronizingly down at her. "When you regain your senses, *leibchen*, have a talk with Ains. What we've done is for your good. We only do the best for you and the children. This is good, Ilsa."

"The two of you wanted to thieve my land," Ilsa spit out at him. "You wanted it all along. I do not allow this! You will not do this to me."

Adam looked down at his niece, a small woman standing in the weeds at the edge of the drive, raging at him. He felt his motives were good, and he needed to have the last word.

"*Armen naiven frau.* What we have done is legal. We have gone before the court and it is recorded. It is the best for you and your family. Even the State of Ohio recognizes that this is for your good."

The young woman, her face distorted by her rage, bent and picked up a stone from the rough drive. She threw it at her uncle's horse. Ilsa's aim was good and her fury gave her strength. The stone carried force. It hit the horse's neck and caused a ripple down the animal's black mane. The animal's hooves shifted to hold balance.

She looked up at Adam and shrieked again, "Leave my farm! Get off my property. Get off!"

The man shook his head at her. He lifted the reins. "*Genug von euch!*" he barked at her. With a grin that was not humorous but somewhere between disgust and sympathy, the man looked away from her and toward Clark Road.

He gee'd his horse as he slapped the reins. The animal moved, and, following Adam's wrench on his bridle, the carriage's wheels turned to the left. The vehicle inscribed a circle in the gravel of the drive, and the horse, in a quick four-beat gait, pulled the Tilbury out to the road in a smooth, unhurried glide and, once on Clark Road, it turned toward town.

O<<>>O

17 ~ Waiting

After Adam Mueller's visit, Ilsa came back across the yard to find everything in it transmuted. She felt shadowy, like a ghost or some wraith-like phantasm. She with no substance, walked on a path that had no definition across an earth that was without enough gravity to hold her to it. As she stepped back into the house, she did not recognize the sound of the clock's chime. She was aware only of some great resounding vibration that four times painfully tore her heart open. She looked at Emil, propped up in his cart and her eyes burned. She had to look away lest she begin to weep. How could what her Papa had bought for her have been so ruthlessly stripped away?

Jacob asked, "Did Uncle Adam leave already? He didn't say goodbye to us."

"He should stay to eat supper with us, Mutti. He has no family to take care of him," Hetti added. "Call him back."

"He's gone. He had work to do." She listened to her voice answer as though it belonged to some other woman. She had no voice so it could not have been hers.

The house should have looked the same, but it wasn't hers any more, and so it wasn't the same. What had given a glowing and golden value to her had been corrupted. The bright colors in it were dulled to brown. Its proud cleanliness was clouded over by grief that seemed blown from a thousand years of dust from her grave. Nothing was the same. The voices of the children, sounding around her in the big room, their mouths still full of candied treats, came to her ears as the frantic noise of a pen of hungry animals. She did not attend to them, for it seemed that their noise was

105

grinding into her ears until she wanted to scream.

She didn't scream. She didn't even cry. She kept control for Emil's sake, hoping that her child could not sense what she felt and choke or tense into spasms of contracture.

Early that afternoon she had been so full of loving thoughts of her husband. Each thought she'd held became a splinter piercing into her. She wanted to climb into the clock case or dissolve into the slates of the floor to hide from this ugly knowledge that her husband had schemed against her. He had made love to her at noon, when he knew what cruelty he had done to her that morning. He had betrayed her in the cruelest way possible. He had danced her like a carved wooden marionette with no mind or heart.

Sans husband, sans uncle, there was not one single person left in the world to whom she could appeal. There was no place where she would find help. Her parents wouldn't help her if they were alive and able. They certainly wouldn't from the graveyard where they had lain for two years. Her sisters could do nothing for her. Their husbands wouldn't allow it. Neither Reverend Johnson nor *Pfaffer* Gruber would side with her against her husband. She had no friends but Elizabeth Buchanan. There was an ugly twist to that fact. An evil conspiracy between Ainslie and Adam Mueller had taken away everything she had worked to achieve. She was only in her twenty-seventh year, but Ilsa knew very well that she was finished. The man she loved ravished her when he grabbed her property away from her. Ainslie was the only person in the world who had vowed to give her his love and protection. Franz made vows to her, and he had kept them. But Franz was in his grave. His people, the Rohes, left him a penniless orphan her Papa had taken in. Franz had no family who could help her. Nor did she, not one person.

But Ilsa would not die the forever working-tending-doing death of a grey and beaten wife. She would face Ainslie and watch his face pale as he listened to her wrath.

Two hours later, it was dark. The tree strippers had finished and gone to their tents and campfires. Their wages were in the crew handler's money belt for division come season's end. Ainslie Buchanan came in at the back of the house. He nodded to Ilsa and greeted the children. There was a clamor from the children as he came in. They rushed to tell him all the exciting news of their day. Then, the greeting over, he moved into the room from the work porch. She watched as he leaned down to lift Emil's limp hand. He lightly roughed the boy's hair and patted his cheek. Only then did he lift his little Johnnie up and swing him around.

Ilsa poised waiting, saying nothing, watching him. Her eyes were dry and narrowed.

As was his daily custom Ainslie went to wash at the back door basin. He took his time at that. He took a rag down from the hook on the basin stand, dampened it, and scrubbed his face and neck and opened his linen shirt to wash under and down his arms, across his chest. Slowly he put his shirt back on. She remembered that she had delighted in watching her husband come in from his work day and wash. Those feelings would never come back. He had thieved her property and her home. Ilsa felt nothing but rage and hate for him.

He carried the basin out to the chill of the yard. He'd moved from her sight, but she knew what he was doing. He would empty the basin under the leafless lilac by the work porch steps. He brought the basin back inside, and put it carefully back in its ring on the washstand at the far side of the fireplace, wiped it out and hung the towel on its bar. She kept watching him through all this. Ainslie would not look up and meet her eyes.

Jacob and Josiah brought the night and morning's wood from outdoors to refill the stove box while Ainslie washed. Andrew helped them by picking up any wood that fell, and by opening and closing doors for the older two boys. The three went back to their checker game on the rug in front of the fire. Johnnie was putting his little toy trinkets in and out of the box where their checkers and its board had been.

Showing nothing of what she was feeling, so not to frighten Emil or alarm the children, Ilsa left the kitchen and crossed the big room to approach Ains before he could join the boys. When she was near her husband, she turned to the children sitting on the rug. "Watch Emil and Johnnie," Ilsa said to the three boys. "Your papa and I will soon be back but we have something to take care of. Supper will not be late." She tried to keep her voice steady, but having to use her voice to talk to the children made her anxious. Tension crowded her throat and tried to block air from coming into her lungs.

"Yes, Mutti," the boys trilled back in triplicate answer, affirming that they heard and would comply. They scarcely glanced up. For all that the boys noticed, she and Ainslie could have been leaving the house to go walking down Clark Road to heathen China. This night seemed the same to them as any other. She wanted it to seem the same. She would not do to them what Ainslie and Adam had done to her. Supper would be on time, no matter how she felt. Soon they would have to put the game away and go to their evening meal. They were crowding in as much play as they could between schoolwork and supper. She saw the family as on a stage where she was not a player.

Ilsa's hand on Ainslie's wrist pulled the tall man toward the storage room door. As they passed behind the girls at the table, Ilsa saw that Hetti was working on multiplication. The child was relentless in her need to be the best student in the school. She had been fonder of Franz than Ilsa. She would ask Anna to help her before she'd ask her mother if she needed a step explained. Ilsa understood her daughter well. Ilsa instructed Anna to keep supper's broth at a steady simmer. She told Hetti to put her books away and to clear and set the table for supper.

The boys paid little attention to Ilsa taking command of Ains, but Anna looked up at her with a questioning expression, and seemed to understand that something was amiss. Ilsa noticed a brief look of concern cross the girl's face. This slim and timid Buchanan girl was not like her sharp-tongued sister Libby. She would not raise a question to what might not be her concern.

Ilsa turned the latch at the storage room door and pulled it opened. She nodded to Ainslie that he should go in. The man's face had a greater look of concern than his daughter's had. She could read his face as easily as a children's primer book. He knew Adam had been here. He knew that he and Adam had killed her. He had known it when he had made love to her just that day. Though her soul was dead, as stone dead as her parents or Franz, she had forced her body to stay upright and her limbs to move. She would act the whole woman until she could face him and show him her anger and curse him for what he'd done.

As she followed him through the door into the small room, she thought how well she had kept her troubles to herself. She congratulated herself that she had gotten through the afternoon without alarming the seven children. Not even Emil seemed to know what had been done to her by any sense that she had given off through her voice or face or through the very pores of her skin.

She would have her anger out with Ainslie, but they were innocent and should be shielded, while she gave back to the man all the pain he had inflicted upon her.

The storage room was no longer crowded with the whisperings of joy and the excited anticipations it had held for her since Ainslie first came to love her. It was just an ugly cluttered room with a sloping ceiling. It was dark in the room, past dusk outside. But the small window showed neither stars nor moon yet beginning to appear in the sky. It was colder in the room than earlier in the day and much darker. Ilsa could scarcely see Ainslie's face in the dim shadowy room. Hulking shapes were all around them.

She stayed near the door and kept her back against it so he could not leave. She waited, and when he walked past her into the room's dark interior, she reached to turn up the lantern that hung from a hook in a high shelf near the door. The lantern flared brightly, and out of habit, she turned it down until it was just light enough. Even in her rage she was careful not to waste its fuel. Even no longer herself, Ilsa Buchanan, her body maintained its role as the *gute Deutsche weibe*. She kept order. She took care of her children. She kept everything to its proper place.

How well her mother had trained her daughters, she thought as her eyes examined where Ainslie stood now, where the bench was where they had touched each other just that noon. She looked up at the window above the bench.

Any possibility of seeing the stars or moon in the window disappeared as the lantern beamed its light outward. All that Ilsa saw in the window now was a reflection of the room and her own face staring back at her.

O<<>>O

~~~O<<>>O~~~

18 ~ Within the Law

She knew better than to try to move the man with sobs or impassioned pleas. Ilsa vowed she would hold tightly to the good control she had shown with the children this day. She would let him see her anger. She wanted it to hurt him, but knew she could not let the passion of that anger best her.

Now that she was finally able to make her accusation, she knew not to scream or rage at him. His people were an icy crowd even with their children. Ilsa was trying to appear calm and reasonable, better to appeal to his reason. But hard as she tried, she couldn't hold against the intensity of her emotion. She wanted to be as strong and frozen-hearted as the most ruthless and brutal of men, as he and Adam had been ruthless and brutal with her. She didn't want him to see her as a pathetic fool.

It was only with a cold heart and an immoveable face that she could bring him down. She knew that. But as soon as she had closed the door and drawn the heavy curtain between the kitchen and the low shed's pantry over it, a fierce fiery anger came and took power over her. It incinerated her careful plan.

Before she could confront her husband with his cruel deed, scalding tears of hatred filled the eyes she had vowed to keep cold. She was struck mute. In this room, where just today she had felt so filled with love for him, its absence stole all her words from her. It was another theft from her on this day of unrecoverable loss.

The man watched her as the blistering tears ran down her face. And then he reached for his kerchief and thrust it into her hands. As though she were upset over no more than a chipped mug or a stain on one of her tea towels, he made light of her. "I know Adam came to visit you today, Ilsa," he said.

She heard the voice he'd used to jolly the children after a bump or scrape. This wound was deadly. It would not heal in a day or two. Ilsa felt like the furies of Hell were dancing in her. She squinted her eyes as she leaned toward him, her mouth drawn into a cruel line. She would let her face speak to him. And it did. Ilsa, with a bitter satisfaction, saw how his posture changed as he responded to what her face was telling him. She dropped the kerchief down on a sealed barrel.

Changing his tone, Ainslie tried to appease her. He gave her a small morsel of honesty. "Ilsa, my lass, Adam asked to come and talk to you. He's of your family. He could tell you what we have done for the family's good better than I. I agreed it would be a good idea that he talk to you first."

Her voice came back, but it had grown thick. With great difficulty, she kept her intent for this confrontation and spoke out accusingly. "I know the two of you, you with my uncle together, conspired against me. Listen to me, Ainslie Buchanan. I do not allow you to do this." Ilsa sucked in air so she could speak strongly. "I do *not* allow it!"

"We worked within the law, lass. I told you long ago that this would be coming after we married and became a family."

"But I said no to what you talked of. We didn't talk. You talked, and I did not agree, Ainslie. I never agreed to what you wanted! It is *my* farm."

"You didn't say no to the marriage, girl. You were prodding me and ever anxious for that." He smiled lovingly at her, as though he remembered their courtship days, as though willing her to come around to his thinking. "My darling lassie, this business your uncle and I have undertaken is a right and sensible thing."

She shook her head. "No. It is not right, and it makes no sense to me. You cannot take my land from me."

The man looked down at his wife as though he wished to ease her distress. He tried to make her listen. "Sweet girl," he said gently. "You must listen to me. These eighty acres, and all on them, once belonged to Franz, not to your father. It matters not to the court where Franz came by the money he paid. He was the recorded property owner. And you were but Franz's wife.

"By the law, lassie, on his death this property came to his children. Franz's property did not come to you."

She sputtered, "No. That is not right. He bought it as my father instructed. Franz bought it for *me*."

"Ilsa, listen to me and try to understand. When Franz bought the property, his name went on its deed, not yours. When Franz died, as is the custom, and the law if any man should die and leave children not yet of age, the court appointed Adam to control that property. He was an honorable man and a relation to you— and to Franz through your marriage. The court appointed Adam as the children's guardian. He is designated to determine what is done with them and with any property coming to them. Surely your uncle sat with you and explained this to you when Franz died."

There was no anger in the words Ainslie spoke to her. He was trying to be gentle and soothing in his speech. That infuriated her more. "Adam told me this was my house. He said it was. He said he would take care of us, but he did not say he owned us. He did not! I bore the children. They are not Adam's children."

She paused, then said, "Emil, Jacob and Hetti are *my* children, not Adam's." The words rushed out of her. "It's *my* house, and it's *my* land. You cannot take it from me. You are wrong."

"But, it isn't yours, Ilsa. It belongs to Franz's children. That is nothing to do with you. Your name is nowhere on the probate records of Franz's estate. Adam as their guardian determines its disposition."

"My uncle Adam Mueller said the house was *mine* until I died! I am standing before you. Do I look to be dead? If it is mine, how can the land it is *on* not be mine?"

He shook his head sadly. "Ilsa, your stubbornness denies sensibility. The house isn't yours. How can you not understand? Did your parents teach you nothing? You are a grown woman, must I teach you the ways of the law?" He looked angry and puzzled.

Then his shoulders loosened and he began to speak again, calmly and in a straightforward manner. "Ilsa, when Franz died, this farm-house became a *dower,* and that is all. It was only a dower house to your use until you died or remarried. It never became your house *by deed.*

"I asked you about this long ago. You assured me that Adam had read the court documents to you when Franz died."

She didn't remember what Adam had read to her when Franz died. She only remembered that she was Franz's widow, and Rohe Farm was hers. "You are a liar," she sputtered. "How could Adam have told me such a thing?

Rohe Farm is mine and my children's." Her voice was becoming louder. "You did this. You wanted my property. You connived and tricked my uncle until you got it."

"Oh, Ilsa, listen to what you say.

"It is ludicrous to think that anyone could trick Adam Mueller. The man is canny and clever. He knows the law. And people trust him. I trust him."

Ainslie was growing tired of this useless dispute. "Ilsa, it was your uncle himself who first suggested that I buy this property from Franz' estate. Think, Ilsa. Think of Adam. Franz' estate has been a sorry burden to your uncle.

"Should anything happen to Benjamin, he would have to insure that good tenants could be got to run the dairy's complicated business. With Benjamin here, he must still make time to run the accounts each month and allot money for the children's maintenance and face court audit that he is trustworthy.

"And, it is a burden to me to go and supervise Thomas on my property, help my father on his place, and also work this place. As it is now, I must account to Adam that all profit from Rohe Farm go to him for the children. He bills Franz's estate for his fee and for the court's yearly audit. He pays the property's taxes, and charges against the estate for that. Then he gives me back money for the children that I support them. It is so much better for our family, yours and mine, that I should purchase it from him. The money stays with us. No one else has a hand in it, and Adam is released from the responsibility."

She was trembling with rage. "You are a liar and a thief. You've done this on your father and brothers' advice that the Buchanans gain all the land in the township. You dare put the blame on my uncle."

He reached toward her and she slapped him away. He stood back, surprised. "Come now, girl. I've done nothing to you. My family knows none of this. I don't talk our business with them. You surely know I don't because then I'd have to listen to their advice. You *know* that to be true. You remember how they thought me the fool to move my family into this house when I had a better one newly purchased."

He slowed his speech, guiding her along as though she were an imbecile. "Think of Adam. This change is far better for him too. Your uncle knows the law, but he knows little about farming.

"Here it is simply put. I pay rent to Adam, as I am Rohe Farm's tenant, he takes his fee, and the money remaining comes back to me, as I am the man who is actually maintaining Franz's children. Under Adam's authority I am appointed provider this past year. You have not asked him for money since we married. I'm that one that gives you all you need for the children but it comes from what this farm earns. Adam must manage the monies of the farm, then make a return to me for the children's need. He charges against the estate for his work at a lawyer's fee, and that is money for the children we lose to his pocket. With this change, I will manage the monies and we retain more."

Through her tears and anger she stared at her husband disbelieving him. He kept explaining, but she could not attend to what his words meant.

"Ilsa, lassie, I agreed with Adam that it has been a wasteful roundabout. The court allowed me to purchase the farm outright from Franz's estate. Adam has lost the fees he takes for managing the estate. That is to our family's advantage. And Adam loses the farm's burden as well, which is to his advantage. The purchase money I gave him is kept for Franz's children. Adam puts it in the bank or into what investment he chooses. It is secured. But he no longer has to fret about the good years and bad years a farmer must deal with to preserve the investment. Dear wife, you must see the logic."

She could not see logic. She saw greed and cunning in her husband's eyes. While he'd been talking, the hate she felt for him this evening grew to more than equal the love she had for him at mid-day. Ilsa's father had been crude with his daughters, even cursed and hit them, but he never slighted their intelligence. Ainslie did. An overwhelming sadness streamed from her over this slighting. It ran as a tributary to the river of her grievances. Her husband had stolen from her and then he had dismissed her as a silly child. Franz, for all her disappointment in him, had never spoken to her as though she were an infant.

Ilsa was shaking and she was afraid she couldn't speak. To her surprise, she spoke clearly. "You wanted my farm and you tricked my uncle into giving it to you. I wish from God's hands a bad, cruel, and painful death will come down to you both for what you have done." She saw from his face that her curse shocked him and it gave her satisfaction. "You never wanted me, just my property. *Ich werde sie in der Hölle!*"

"Lassie, I'll tell you truly. It was never your barn or this farm I wanted. It was only you."

His voice was weary. She felt a change. He was going to walk away, out of the storage room, not let her finish. "Liar," she wailed. "Liar! Liar! Liar! When Franz died, Adam *told* me the house was mine."

Ilsa struck out at Ains with her fist clenched and all her strength behind it. All that happened was that she caught her knuckles on a sharp metal button on his work shirt. She brought her hand to her mouth and tasted the salt and iron in her blood.

They both stopped and stared at each other for a few moments. Then slowly, he shook his head.

"I have not done what you accuse me of doing, Ilsa. In Deuteronomy there is forbiddance of doing any evil to widows or fatherless children. I would never take from you or from Franz's children —or from any other such."

"You have! You have taken my house and my land," she spit at him.

"The house was only yours by dower, Ilsa," he repeated. "It was only *to your use* by dower. It was never yours by deed. I could not take from you what wasn't yours. The land was never yours." He reached down to put his arms around her as he did when comforting her from minor annoyances, little disagreements with Hetti or Tanzie, or an arm burnt by a frying pan's grease splatter.

She flinched away. "Thief! This is my house. The land is mine. It belongs to my children and to me. It is not yours to leave to your children."

"Don't you understand that we are a family, Ilsa? Do you not see that?"

She looked at him and thought that if she had the means, she would kill him. She couldn't articulate what was twirling around in her mind. But she was not stupid. She knew her numbers. Her children would each only inherit an eighth part of Rohe Farm. It would be split with his children. Rohe Farm should be theirs in full, not in part. It came from her Papa.

The argument was over for him. "Blame Franz, Ilsa," Ainslie said, his voice sounding raw and tired. "If your husband had wanted it otherwise, he would have recorded a will." He leaned back against a tall barrel, and looked at her. "If he had named you his heir, within the law, the court would have recorded the deed in your name. He could have assigned you as the children's guardian. But he did not. It assigned them to Adam. Blame

Franz, if you must cast blame. This has naught to do with me." He took his kerchief from where she had placed it on the barrel and tried to hand it to her.

The fury on her face didn't diminish, but she arched back to put more space between them as he kept talking.

"It is done, Ilsa. The contract recorded. Make your adjustment. You have no choice. Soothe yourself down now. You need to see to your family's supper." He moved past her and pulled the curtain at the door aside.

Ains looked back at her and indicated that she go through the door before him. She stood in front of the meal bins, red-faced, and angry that she had been reduced to sobbing.

"I would not hurt you, Ilsa," he said, holding out the kerchief again. "Wipe your face and hush yourself, lassie. You'll disturb the children. They may have been listening. You know what happens to Emil when there is strife. Think of your poor boy."

Ilsa looked at the handkerchief but did not pick it up. It drifted to the floor. She pulled the edge of her skirt away from the crumpled square of fabric. She raised her chin and looked at him with wintry eyes. He had stolen from her, treated her as if she were a child, and worse he had used Emil against her. She would not touch his handkerchief. She wanted nothing he had touched to touch her.

"Thief," she cried.

"Quiet now." Ains cautioned, moving to where she had first been standing and using his body to block her voice from penetrating the door and reaching the children. "Think of Jacob and Hetti if you do not worry for Emil. Think of my sweet children too. They are none to do with this. Anna is older, and she may reason we are only quarreling, but those younger will grow upset with your noise. You know I'll take care of you and your children. This complaint you bring me is nothing, and it is nothing that you can change. This affair has gone to the county record and Adam has filed it with the court.

"It is time to take care of your family. The children wait for us." He pushed aside the curtain, opened the door and went through. She was left alone.

Warmth from the kitchen stove drifted in through the door, still ajar. He had walked away from her and left it open for her to follow.

———

117

Ilsa heard Ains talking to the children. His voice was low. Anna's voice chirped. Jacob and Hetti laughed. He was the one soothing them. Everything in her life had gone topsy-turvy. There was nothing for Ilsa to do but wipe her face on her apron and compose herself. But from this moment, she denied everything from the man. She denied her love for him. She denied her love for his children. She denied his name. Under the true light and justice of God's Heaven, she was Ilsa Rohe

19~ Another Theft

Ilsa came out of the storage room. She kept her head down, but stood straightly. Before she set about preparing the family's supper, she picked up a tray and napkin and went down into the cellar as though she were going down to find something she needed. She lay the tray down and pulled the heavy lid from the small well. She drew up a bucket of its cold water to wash her face and cool her forehead. She knew her eyes were swollen and hoped the children wouldn't notice. The cold water would help. She breathed deeply. Her eyes stopped burning.

She left the napkin hanging from a shelf's edge to dry, and then she put a spice tin and a jar of condiments on the tray and went back up the stairs.

Anna looked at her. She made herself smile as she normally would. Anna and Hetti set serving bowls on the table as they chattered about some school happening. When the meal was ready, Ilsa said, "Wash your hands, and come."

Jacob rolled Emil's cart to the table and each member of the family took his or her stool. Ainslie, at the head of the long table, led the grace. Around the table all heads bowed but Ilsa's. She raised her head and stared across the table at her husband with her lips stiffened. She'd not join in the prayers of a thief.

Emil couldn't sit upright in a chair. The boy was propped on pillows in a small cart beside her. He ate very little other than milk-gruel, but it had become their custom during the past year that he share family meals like any other child, whether or not he could eat much more than gruel and softened vegetables. Ilsa, at each suppertime since the Buchanans came to live in her home, had the children move Emil's cart so he would be with the family. He seemed to respond well to the ritual. She put food on her plate, then separated it out and forked it into a pudding soft enough that Emil could swallow. It was her custom to spoon the mash to him between her own bites of the family's supper.

The boy was tolerating the food, and eating better than he usually did. She had to think of her child. She was his mother. She had to be no different this evening.

Turning toward the child helped. Ilsa didn't have to see her husband across the table. There would be no accidental meeting of eyes. For the child's sake, she worked to remain calm. The repetition of scooping up tiny bits of food and coaxing them into her boy's mouth calmed her. She feared he might sense her anger, feel it directed at him and become ill.

Conversation flowed around the table that evening. The children didn't seem to notice that she took no part of it. Jacob and Josiah complained that Hetti had told tales on them at school. Andrew, the six-year-old, who would start school soon, interjected that Hetti was also bossy and wouldn't let him sit where he wanted on the rug that day. They spoke of trivial things, the annoyances of children. Their innocent school talk and jokes moved around her like soft wind, but instead of helping cool her temper, it maddened her and she grew more and more inflamed with anger.

The man had not only robbed her. He had robbed her children of what was theirs. Papa had provided for Jacob's future in spite of his disregard for her by buying Rohe Farm. She had unwittingly, unknowingly, handed it over to Ainslie. The horror of it was that the children were robbed as well as she. They shared the cruel future that her stupidity and Ainslie's greed brought. She acted in anger. Ainslie had no right to sit at her table. Without realizing what she was doing, Ilsa gripped the spoon tightly, and then thrust it into Emil's mouth with too much vigor. He made a shrill sound, but all she could think of was how she had hated the man who had shamed and robbed her.

Not completely conscious of her actions, she roughly wiped the pitiful boy's mouth. Emil made a gagging sound and tried to move his head away from her but it was not an escape he could complete. In horror she saw what she had done. A small streak of saliva and blood on the napkin showed that she cut the corner of the boy's mouth with the edge of the spoon. She dropped the napkin and spoon. The silver clanged on the slates. She pulled Emil's head back toward her and crooned to him. Tears filled her eyes.

Andrew jumped from his stool and ran around the table to Ilsa. He put his hand on her back and tenderly said, "Don't cry, Mutti Ilsa. Emil knows you didn't mean to hurt him."

Anna came around the table to speak to Ilsa in her soft way. "Maybe you are tired, Mutti Ilsa. Let me feed him for you. I'll be careful."

Hetti was right behind Anna, patting Emil's face and dabbing at his mouth with her napkin. Ilsa made no response to Anna or the other children. She wouldn't look at them. Instead, she kept spooning mash into the boy's mouth. She felt movement and saw Andrew beside the cart, opposite from Anna. The boy picked up Emil's limp hand and gave it a kiss.

"You are all right, Emil," Andrew said, "Mutti didn't mean to hurt you." He trudged back around the table back to his stool and his supper.

Anna, to make herself useful in some way, went to get the milk pitcher. She went around the table refilling glasses. "No more for you, Johnnie. You'll wet your quilt tonight." The children laughed, Emil didn't cry out again. Ilsa used a pap bowl to give him a little milk.

In a few minutes everything went back to normal.

"Uncle Adam came to see us today after school today, Papa. You were still working." Josiah had said.

Ilsa's anger flared up again, and she knew she flushed, thinking of what had been done to her that evil day. Her hand shook and she almost spilled the spoon's contents onto Emil's bib cloth.

"What did he have to say, Josie?" Ainslie asked his son in a smooth, even voice. It was too smooth, too even.

The evil man was playing against her trying to prove to himself that he was the good parent, not her. At one end of the table her children would see a calm father and at the table opposite, a tense and frowning mother. She willed herself to breathe deeply and slowly.

"He brought us peppermints," the boy answered. "And he said Mutti Ilsa was his 'pretty little *madchen*.' Tansie fixed tea but he wouldn't stay."

"He showed his new little carriage to Mutti. I hope he comes back on Sunday and takes us for a ride. He never has yet," Jacob complained.

Andrew smiled and Jacob giggled, but Hetti sniped at Josiah. "You called him Uncle Adam, Josie. He's *not* your uncle, he's ours."

"You are wrong, sister. Uncle Adam is theirs too. He is their uncle now by marriage," Jacob smugly corrected. The boy looked around the table making sure that Anna, Andrew and Baby Johnnie knew that he was correct in his opposition to his sister and had defended their status as well.

"Thank you, son," Ainslie said. "You are correct. I am father to you, Jacob, and to Hetti and Emil. If it is not by blood, it is by vow and just as binding. And I shall be as good a father to you as I am to Libby, Anna, Josiah, Andrew and Johnnie. I shall make your born father proud in his Heaven."

"He is there, Jacob," Josie said. "Reverend Johnson says that our mother can look down and watch over us, so your father must be able to."

"I wish he were still here. I miss my Papa," Hetti whined.

Ainslie looked down the table at the little girl. "We know you do, little lassie. But we canna help what happens in the world. We must just make the best of it. I'm not your truly born Papa, but I promised your mother on our wedding day that I will love you and take care of you and your brothers as I do my own."

"Will you love me as much as you love Anna?" Hetti put the question to him, and he blew her a kiss.

Ainslie grinned and raised his hand. "As much, but no more, little lassie, And Jacob and Emil as much as Josiah, Andrew and Johnnie."

Josie spoke up to make the other children giggle. "As much but *no more*, Da."

Ilsa clenched her jaw at the easy interaction between her children and her husband, and she ground her teeth at his distortion of what was true. The loyalties in her home were quickly shifting from her control. She grew more sullen. She was silently raging, too distracted to notice that she was pushing an overly full spoon into Emil's mouth. The boy began choking.

Anger dissolved into anguish. She spun to her feet and tried to lift the boy from the cart to clear his breathing. Quickly Anna slid two-year-old Johnnie from her lap. Her rush to help knocked the stool they were sitting on down. Ainslie was already on his feet, stepping around the table. The tall man had swiftly scooped up the boy. He turned Emil over and held him with his head down. Anna was there at his side and a pat from Anna's hand dislodged the food blocking Emil's breathing. The girl had helped do this before, living at Rohe Farm, as had Josiah and Jacob. They all were loyally protective of their brother Emil.

The stricken child blubbered and coughed. Soon, his breathing became less ragged. Finally he was calm.

Little Johnnie watched. "Da take care of Emil," he said, smiling at everyone around the table.

Andrew was smiling too, as were Jacob and Josiah. The panic was over.

Pushed aside, Ilsa watched the drama with narrowed eyes. It was as though the family had dismissed its connection with her. Ainslie Buchanan had shoved her away from her son. He had not only stolen her property, but also her children.

O<<>>O

~~~O<<>>O~~~

IV

ILSA ROHE
~~~1845~~~

Josiah Buchanan's Home

20 ~ Anna's List

14 March 1845, Friday afternoon

There is something I should have given you earlier. I made a list for you with our birthdays, that you may see how the newspapers were wrong. But I don't want Gran to see my writing. She thinks it is shameful.

I do everything easier with my left, but Gran and my mother Fiona believe that the left hand is the Devil's hand. They tied my left hand behind me when I was little, to force me to eat with my right. I can do that well now, and I do not spill my food. Mr. Herbert says it is what is in our minds that is his interest, not what is in our hands. As long as he can read that what we write is correct on our papers, he won't mark us down for how it is written.

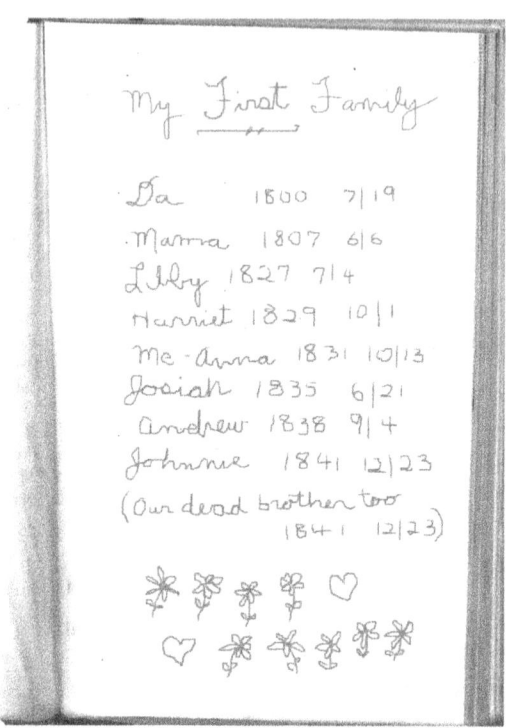

My First Family

Da   1800   7/19
Mamma   1807   6/6
Libby   1827   7/4
Harriet 1829   10/1
Me - Anna 1831   10/13
Josiah 1835   6/21
Andrew 1838   9/4
Johnnie   1841   12/23
(Our dead brother too
              1841   12/23)

Mr. Herbert does grade me down in handwriting, but that is fair. Even I can see it isn't good. In Iwahata, the shapes of our letters had to be written perfectly or we were marked down in the *subject* of our essays and themes.

But this isn't what I planned to tell you. I must tell you of our life. You'll see that on the list, one of my brothers has no name. He didn't live long enough to go to church and be welcomed. That is when we are named. He was Johnnie's twin, and we never knew him as a *living* person. At first when he was born, we didn't know about him. Libby and I weren't allowed into Mama's room. Later we learned that he was the first twin born.

Johnnie was born a few minutes later and cried so loudly Libby and I could hear him from the hallway. We thought there was only one baby. Mrs. Cochran, the mid-wife, called our Da and he went into the bedroom, but we couldn't go in yet to see the baby. Da had to have his own time with Mama. Mrs. Cochran stood at the door with us for a few minutes and told us that we had a fine baby brother. She told us to go and tell our little brothers. She didn't tell us about the first baby. The weather had made our Gran late getting to our house, but she had finally arrived.

Da came out a little while later, holding Johnnie. Andrew was young enough that he wasn't very interested in the baby. But Libby, Josie and I were. I couldn't help thinking that it would be my turn to hold a baby for his church welcome. I didn't say anything because I didn't want anyone else to feel sad on Johnnie's birthday by remembering how Harriet held Andrew on his welcoming day. We were excited that a baby was coming.

I remember that Da didn't seem as happy as I'd expected. I thought he was still worried about our mother Fiona, though she had never had troubles when any of us were born like some women did. But he was very solemn. Da called Libby to take the baby and go and sit with our mother. He said he would need Josie to help him that afternoon, and I should make sure Josie dressed warmly and had his boots on. I thought that they were going to go riding, maybe to our uncle Johnnie Reid's farm to tell the good news, though the weather was bad.

After they left, Mrs. Cochran had let Andrew and me in to see our mother, and Mama told Gran and Mrs. Cochran to let us see the poor wee boy who was gone, so he'd have family to remember him. She did, and he looked like he was sleeping. Mrs. Cochran had dressed him in a gown so sweetly. He looked just like our live new brother. Little bits of dark hair came to a point on their foreheads and they both had eyebrows like Gran Da and Da. So much sad had happened that year. We lost our sister Harriet, and now we lost a baby brother before he even lived.

It was nearly Christmas. Josiah and Da went out to the barn and were gone for quite a long while. When they came in, they had a little cedar wood box that they had made together. Josiah showed us the nails he had hammered himself, and Dad explained to us what our little brother Josie already knew. The box was for our tiny dead brother's burial.

We kept the little dead baby in the cedar box in the parlor until early the next day. Libby was helping Gran and Mrs. Cochran with Mama and our new baby brother Johnnie. The women thought Libby was old enough to help, but they didn't think I was. I played with Andrew until he took a nap, and then I went down to the parlor and sat with our dead brother. In my mind I told him that he should be happy because he had a sister named Harriet waiting in Heaven for him.

It's quiet in the parlor, and because we didn't use it very often, there was no fire lit. It was cold. But it didn't seem right to leave him alone. After a while, Gran came in too. She had a pretty piece of lace in her hand. Gran puffed the quilts between our dead baby and the edges of the box and took the lace from over her arm and placed it over him. Then she sat beside me on the blue sofa and put her arm around me. We didn't talk. Gran understands about when not to talk. After a while, we went to the kitchen and had tea with Mrs. Cochran.

Early the next morning, Da and Josiah bundled up and took the baby in his cherry wood box to Anderson Township in the carriage. He was to be buried in the Kirkpatrick Cemetery. It was a long way there and back, and they were gone most of the day. Josiah was proud that Da had taken him to do important work.

All that day, Libby and I kept going in to see our mother and to look at our new brother. Andrew stayed in the kitchen with Celine, our hired girl. He was so young he'd rather play with the pots and pans than see a new human being. Mama didn't seem to miss our dead brother. She was so proud of how Baby Johnnie was already looking toward the window's light even when we turned him away from it. She said he was going to be a clever and observant man someday. She hadn't expected that there be two babies so maybe she didn't miss him very much. Da seemed sadder about the lost boy than Mama did. But then, Da had to build the box and do the burying while Mama, Gran, Libby and I were occupied with our sweet baby Johnnie who was living.

Our baby who died is at the Kirkpatrick Cemetery. He has a stone now that says Baby Boy Buchanan, 12-23-1841. He didn't get a name. But I love him still for he was ours. I don't understand that custom, waiting to do the naming in church. I gave him a name of my own, but I've never said it aloud for it couldn't ever be his real name.

Josiah was only six, but Da said he had taken Josie to help him build the coffin and bury our brother because it was "never too early for a boy to learn the work a man must do, and the sorrows he will know."

It wasn't very long after that, on our saddest day, that we saw our baby's grave. Mama died on the night of the third of January. Her funeral was on the fifth of January. Our baby didn't have a stone in the cemetery yet, but we could see the little mound where he was. It was right beside Harriet's grave. We buried our mother on Harriet's other side. Gran put her arms around Da after the burial, and she said, "We'll mark this plot next to Fiona Buchanan for you, my dear son. Have no fear it will go to any other."

Gran Da came and shook my da's hand, and Da was so overcome that he fell onto Gran Da. It is good my grandfather was strong enough to hold his weight. My uncles had to help my father back to the carriage. It scared me a little to see my dad weep so hard. He had seemed ever brave to me, and although he ran tears for Harriet, I had never seen him sob as he did at the cemetery that day.

Uncle Andrew's wife Rachel stayed at our Iwahata house to care for baby Johnnie, and Mrs. Cochran came to help her. It took so long to try to feed him. One of them had to sit for the better part of an hour trying to get him to take milk from the pap bowl and a straw. He'd sleep for a little while, and then they would feed him again. If he slept two hours, they would wake him up and work to feed him more.

It was January 5th, 1842. It was a new year, and a Wednesday. I kept Andrew close to Josiah and me on our long drive home, and he didn't take cold.

I will need to stop talking now, Mr. Laughton, for I am tired. Excuse me, but did you copy the list I made into your journal? I must take the list I made with me so Gran doesn't see how I wrote it so unevenly.

O<<>>O

~~~O<<>>O~~~

21 ~ Reading the Bible

March 17,1845, Monday afternoon

Yes, I'm here. I'm sorry I was late. I was helping Mary and Tillie in the kitchen and not watching the time.

I remember I was telling you about our mother's death last week. If you please, I will continue from what I was telling you.

Everything went topsy-turvy when Mama died. Of course you would understand that Libby, Josiah and I didn't go to school the week our mother died. She had turned so sick. Johnnie was yet newborn, and the weather was terribly bad. It was so cold. There were deep, low clouds but snow hadn't fallen yet. The trees were all bare and the fields had that rattie look that they have when the crops were long harvested and nothing alive was showing. It was all black and brown in the fields and the patches of woods looked weedy and raw. Gran said we could stay home and help her by distracting Andrew.

We'd hardly celebrated Christmas at all. Da brought in a tree, and Libby and I decorated it. The boys were happy with their presents, but I don't think Libby and I were very excited. There had been so much that happened the two days before. Mama was already not well and we knew that. Da had to carry her down the stairs for our Christmas. She had fever.

Gran showed Libby and me how to feed Johnnie by using milk and boiled water and adding three grains of salt and a half-pinch of sugar so it would be more like our mother's milk. Our mother was too sick to feed him proper. One must be very clean with babies' food and drink and must boil the teakettle to rinse the pap bowl each time to make sure it is well cleaned. Gran was afraid that hired women wouldn't do it properly. Mr. Laughton, this may not be interesting to you, since you are a man. But women's work is important. With respect to you sir, I think it is more important than man's work. What is building barns compared to keeping people alive through good care? I'd never be jealous of men's work.

Ah, I see you agree with me.

But men's work can be very important too. It was my Uncle Cameron, when he found how sick Mama was, who had taken two fast horses with him and gone for a doctor that Monday. My da asked his help for he was afraid to leave our mother for so long. It was far Uncle Cameron had to go, for there is no proper doctor in Cossette. By the time they got back, my mother was dead.

The Kirkpatricks own our family's cemetery. They are distant kin to us. Gran explained it to me once. It is through the McCreas. Gran was a McCrea before she married Gran Da. She says that's how ginger hair came down to my sister Harriet.

Who we are as a family is written down in the big McCrea family Bible Gran keeps in her room. That Bible is very old. Its leather is peeling, but it is her treasure. If the house burned down, I think she might save it before she saved any of us. I hope she leaves it to me when she dies. Libby wouldn't be interested in it, and the boys might not care. But then, Gran has other grandchildren older than we are. One of them might want her Bible and be more entitled.

My da's Bible is here now. I have all his books. They are in the second parlor, on the shelf beneath Gran Da's old Buchanan Bible and his box of maps. I can hold it and read from it any time I want. My da bought it in Dayton when he and my mother were on their wedding trip. I think he was already planning for us to enter the world from when he was a young man, long before he ever met my mother Fiona, because as soon as they were married, he bought the Bible. I looked at it soon after we had moved to Rohe Farm, and Da had added our dead baby brother. Just beneath Johnnie's name it says: "a son, twin to John Reid Buchanan, still-born, 23 December, 1841." My da had lovely writing and I like to look at our names in his script.

But I want to tell you about the Kirkpatrick Cemetery and I'm not doing as I planned. The cemetery where our family is buried has lots of space. The Kirkpatrick family donated the cemetery land for the neighborhood's use. The Kirkpatricks had lost so many in their family already that they cleared an acre section of their land for other friends and kinfolk. Everyone who has family there goes out to keep the path clear and to clean the markers every spring and fall. Gran Da and the men and their families got together and they put up a fence around the cemetery, and he edged the path up from Roselle Road with fieldstones. Some people who lie there have wooden crosses rather than gravestones.

I imagine it is the same in Boston where you live. We have a stonecutter in Cossette even though it is a small town. Mr. Bernier does mortar work too. He built the big stone fireplace in the house across the street. His daughter Vallerie used to work at Rohe Farm. Hetti told me she liked her very much and still misses her.

My uncle Cameron's wife, Matilda, lost three children before she had Susannah and Corey. Uncle Andrew's first wife is buried there with two of her children. I never had a chance to meet them, but his other children who are my cousins have come to visit me since I've been here. Everyone says that my other cousin named Suzanna looks like her mother did, so I feel I know Aunt Louisa a little. Uncle Francis is there too. He owned our brick house across the road once, but he was killed when he was thrown from a horse. He was the second of Gran's sons. Uncle James was the first and he is still alive. Da didn't want Harriet buried close to our other family members, because years from now people might think that Harriet was part of Cameron, James, or Andrew Buchanan's families, not *Ainslie* Buchanan's family. So my own family is buried on the north side of the oak tree away from all the other Buchanans buried on the south side. Our family has five graves now in the Kirkpatrick Cemetery.

Gran is daft afraid that I will get consumption like my mother and Harriet. She makes me drink cream in my tea every day to fatten me up, and insists that I eat a boiled egg for my breakfast, not just bread and jam. She's afraid I'll get sick and die like my mother and sister. But I won't. Nothing will hurt me. I know that now. She thinks fat on one's bones keeps the consumption disease away. Maybe she is right, but none of us have been fat and only two ever got sick. My da, Libby, Josie, Andrew, Johnnie and I never had a cough at all, unless hay was being cut, or grain winnowed, to raise a dust. I've never been sick enough to get out of doing my share of household tasks. Which proves I'm very healthy. Still, Gran worries.

Da worried the same way about all of us. He hired Mrs. Sullivan to come in and do more for us than our housemaid did after Harriet died. On that last Christmas, Da carried our mother Fiona up and down the stairs as though she had but the weight of newborn Johnnie. We wanted her to see how our tree looked. He even cleaned up after her when she was the sickest on the last days, just as the best nurse ever could.

Once our father moved us into Uncle Francis' house, Gran was just across the road where she could make sure all was right with baby Johnnie, Andrew and our da. She worried most about Da, for he was still broken-hearted.

Mrs. Fournier and her daughter Celine, who had worked for us in Iwahata, didn't suit Gran, and they didn't want to travel so far from their friends, so they didn't come here with us. Instead, Gran's maid Mary's sister, Tillie Kelso came to be our cook and help with the baby. Gran was just across the road. She was with us every day. She stayed the night when Johnnie was teething, but it was much easier for her and Gran Da once we moved here. Tillie works here at Gran's now with Mary. She's crotchety and sharp, but she helps Gran take care of Gran Da and Uncle Johnnie Reid. She helped take care of me too when I was sick. I've learned to get along with her better than Libby did.

It took Da a long time to get back to taking charge of our family after our mother died, even after we moved here. Gran Da said that Uncle Francis' farm crops would have gone to "wrack and ruin" if it hadn't been winter when my mother died. But after that winter Gran Da was happy and he told us, "The Almighty protected the ground with a white blanket to be saving it for our Ainslie to recover his senses by spring planting." Gran Da is too feeble now to talk very much, but he did once say colorful things. I may not have quoted him exactly, but it is about what he said.

My grandfather didn't learn his fine way of talking by going to school, Mr. Laughton. His own mother taught him to read using a *Bible* and *The Works of Mr. William Shakespeare*. That gave him a grand manner of speech without schooling at all. I think I could learn like Gran Da did. I read Da's *King James* every day. Even the book called *Chronicles* in it, and those pages are mostly a listing of names. I like to read them out loud like my da did, just for the sound of it. One of my father's books I have true affection for is *Poems, Chiefly In The Scottish Dialect.* Do you know it? It is by Robert Burns. Da called Mr. Burns "Robbie", as though he were his own brother.

Gran Da gave that book of poems to my father on Christmas before last, when Da married Ilsa Rohe. Gran Da was afraid that if our family lived at Rohe Farm, we would become Germans and forget who we really were. Da would never have let us forget. Gran Da told us to always remember we were proud Scots no matter where in the world we might live. Mr. Laughton, the truth is that our Buchanan ancestors came here from Ireland, not from Scotland. Da told us his family came from Ulster, just like my mother Fiona's did. There had been years of fighting and contention between the Scots who lived in Ulster and the Irish natives, so our family and many other families moved here to America to be free of the strife. He thought it amusing to tell us that no sooner had our family arrived here but they had to go to fighting wild American natives and the vile British.

I do have to go back to school, though I don't want to. My father promised my mother Fiona that he'd make sure my sisters and I had the same education as our little brothers would have. Our mother Fiona demanded that we go to school. It was because she couldn't even read a letter from Da or a road marker without help from my sisters and me.

Our mother Fiona went to Dayton with Da for the racing, but she wouldn't leave us to go so far as Cincinnati or Louisville. When Da was gone to those places, he wrote long lovely letters to her that she could not read. She knew her sums and could calculate. It was only reading she lost by not ever being sent to school when she was a child. Oh, but my mother Fiona could sing every hymn she memorized in church and never forget a word. And so beautiful was her voice. All we Buchanans like to sing, but only Harriet could sing as beautifully as our mother. It makes me think that people who sing high and beautifully like birds are doomed to have short lives. They are like the songbirds we find fallen from the trees when we take walks in the patches of woods. We almost never find the bodies of hawks or crows fallen on our path, just little songbirds. I suppose that seems very fanciful to you, and I should get back to what I'm supposed to be telling you.

Ilsa Rohe, our second mother, could read and write very well. She didn't go to school very many years, but she told me her Papa hired a tutor for his daughters until they were thirteen. He wanted them to speak perfect

English and didn't want them to have a German sound in their voices. She said that her mother had that sound, and her Papa thought it made her mother sound ignorant. He wouldn't let her mother speak if they were out in public. Things must be different in Pennsylvania if her Papa worried so, but then my mother Fiona worried about my handwriting, as Gran does.

Gran speaks with a Scot sound, and no one would ever think she was ignorant. Mr. Bernier, the stonecutter, speaks French more than English. Hetti told me that the Bernier family has been here since there were only Indians in Ohio. They thought we were the newcomers here, as we thought that the Germans were. Mr. Herbert says that the Indians would think that we Americans all were barbarians as well as newcomers, but that they were driven west and off this land. But we should remember that they were the first people here.

It is because of my mother Fiona that I can't just stay here as I'd like but must go back to school. She wanted us to have an education. She would have liked Mr. Herbert, so for her I must go back. I'd be more happy to stay home and help my gran care for Gran Da and Uncle Johnnie. I could take walks and read the Bible, and see my family on Sundays. I do like to read my da's Bible. It is a great comfort to me. Horrible things happen in it. If you have read it, you know.

It tells of plagues and slayings and of great tribulations. It tells of the murder of innocents in the land of Israel. That makes it not so strange that horrible things can happen in Ohio.

And now I'll leave you, Mr. Laughton.

O<<>>O

22 ~ Mr. Rohe

19 March 1845, Wednesday afternoon

I'll tell you about Mr. Rohe today. I have been thinking of him since yesterday, but I don't know why.

My father and my grandfather knew Mr. Rohe long before the day he came to thank us for befriending Jacob. But Da didn't become friends with him until after we lived here. They weren't friends like people who live in towns and cities and see each other every day. Farmers are always so busy doing their work they have little time to visit, but farming men know each other from church or from giving help to each other when there is need. All the men in the neighborhood gather to help each other build houses, sheds and barns and at harvesting. And Mr. Rohe never failed to help.

Da liked Mr. Rohe. Gran Da liked him also, even though he didn't admire him for his good sense. Mr. Rohe had much good land going to waste, and Gran Da hates waste. Gran Da thought Mr. Rohe should clear and then plant most of his open pastures and woods to grain, and he said so to my uncles and my da.

That first spring that we were here, not long after we moved into Uncle Francis' house, the wagon bridge over Indian Creek washed out and people who lived on our end of Clark Road couldn't get to town without fording the creek. Josiah and I, along with Abe and John Tyler and Jacob Rohe, couldn't get to school for the flooding. So, the farmers and their workmen on both sides of the creek went to work rebuilding the bridge so the schoolhouse wagon could return to transporting us the whole distance of Clark Road.

Without the bridge, Mr. Higgins could only bring the wagon to the other bank of the creek, so our fathers strung a line from a sturdy tree on our side across to one on the other side of the creek. They added small wheels to make a pulley. Then they hung a seat from a hook on the line, and we could pull ourselves across.

It was more than a little frightening, but it was great fun. I was in fifth grade and thought it was an adventure. I felt I was Aladdin, or an angel like Gabriel, or like Elijah in God's fiery chariot sailing through the sky.

Josie and Jacob were only in second grade. The men insisted that they each go across with one of the Tyler boys who were older and would make sure that they didn't slip. I was proud of my brother Josiah. He was only seven then, but he didn't want to ride with one of the Tylers, or with me either— like some wee baby— so he showed Da and the men that they could put a belt's buckle strap around the back of the seat and buckle Jacob and him in. They would be safe and could swing across on the line alone like the bigger children did. I used Josiah's belt invention too. It made me feel safer, though I'd have clung to the ropes if I slipped, and I don't think I would have fallen to the water.

While the bridge was being rebuilt, Mr. Tyler, Da, or Mr. Rohe, one or the other, would take us by wagon to the pulley and make sure we went across safely in the morning, and in turn do the same in the afternoon when we came home. It was the most fun we had ever had. We wished that the bridge had never been rebuilt at all. When it was done, there was a get-together on a Sunday after church at Dry Creek school for all the families of Clark Road whose men had worked on the bridge, and all those others who contributed money or logs or the big, heavy bolts that they needed.

Mr. Rohe came with Jacob and Hetti. We didn't meet Mrs. Rohe or Emil at that bridge building celebration. But that is where I first met Hetti. She was still too young for school. Jacob told us about his brother who couldn't walk or talk. He explained that his *Mutti* had to stay home and take care of Emil. That was the first time I ever heard anyone call his mother that word. It is German for Mother.

Hetti was very pretty and very forward for someone so young. She wanted to go to school so much, but she couldn't yet. Jacob and Hetti went to the German church with their father on Sundays when they could. It is in Taylorsville, and too far to travel every week. I told Jacob I knew that his mother painted the pretty designs on their house, and I asked him if she spoke English. Jacob laughed at me and bragged that his mother spoke better English than Mr. Herbert. He said that his uncle was Adam Mueller, Esquire.

I felt ignorant because I didn't know who Adam Mueller, Esquire, was, but I didn't ask. I was embarrassed too, because when my gran called Mrs. Rohe "the German woman," I thought it meant that she had come from Germany. I didn't realize she was American, the same as we were. I thought that Mr. Rohe came from Germany and that was why he sounded funny on some words. He would say *ver* instead of were, and to him a wagon was a *vaagon*. But he was born here too.

Afterward, Libby told me Adam Mueller was a lawyer in Anderson, and an elder in the German church. He drove the beautiful little one horse carriage we sometimes saw on Clark Road, and he lived in the Roberson's boarding house and paid for four rooms there just for himself. "Everyone knows that," she said, and smirked at me. She told me that Mrs. Roberson made a lot of money on Mr. Mueller because she could collect rent on four rooms and only have to feed and provide bedding for one tenant. I met him later on, but I admit I am not very fond of Adam Mueller, Esquire. He is probably a good man, but he isn't like the men in my family, Mr. Herbert, or you.

Mr. Rohe was ever kind to us. Josie and I liked him very much. He let Mr. Higgins bring our school's older students out to his big barn and he showed us how a dairy worked and how cheeses were made for sale. It was different from how our families made German cheeses. Mr. Rohe's workman, Benjamin Wilson, lived there at the farm, but Mr. Rohe hired other men too. One of the girls in my grade's father worked for Mr. Rohe. There was a huge cellar beneath the back end of the barn where they made cheeses. Mr. Rohe let us all eat a slice from one of the rounds before Mr. Higgins drove us back to school.

Though the milking and cheese sheds were kept as clean as our kitchen, so many cows in one barn made it smell out near the barn. We kept but one milk cow at home. Not twenty of them. And I was glad. Da kept many horses; plow horses, carriage horses, the racing and riding horses he sold. They didn't smell so badly as the cows. But perhaps it was because I was used to them.

Da told Josie and me to respect Jacob's father. Da said that a dairyman *never* had a season to rest and make repairs as winter gave a crop farmer. My father truly admired Mr. Rohe for his willingness to do hard work — and that he took good care of his family.

Late that very spring, before school was out, Mr. Rohe was killed in an accident. He had gone up onto the roof of his house to fix some loose shakes and had fallen. The constable said Mr. Rohe must have turned as he started to come down the ladder and it must have slipped, for it came down on top of him, and his tools were still on the roof. No one heard him fall. Jacob was in school and Hetti was there with her mother and Emil. But they were all indoors. Hetti had measles and was kept in bed in a little tent where light couldn't hurt her eyes. The log walls at Rohe Farm are so thick, no one heard Mr. Rohe fall.

Libby knew everything that happened. When Mr. Rohe didn't come in for his dinner at noon, Mrs. Rohe thought it odd. After she fed Emil and Hetti, she went looking for him because she didn't want the meal she'd prepared to be spoiled. She found him dead on the ground, the ladder beside him. It was the worst thing that we'd known to have happened to someone we knew.

Our Uncle Francis died in an accident, when he was thrown from his horse. Josie and I weren't born yet. Everyone we'd known who died, had died of sickness. It hadn't been so sudden.

Libby told me that Mrs. Rohe had put her apron over his face when she found him dead, because she was afraid that Hetti would get up and wander out looking for her and find her father dead. Then Mrs. Rohe ran to the barn get Mr. Wilson and the men. Libby had heard all that from someone who heard it from Constable Davies. I don't know if it is true or not, Mr. Laughton. And I never talked to Jacob or his mother about it to know for sure. You ought not put it down. It is probably correct, but there is a chance Libby might not have heard the exact truth of the story. This part, my da told us so I know it is correct. The Rohe's man Benjamin sent for help but it was too late. And by the time someone thought to come and get Jacob out of school, his father's body had been taken to Cossette. Members of the German Church in Taylorsville were going get to it and do the laying out there, so poor Mrs. Rohe didn't have to manage her sorrow and trouble with people coming to pay their respects in her home.

Gran and Gran Da and Mr. and Mrs. McFarland and the other neighbors went to call on her and take food. She thanked them, but she didn't invite them in, and she said that she had help enough from the family's church. Gran said no one was offended because Mrs. Rohe was in shock and a sudden death is harder to bear than a slow death.

My Uncle James took us to the German church for Mr. Rohe's funeral. That was the first time I ever saw Mutti Ilsa and Emil from closer than the road. The German church's pastor and Benjamin, the Rohe's foreman, brought Mutti Ilsa and Emil in a wagon by making a ramp so the cart could get up into it. Gran and Grandpa rode to the funeral with the Montgomerys who live farther down Clark Road and have been their friends for many years.

We went to the funeral with our uncle and aunt because Da was in Louisville to buy and bring home two new mares when Mr. Rohe died. Da didn't know about Mr. Rohe until he came home the week after. Before the funeral started, I went up with the rest of my family and paid my respects to the Rohe family where they sat near the coffin. I didn't know that Mrs. Rohe would someday be my mother. I couldn't feel like smiling that day, but not just because of Mr. Rohe dying. More because I knew Jacob and Hetti would miss him as I did my mother and Harriet. I thought I'd miss him too, even though I knew him such a little. I knew my da would. They often talked when passing on the road, like men do. My da had many business friends, and he had brothers. But Mr. Montgomery and Mr. McFarland in the neighborhood are old like Gran Da. Mr. Rohe was right here in the neighborhood and a young man, younger than Da, but more his age than the others.

 At Mr. Rohe's funeral, I was especially sad for Emil. I had seen his cart in front of their house once or twice on sunny afternoons, but seeing him close for the first time made me realize what a tragical boy he is. He is like none I'd ever seen before. He is a boy just like my brothers, a year older than Josiah. But his body can't do what he wants it to do.

Good afternoon, Mr. Laughton. I've talked too much. You've had to write too much. Today I think you are the one who is tired.

O<<>>O

~~~O<<>>O~~~

V

ILSA ROHE

Rohe Farm, Anderson Township, Ohio
1844

23 ~ In a Poet's Words

Ilsa looked at the Buchanan children quietly busy in the room. Jacob and Josiah were teaching Andrew to play checkers. Anna was sitting patiently, helping Hetti with her school essay. Anna never complained. She never shied away from helping wherever it was needed. Ilsa recognized that. But when she looked at the Buchanan children, even Anna, what she saw was small grasping hands reaching up to take everything she and Franz had worked to gain. His children were wresting Rohe Farm away from her children.

She knew that Ainslie's young ones could not be faulted. Yet they carried the blood of their father and therefore were tainted with his guilt. She had found no crime in them, but criminals they were. It was a conundrum she couldn't solve. She stayed in the kitchen long that evening, finding things for her hands to do so she had excuse not to be nearer to Ainslie by moving into the big room.

She felt numb, and her movements were awkward. The devastation she felt made her work take long, but the work seemed to give her some ease.

"Mutti?" Ilsa felt a tug at her arm. She looked down to see Jacob standing eside her. "Mutti you must be dreaming. You are not watching the clock. It is past Emil's bedtime."

Ilsa was slow to move, but she went to Emil and saw that he had grown restless. It was well past time for him to be bathed and put down for his night's sleep. She looked around for Johnnie and didn't see him. Then, and only vaguely, she remembered that Anna put Johnnie into his woolen nightdress. She brought him to Ilsa for a mother's good night kiss before the girl put him into his crib. Ilsa looked around at the children and felt that she was far away from them looking at them as though through a telescope inverted, or as though they were players on a stage or in a circus ring and she was far off in the audience.

She looked at them and an odd memory came to her. She remembered that before her sister Maria was born, Papa had taken the family to Brown's Traveling Circus when it came to Maryland. It was a long way to go, but it was the nearest a circus had ever come to Waynesboro. The family stayed with Mutti's parents and other relatives, both going and coming back home. Liesl was so young, that she was left home with *Grossmutti* Mueller.

Ilsa, Hetti, and Greta were amazed by what they saw. There was a big tent and inside was a ring with acrobats and trick riders, and clowns. There were monkeys and a Bengal tiger from the Orient. What Ilsa remembered most, was an automaton in one of the booths around the outside of the tent. In the booth was a famous invention, an eerie, mysterious, frightening huge doll of a woman, as big as the girls' mother. The doll was wearing a dress of green and gold and black. She sat up on a dais behind a rope fence. She slowly moved her arms and her head for the audience. She was too big to be a puppet and no one could be seen moving her. When the automaton turned her head to look right at Ilsa, it scared her. Ilsa ducked behind Papa. Her sisters piled in right behind her grabbing at her skirts, just as she grabbed Papa's pants.

She annoyed her mother afterward when she had dreams of that woman, her big eyes and long nose. She had frightening dreams of the automaton for a very long time. The noise she remembered, a grinding sound, as the woman turned to look at Ilsa, could make her shiver in recollection. It was worse than the sound of the Bengal tiger who roared as Papa led them past his cage. On this night, she felt she had become the automaton. When she turned her head or lifted her arms there ought to be a grinding sound.

There was no rope fence between her and the children but there might as well be. An insurmountable distance was between them.

Ainslie, seeing that she was finally going toward Emil, got up from his chair and said, "Let me carry him for you, lassie. He is growing too heavy for you. I tell you to always let me carry him if I'm here."

She didn't answer, but let him carry the helpless boy to the sleeping room. While Ilsa washed her son and put him in a sleeping gown, Ains went back to the fireplace. It was time for him to read to the children.

Before Emil was tucked down, she could hear her husband reading to the children through the open door. Ainslie was reading rhyme tonight. Yesterday, when she loved him, she had been fond of listening to him as he read from the Bible or the Bard, or even from this poet he liked.

Tonight she wanted to hear of plagues of locusts, or fiery chariots, or the monster Caliban, anything that would distract her from the wildness of her thoughts and what had happened to her today. She didn't want this fool's common and simple poems.

She took up her sewing basket and pulled her chair farther away from Ainslie's. The children were sitting on the rug, staring up at him, rapt in his reading. The sound of Ainslie's voice made Ilsa want to scream. She thought about going into the wash closet or the sleeping room and waiting until his voice stopped. But that would be noticed. Her troubles were enough without children set to worrying, or whimpering, or expecting explanations.

And then from the Robbie Burns that Ainslie was reading came words:

> Here Poesy might wake her heav'n-taught lyre,
> And look through Nature with creative fire;
> Here, to the wrongs of fate half reconcil'd,
> Misfortune's lighten'd steps might wander wild;
> And Disappointment, in these lonely bounds,
> Find balm to soothe her bitter—rankling wounds:
> Here heart-struck Grief might heav'nward stretch her scan,
> And injur'd Worth forget and pardon man.

Ilsa listened. She knew herself, Ilsa Rohe, as a creature made from *Misfortune, Disappointment, Grief,* and *Worth.* And she would never pardon the man who had destroyed her, nor would she forget what he had done.

———

145

When the clock struck nine, he got up to go to his bed. It was his usual time. Ilsa had almost gagged when, after he kissed his daughter goodnight, he came to her chair to say goodnight to her. She grew rigid and turned her head from his kiss.

Ainslie bent to her ear and whispered, "You'll see, dearest girl, all will be well. You'll feel better in a day or two."

She writhed away from his touch. She would never feel better. There was no balm for the "bitter— rankling wounds" he had inflicted on her.

She wanted to rip at his face with her nails. He had ripped away her home and her children. What more could he take? Her clothes? Her shoes? The utensils she used to prepare his meals? Ilsa had nothing left of value after his theft of her property but her children. This night, the evil man had made her watch how cunningly he had stolen them from her too. She had nothing left.

O<<>>O

24 ~ Chasing Numbers

The lantern was low, but the fire behind the screen flickered and reflections from metal buttons by the basket glimmered at Ilsa. They brought her back to awareness of where she was. She had not noticed that Anna had left her to go to bed, but the buttons on Jacob's second best britches were shining. Anna had neatly folded them and left them near the sewing basket.

Ilsa had been alternately rocking or pacing in the big hollow room. The clock ticked, the log in the fireplace cracked. The Franklin stove in the kitchen corner's coals popped. She could not remember what else she might have done that evening, but there was no completed work on her side of the basket. She went to pull the gingham curtains aside and look out the front window. There were no answers there, nothing to give her comfort on this night. The evening's torments came back to her. It was near full moon and she saw leaves blowing past the glass, dark shapes in a brightly lit night. They were gathering in the wind eddy at the steps to the door. Her children were like dead leaves tumbling from their trees. She wondered what would become of them and of her. She paced in the big room, not able to sew or take up the darning that the boys' stockings needed.

When the clock sounded quarter past midnight, the woman finally retired to the bed she shared with her son. Her body was demanding rest. Ilsa shut the lantern, and went to the wash closet and stripped down to her shift, put her clothing and petticoats on their hook, and went to lie down next to her son. The usual sounds in the room, sounds that woke no one who was sleeping, pounded into Ilsa's ears. The crackles from the fireplace, and the coals banked in the Franklin stove in the other room, hurt her ears and seemed to prick at her head. The critching of a cricket's chirp tormented her. The wind had grown and was whining around her house.

The wind increased. It sounded as though it were crying for her, crooning the sounds of her husband's betrayal. The clock kept ticking but the wind grew louder until she couldn't hear the cricket or the clock. The whining coloratura shrieked an aria of her rage, high killing notes crying out at the mockery Ainslie made of their life. He stole her father's parting gift to her. He knew how she valued Rohe Farm and he dared steal it from her. Five years of her life had gone into advising and counseling Franz into working harder and better, encouraging the dull man to make improvements to the outbuildings to then improve profit. It was her wit and cleverness that convinced him that his precious cows could be used to make the seeded and herbed cheeses that gave Rohe Farm its greatest profit and least risk. She talked him into the expansion of the dairy. It had taken years and all her persuasiveness to keep Franz from making foolish decisions.

She built Rohe Farm to what it was. And now, just when everything she had wished for had gloriously come about, Ainslie used her uncle to betray her. In her twenty-sixth year, all she had created to secure her own and her children's future was gone. He stole away everything she owned to puff up his own wealth and increase *his* children's security. Did the Buchanan children deserve more than hers? Did they deserve to inherit a farm bought by *her* children's grandfather? It was a man's vicious crime backed by a man's help and men's vicious laws.

Ainslie and Adam might know the law, but she knew the numbers. They couldn't convince her it was best for her children. If her children someday inherited Rohe Farm as they should, each would inherit one-third its value.

If she were able to persuade Ainslie to take her children as wards under the law, equal to his own children, they would inherit from him along with his own children. But then the joint properties, the two farms and his stables, would be split into eighths. His children would take five parts to her children's two. One eighth of all was not worth one third of Rohe Farm. And, the courts wouldn't let Emil inherit. What would happen to Emil?

Bitterly, Ilsa reflected on an answer to that question. She had seen and smelled the horrors of a public infirmary in Maryland once when Dr. Bentzinger took her there. He wanted her to see why he was so compelled to open private clinics. Ohio's state infirmary would be no better, likely it would be worse.

Hetti wrote her that Dr. Bentzinger had taken ill and gone back to Austria. She didn't know if the clinics he had established in America still existed. She clutched the quilt and began to weep soundless salty tears into it. Only one person in the world was left who would try to help Emil.

Her sister, Hetti Mueller Schubel, would scramble to try to find money to come to Ohio and get him. But her sister already had five children and Otto was just a poor man. Sister Hetti's heart would be willing, but how would it be possible for her to get to Ohio or to transport a helpless child back with her to Waynesboro?

As the night passed, Ilsa's mind began rambling through a brittle, thorn-filled and dangerous forest of memory. She counted her husband's smaller betrayals. Anna, it started with Anna. Ainslie had denied her the use of his daughter when she, his wife, was in need. He had refused her when she needed Anna to stay home in September. He chose his daughter over her in September. And worse came the next day. He interfered when she told Hetti to stay home and help her and Tansie with the kitchen work. Hetti was Ilsa's child, but Ainslie took the girl away from her. He dared lift her in his arms and carry Hetti out of the house. It was the end of her then, but she was blind to knowing how grave it was to become that he take what was hers.

 She was a better mother to his children than they had before, anyone could see that. His children were thriving under her care. Their hair was glossy, their cheeks fuller and rosy. They laughed and played. She knew what was best for children, yet he had defied and bullied her. And she could not understand why she didn't fight him that day. Ilsa saw herself as *ein narr*, a woman bewitched into stupidity by the man she loved.

She should have thrust her fingernails into his eyes, torn his skin and thrown him out of her house the day he carried Hetti to the school wagon. She shamed herself when she had forgiven him. She was only a whorish servant in his eyes. No, she was not so high as servant to him. She had lowered herself to become his whore. She became his pasture beast to do with what he wanted. He had taken her milk, and then when he found her meat gave him better profit, he had led her to the butchering slab. Ains had killed her. Adam handed him the weapon, but Ains did the killing.

During that long night, Ilsa's anger flamed against her husband. Her fists closed so tightly that her nails cut into the palms of her hands. She felt them bringing sliver moons of blood up and the pain brought her back to where she lay on the bed, her mind no easier. It was her punishment for being such a gullible fool that she allowed him to bewitch her.

She looked around the shadowed darkness of the sleeping room. In a lucid, practical window that opened in her angry thoughts, Ilsa knew she needed rest. Morning would come and Emil would need her. She had to be alert for him. There was so much work and her days so long. She had to sleep, but she felt tense, wild and strong. She wanted to go out into the middle of

———

149

Clark Road and scream at the stars and moon, not to sleep.

In the illumination leaking through the doorway from the brighter big room's banked fire, she could see Ainslie's long blanketed shape. Around the room the slight, smaller mounds of the children lay in cot and crib. To coax sleep, Ilsa tried to make a game for herself, the kind of game she taught herself as a child to conjure *der sandman* when she and her sisters were sent to bed so early in the summer that light still filled their room. The child Ilsa would close her eyes and play with numbers, moving them about, adding and subtracting.

Watching the numbers grow or shrink always helped her grow sleepy. She would close her eyes and begin by counting the room's sleeping children. She'd slowly count them and count again until she went around the room seven times counting, for seven was a lucky number. Her papa had seven daughters. There were seven children in the room. She'd double the number she'd reached, and keep doubling it, again and again calculating to larger and larger numbers, each multiple being lucky for having begun with seven. Ainslie would then be banished from her mind. Sleep would come. She had to sleep for the children. They were good children. The woman tried to grasp the memory of warm summer nights in Waynesboro to find a distraction and let her mind go into the constancy of numbers.

Ein, Emil, her helpless firstborn she would give her life to protect. Emil was always first, before Jacob, before Hetti, before all else.

Zwei, Jacob lay on a narrow cot pushed against the open side of her bed lest Emil fall in the night. Jacob was her helper, always ready to help her lift or turn his brother. He was a good boy.

Drei, Baby Johnnie was in the crib on one side of Ainslie's bed. He killed his mother, but he was innocent. His father's evil was not his.

Vier, Josiah was on the trundle on the opposite side. Jacob took Josie as his friend long ago. He was loyal to her son, never rude or naughty with her.

Funf, little Andrew was a thin, kind-natured child. He'd begin school after Christmas this year. His cot was near the back wall of the fireplace where the stones warmed the room.

Of the Buchanan children, she had felt such kinship with Andrew. He was not of her blood, but he too liked to count. He could have been a Mueller or Rohe boy if his hair had not been so dark. He talked little and was happier to stay in the house and measure out flour and sugar with her, working in the kitchen, than to run outdoors with Jacob and Josie.

She found no crime in Ainslie's children, no betrayal. But how could there not be? He was their father.

Even if there had been better light in the dim room, Ilsa couldn't see the girls from her bed. They were behind the shallow waist-high partition Ains had erected for them. Anna was old enough to want privacy from the boys, and Hetti had been fond of Anna from their days in school, and she had formed a strong attachment since the older girl was now her sister. Hetti had demanded that her cot be next to Anna's next to Ilsa's. Ains moved her cot and erected a child's version of a wall. He obeyed a child's silly whim.

Ilsa's mind scrambled again. She could not think how to count Hetti and Anna. Ainslie was in the room. His presence seemed to fill all its space. She could not banish him and he blocked her thoughts of all else, stifled her comprehension of all else. How could she count? How could she sleep?

"Stupid. *Dummkopf*," she angrily whispered, cursing herself. She had sold her children's future for a man's good looks and polished boots.

O<<>>O

~~~O<<>>O~~~

25 ~ *Rübezahl*

Ilsa's sleepless thoughts swung out in a wider arc. No one could help her, not even God. *Gott* had again chosen against her. He had abandoned her. She had seen Him cast his favor on other women, homely women and ugly women, women with voices like donkeys braying, and women she had seen when she was a child who were so fat that they couldn't fit into their own kitchens. God cast his favor on them but not her.

Her Papa was a brute devil who had thrown her away. Uncle Adam was a man who broke his promises. Franz was too weak to be of any use to her. Dr. Bentzinger was a good man, but his kindness brought her to ruin.

Why had she ever prayed to Gott? He was just another man, and who but God had put Ains in her way?

She'd pulled the spread that covered her and Emil higher, lest her son take a chill. From across the room she heard Ainslie groan in his sleep. She cursed the God who brought her to this. He didn't listen to her prayers when Emil was born limp and prone to fits, or when Hetti was born vigorous and perfect but announcing to the world in her very looks that she wasn't Franz's child. God hadn't listened when Papa banished her, giving Franz money to take her, and her imbecile son and her dark haired daughter far away lest the sight of them shame the family.

Her eyes squinted down, and her lips were tight across her teeth. Ilsa knew *Rübezahl*, the trickster, was in the room with them. He was in the big bed, not eighteen feet away, pretending to be asleep, pretending to be a man named Ainslie. It was the trickster's doing, not God's, that she had lost everything that Franz and she had built. And it was not her doing. She was not to blame. She was guilty of no vice but one. The trickster, the ugly gnome-faced giant changed his appearance to a fox, to a tree, to a man. Ilsa was fooled by the trickster. He changed himself into Ainslie and she had loved the image of him to the point of deafness, of blindness and to madness.

As though she were a little child again seeing monsters in the dark, Ilsa saw Ainslie's form hiding the sly trickster from her *Grossmutti* Mueller's Old World stories. She knew she was awake, and that she, a woman grown and the mother of children, had fallen into a child's dreadful nightmare of a life.

In *Grosmutti's* stories, *Rübezahl* disguised himself as an ass, or a spear, or a stick of wood, to make fools of innocent people. This time, he'd disguised himself as a man and she was his innocent victim. She played the role of the fool.

She wanted to conjure the magic of those old stories to her own use. She wished she could click her fingers and cast Ainslie and all that was his: furniture, children, clothing, shoes, and the very smell of him, from her house. But she had no magic. She could change nothing. Her wishes had no power. She could do nothing but rage. She carried the weight of her children. She was unable to run, unable to fight. She had no friends who would side with her or could give her help. Behind her rage, something Ilsa tried to dismiss kept coming back into her night thoughts to torture her. Her tragedy had always been that whatever she most wanted came to her. But an ugly hook was attached to her desires. As soon as she took possession of the object of her desire, it twisted into something else, something she least wanted, something hateful and horrible. She had wanted Ainslie Buchanan.

Ilsa's *Grosmutti* Mueller had been born far away, across an ocean and up a wide river, deep in the forests of the *Oder River*. She'd come to America as a girl. *Mutti* cautioned Ilsa and her sisters that they should not believe their grandmother's stories. Mutti had scolded the old woman. "Old tales belong to the Old World, not to the New," Mutti had scoffed. "*Lächerlich!* This is America. It has no place for ridiculous tales to scare children."

The stories had not been ridiculous. *Rübezahl*, the trickster, was not in the Old World. He had been in Ohio all the time, waiting for her. Ilsa's imagination leapt from anger to fear. Her senses, dulled after Adam's visit, came alert. She heard a noise that wasn't just one of the usual nighttime sounds. The scratching noise from the roof might have been a possum or a cat, but Ilsa saw hordes of rats marauding down into the attic after the food she'd so carefully dried and preserved for the season ahead. What would her children eat, if gangs of rats stole their food? A whirl of night wind

---

154

echoed down the chimney. She heard it as the ominous forewarning of an out-of-season tornado. The house was stronger than most, but only God knew the strength of a tornado. She and her children might be killed or buried in rubble to die slowly of injury and thirst.

From the time she was a girl in her father's house, she had welcomed night. Sleep seemed to nourish her body better and quicker than food or drink. Sleep would not come this night. *Rübezahl* was here in the room. Swallowed-down anger and fear combined to become a poison in her mouth. She bitterly analyzed what was happening and felt it in her throat poisoning her, while the trickster lay at ease. She needed to scream the poison out.

Mutti said that sleep came from *"guten arbeit und gewissens,"* good work and good conscience. Ilsa had earned rest, but sleep was denied her. She heard the light, quick breathing of the children in the room. His, deep and steady, in-and-out breathing, infuriated her. His conscience should keep him awake and pacing, red-eyed, hollow-cheeked. He should be kneeling at the side of her bed, pleading with her to forgive him, and making promises to her that he would put things between them right again.

In the dark but moving toward morning, Emil cried out in his sleep. Careful not to disturb her restless son, Ilsa left the bed they shared. From the day of his birth the child had shared all his mother's feelings. Though she'd tried to keep it from him, the turmoil she felt the torturous evening past had disturbed him. His night had been almost as restless as hers. She'd had to fix his pillow and turn him. He'd cried out too often with his raspy call. The room's air, thickened with the exhalations of the family sleeping in the room, stifled her. She went to a window to push it open. The night air rushed in. It was clean and fresh, but brought the chill of November. She tried to fill her lungs with the chill of night, but felt no better for the deep breaths she took. Before the children felt the cold, she drew the window closed and returned to the bed. Her mind, overflowing, repelled what moments of rest might have come to her.

Ilsa found no peace during the long night. If she had slept at all, it was fitfully. She cast her quilts away, then pulled them back, turned her pillow over, then over again. Fragments of dreams came to mimic sleep. In them, cruel visions fractured into kaleidoscope segments of her past day and magnified its betrayals. She'd startle back to wakefulness.

Before dawn, she came awake to what seemed more vision than dream. She was outdoors. A frightful rain descended from weirdly earth-colored clouds.

The rain was falling in the form of rough broken stones and burning coals, twigs and sticks, spoons and knives, sheep shears, spools of yarn, garden tools. They pelted down on her, then all the debris swirled up around her by some eerie ground wind. She was raging, hitting, and fighting the objects pelting down on her. Her hands were burned and cut. In the sly sliding way of dreams, a large garden trowel was in her right hand. Her children were there beside her. Emil was there, Hetti and Jacob with him.

She began lashing at the objects pelting down, while with her left hand, she tried to shield her children by pushing them back where the protection of her body might shield them. But in the way of dreams, when she glanced to see if the children were safe, the cart was gone and Emil had the use of his legs and his arms. He could run like any other child. He waved at her then ran in great loping strides into the wind and dark brown wall of jabbing rain. She watched him go and the rain grew browner and harder, and the trowel disappeared. Her hands were empty. She felt a void, a disturbing emptiness. The sounds of the storm clanking and banging stopped. She was looking at her empty hands.

Jacob and Hetti were gone. They weren't behind her. She realized that time, in her dream, had passed and she had forgotten them in her concern for Emil, she felt an enormous guilt. She went searching for them. She looked for the children though the painful jabbing rain was battering her.

She looked and looked and saw only rain. Then she saw the two children, but they were far away. They were also changed, but not as Emil had been. Jacob and Hetti were transformed into tiny figures, doll children, miniatures made of hardened clay or some Albrechtsburg china. Amid the debris falling she saw her son and daughter break apart, swirl into the wind and become pieces in the storm's rain of debris. She needed to put them back together. She tried to run and gather her children's parts, but her arms and legs wouldn't move. The hellish rain came falling harder. In it, her two beautiful and unafflicted children's legs, arms, hands, and heads were multiplying so that parts of hundreds of tiny children were falling amid the stones, twigs, scissors and sticks in the rain. She tried to call out her own true children from the mass falling, to gather their parts to her so she could piece them back together again, but no voice came from her throat.

Emil was talking to her. But she didn't know what he was saying. He was laughing like a healthy child and she knew from his expression that he, the son of her heart, refused help her find her other children, and she woke to

her son flailing out on the cot beside her. His thin legs had stiffened out and scissored, twisting his blankets. With his head flopped toward her, one of his arms was rigid and jerking up above the cot repeatedly banging its wooden frame. The boy was in spasm. She rose from her pillow, sat up and pulled him onto her lap. Her practiced body did what needed to be done.

She pulled back the knot of covers and forced his legs apart. She whispered gently to him as she worked to flex the boy's knees and massage his calves and thighs until his joints were pliable and his muscles relaxed again. It seemed a long time before Emil's stiff extended arm flopped down across his belly and was no longer rigid and he fell back into the rhythm of his body's normal sleep. Her back hurt, and her legs were numbed from the pressure of his weight.

Still, Ilsa held him. She listened to the clock in the other room ping a quarter hour. The wind whistled outside; the breathing of the children was even. She was afraid to close her eyes. If she slept, she would dream. Dreams had become her enemy, but she didn't know a way to bar them if she slept.

O<<>>O

~~~O<<>>O~~~

26 ~ In the Dark of Morning

The room's temperature dropped, and she knew, with a sense of desperate relief, that morning would come soon. Ilsa rose and moved from the cot to the high cupboard to get new padding for Emil. Her child had almost soaked through what he wore, and she'd need a fresh gown and clean, dry pad to put under him. Better, she might as well wash and dress for the day. It would be light soon. First, she'd freshen her besieged son's garments and his bed. She could do that in the dark, she had done it so many times before; the quality of light, or time of day, mattered little.

The others in the room slept on as she worked to change him and her hands, always gentle, didn't wake the boy. He slept restlessly and often interrupted by spasms or fits, but he slept long, like a small baby does. It made her work easier. The other children would be up and tended before he woke. Her family was as used to the sounds of caregiving during the night. It wouldn't wake them. The steady nasal rattle of Baby Johnnie's breathing in the crib beside his father's bed and the peaceful occasional turnings of the other children on their cots, gave her no comfort. Anna usually helped the baby get ready for the day. The girl went to her baby brother in his crib as soon as she was awake. Anna liked playing little mother, and Ilsa knew it helped her to have the girl willing to work.

There was only faint light coming through the doorway from the fireplace's illumination, but Ilsa knew her way around her house in dark or light. She could go and stir the fire, add wood to the Franklin stove and start the teakettle to boil. Until she had settled her own mind on what she would do, she didn't want the children alarmed. She would act the same wife that she had been these past eleven months, at least until she planned out what she must do.

Washed and dressed, Ilsa slipped through the doorway into the big room. She carefully closed the door between so no squeak would wake Ainslie or the children. He got up so early, usually before she did. She didn't want him near her. The benefit of her night of wakefulness was that she had risen first, before that evil presence was awake. For this short time she could pretend that she was still mistress of her home. She went around the fireplace and took a lantern and went out through the back door. At the woodshed she put the light down on the chopping block for a moment while she hoisted an armful of small logs already cut to fit the stove, then and went back to the house. The wind had stopped. It was still and dark outside. The only sounds came from her shoes on the gravel of the work yard.

At the kitchen end of the big room, the firebox in the Franklin had coals enough to ignite the new wood. Ilsa took her kitchen apron from its hook by the storage room door. She looked as tired as the night had left her, but within she felt the fury of the angels who had been cast from Heaven. "*Gott im Himmel*," her mother cried so often, more as a curse at her children's errors in doing their tasks, than as a prayer. *Gott* had never turned *Mutti* out of his sight. He had saved that insult for Ilsa. Ilsa began the early preparations of breakfast for the family in the dark pre-dawn kitchen corner of the room. She found it strange that she could hold this violent anger within her, and still carefully ladle water from bucket to pot, measure grain and salt, and observe the flame of the stove. Her body worked as it always did. The benefit of the good order she maintained was that she needn't think of what she was doing. It carried her through what she did every morning since she came to Rohe Farm.

While her body did the work, her mind would not stay with what her hands were doing. It filled, with images of Ainslie, not as *Rübezahl,* the night effigy, and not as he was during their confrontation yesterday's evening. Alone, in the dark kitchen, she was thinking of her husband as he was yesterday at noon. She was thinking not of his words or his treachery, but of his touch and smell and what he did with her. She was aroused and no matter how she tried to rid herself of sensation, it spread from her mind to her body. She couldn't let it go. Ilsa's dry mouth moistened. Sparks circled in her low belly. She felt a flow of liquid. She hated Ainslie, wanted him dead, yet her body was opening to the thought of him. Yet as her hands pumped water into the kettle, she delighted in the memory of how his size had grown to fill her, and how he'd not moved while she'd danced under him. Perversely, the thought that he could be the trickster excited her more. An ugly giant with a gnomish nose and wild eyes was in her kitchen making her body do what he wanted. She felt *Rübezahl* come into her, the monster's spiked penis filling her. With slow jerks and tight spirals he made her convulse again and again, over and over. She knew she would die.

Ilsa stood in the still dark of morning and realized what she was doing. She was using the fire rod in her hand to poke at the kindle in the banked stove. Her hand was repeating the rhythm of her dream, moving and moving into the brightening coals. She was imitating the monster, *ficken* a real fire just as he had done to the fires of her body. The trickster had thieved a path into her thoughts.

Here in the lantern-lit kitchen corner of her house, on a day so new light hadn't yet broken the sky, the trickster was still trying to thieve everything that was hers and make it his, even her flesh. She felt herself wanting to vomit up all the ire and outrage she had ever felt. She wanted to spew it on Ainslie, the man, as he lay in his bed at the other side of the house. Stupid, stupid fool she was. She'd been trickster-deluded into this deviant passion for him. She wouldn't allow that her body do this today, now that she knew what her husband was. Damn him to Hell!

She dropped the poker and jittered back from the stove clanging its firebox door closed. She vowed to the death of her that she would use the splintered piece of a broken broom handle to pleasure herself, before she'd ever let Rübezahl touch her body or inhabit her mind again. The joke in yesterday was that after he'd pleasured her, while she was still feeling the gentle lassitude that comes afterward, Ain's had set her uncle to tear her belly open for him to pull her guts out of her. Remembering yesterday and how she had wanted Ainslie brought another truth to her. The man masked concern for her in his false denial. She'd asked for his child. He had withheld himself from her, not because he was afraid she'd die in childbirth, but because he was afraid she'd bear another like Emil— carrying Buchanan as his name.

As Ains had left her that noontime, he must have shown cocky and gloating, *Rübezahl's* face. The crew down in the orchard must have seen his depravity. How could they not?

She remembered the smugness she had seen on Adam Mueller's face as he let his horse turn his carriage back to town. She was nothing to either of them. She might have been a stick or a table, herself of no more importance than a butter churn.

Foul, vicious thoughts came to her. If she couldn't rid herself of the spirit creature from her grandmother's tales, she could take her vengeance on the man. A man could die. She stood in the kitchen looking at her cupboards. Since she was preparing what Ainslie would take as his breakfast, she entertained the idea that it was simple for a woman who worked in a kitchen to poison a man who sat at her table. But then again, poisons take time to work. They often fail even to kill mice. How much would it take to kill a man? Perhaps there were better, simpler ways to kill a monster.

———

161

It seemed quickly that light began glaring into the room. It burned her eyes. Ilsa looked at the clock, though she knew the time by the window. She reached into the cupboard and took out the left over *stollen* unwrapped from its towel, and set it on the breadboard it to slice, then went to the cellar to bring up milk and butter, and a basket of eggs. Ains was undoubtedly sitting at the edge of his bed reaching for his britches. He would be rested. His sleep had been easy. He would do what he did every morning of the week. He'd slip out to the privy through the small door, come back to wash, dress, and in ten minutes, he'd creep out into the big room and put his boots on so silently that the children could sleep a little longer. Every day but Sunday and his business days when he traveled, he liked to be out at work before the children began to scuttle about full of banter and noisy jibes.

She heard the click of the door opening. His footsteps into the room were soft. She had imagined he walked softly in the morning so the children could sleep longer, when he merely wanted his day to start without confusion or childish noise. More the fool she had been to give a nobler place to his intentions. He didn't carry a mother's concern for the children. Only *"Eine Mutter die Liebe"* was unending and unselfish. It was their mother who washed up children's foul messes and found their mittens, cleaned behind their ears and set them to their schoolwork. Her beguiled children chose to listen to his stories and love him. They set her away from them and into the background of their lives. He had seduced them as he had her. She could not blame the children. She, too, had loved what was false.

Ains came into the big room and carefully set the clock's pendulum. He said nothing to her. She said nothing to him. She fixed his breakfast. His routine was that he would eat and afterward he'd go first to check all his horses. He'd stop at the barn to leave a chalk slate full of instructions for Benjamin. He'd walk the perimeter of the eighty acres inspecting the condition of the land. Then he'd ride to his own farm to meet with Thomas, the crop foreman for both farms. Ilsa gave him no kiss as she placed his breakfast before him. He seemed not to notice. She thought that it was good that he would play against her at this game of silence. She walked to the window above the sink and looked out. The trees looked bare and black. Their boney limbs were sharp against the still dawning sky.

She had come out of her bad dreams. Ainslie was not a creature from a children's story. He was only a man. He was as ugly in his heart as any other man she had ever known. She knew what to do to men. Her body was not so strong as a man's was, but she had a clear and fearless mind. It could find ways to circumvent the limitations of her smaller, weaker body.

O<<>>O

162

27~ Emil

The children came out of the bedroom washed and dressed for school. Anna was carrying Johnnie and took him to the seat Ains had made for his children's toddler years by affixing a big round of hickory on the seat of a stool with iron brads. It was Hetti's job to get the children's bibs from the hooks in the storage room. She passed them around, helping Andrew and Johnnie by tying theirs for them. Ilsa served porridge into their bowls. Anna passed butter around quickly so it would rotate among the children while the meal was hot enough to melt it. Then the milk jug and honey were passed. Ilsa went back and brought the teapot. Jacob poured for Andrew, and it was then passed around the table too.

Before she went to get Emil washed and dressed, Ains had his hat on and left the house. He'd kissed the children, told them to be good to their teacher and their mother, then he asked her if she could manage Emil this morning without him.

Ainslie put his arms around her and softly said, "I'll be at my da's farm today. He's down with his back and needs Cam and me both to help him. Don't fret about this other so much. You'll see it's for the best, my love."

She stiffened in his arms, and said nothing. He let her loose. When he was gone, Ilsa went to tend to Emil. He was awake and ready for the day. She put her arms around him and tugged until she could stand upright with him, and drag-carried him into the wash closet. He was soon going to be too heavy for her. While she cared for Emil, the children cleared, scraped, and stacked their mugs, bowls and spoons. Hetti was sitting in Ain's chair. Josiah was setting out toys for Johnnie and Andrew's delight. And then, the older four kissed her goodbye and went to meet the wagon.

In spite of Ilsa's distress and fatigue, the woman sat by her son's cart and carefully, patiently fed him the mixture of boiled meal, milk, sugar and cinnamon that he seemed to like. He was learning to chew, though he often tore his cheek with his teeth when he tried. If she put small chunks of apple into the mix he would look at her in a way that let her know he liked tonguing the bits. He was controlling his mouth better, and he was more able to look in the direction he heard sound. Dr. Bentzinger thought he was deaf, but he wasn't. But she knew that this child, so precious to her, would never reach to pat her cheek or have language to tell her he loved her.

Benjamin came to the house with a message that Tansie would not be able to come to work for a few days. Tansie had been called to her daughter's house in town during the night. Her daughter's labor had begun and she needed her mother. Ilsa had known that the girl would call on Tansie when her time came. The woman had talked of little other than her first grandchild's arrival. Ilsa felt relief that the woman would be gone. She could not think. She could not direct a maid.

The big room swallowed up the slight noises that came from the popping and crackles of the wood burning in the fireplace. Johnnie was drumming on the slates with an old splintery wooden spoon she had long ago given him as a plaything.

Emil seemed to be watching from the cart. His lower lip seemed to be keeping time with the sounds of the spoon against the slates by moving rhythmically. She had once thought he could hear from his earliest months. He would startle at loud sounds but Dr. Bentzinger had said that was sensing sound vibrations, not hearing in a way that would matter.

Emil was making the weak sounds. Andrew called them singing. Emil had seemed to benefit from the greater stimulation of having the Buchanan children around him. Emil seeming to know when they were leaving for school and when they were due home, seemed to connect with two year old Johnnie during the long hours that the children were gone. Jacob and Hetti had never given him so much attention as he received now with the Buchanan children added to the household. She knew she should have been exhilarated at the sight of Emil seem to be attending to another child's play. He was showing something new, advancement in what he could do. But she felt remote from all that was happening. It was as though there were a thick wall of water between her and all human interaction—even that which gave her hope for her child's progress.

When Emil was clean and fed, she walked away from him. She went as far across the big room as she could so he wouldn't perceive how angry she was or feel her tension in some way beyond her understanding. She wanted to go outside and scream. No house could contain the space of that anger. She wanted to scream so loudly that the sound of her voice would penetrate the walls, shake the trees, and echo across the fields on the other side of Clark Road.

She couldn't scream. She wanted to scream so loud that her screams would penetrate the stables and tear into Ainsley and pin him to the walls like spears. She couldn't. If her body's moves as she worked through the day weren't as measured and graceful as a dancer's, Emil would begin his piteous noises. Her boy would grow upset if any sound that came from her wasn't soft speech, cooing, or melodies. Her lips had to stay soft, her face at ease, as she restrained all that she felt. No frown could tense her face. She could not lash out, even against a pillow or her own belly. Her limbs had to move easily, slowly. Words would never come from his throat. But his anxious, and gutteral noises tore at her heart. She had never been able to show what she felt, and she could never leave the surroundings of the house. This had been her life from the morning when he was born. If Emil's eyes cried and his nose ran strings of mucus, he might also begin to choke. Sometimes she had to clear his mouth and pat his back so he could breathe. Day or night she was always listening for him.

He had been so perfect at his birth. When her mother held lifted him to let Hetti cut the cord, Ilsa could see he had a small nose, two eyes, a little mouth, fine hair like summer's wind-blown lint. He had all his parts. He did not cry and that had frightened her. She had labored two days and two nights already. The midwife had shaken her head before daybreak on the third day's morning. The exhausted woman had gone home saying, "It is too long now, for this one to live."

It was left to Mutti to bring Emil out from her body. Her mother called Hetti out of bed with the morning still dark to come and help her with the delivery. Hetti was just fifteen, large and clumsy, but a reliable girl. In spite of the duration of Ilsa's labor and the intensity of the pains, she was happier once Hetti was there with her. If she and her baby had to die because her body could not let loose of the child, at least her sister was with her to hold her hand and wipe her brow until they were safely gone from this pain to heaven. And then she'd felt the baby move in her. Her stomach welled up in a hard knot, she tore apart and her mother was able to wrest the baby out of her.

Ilsa wanted the feel of her child, but Mutti held the baby out away from the bed. She asked Hetti for a towel and put it under the wet, bluish infant. Ilsa's mother moved away from bed. The woman went to the window and held the baby up to the early light of Ilsa's baby's first day. Ilsa was so tired but she saw her mother frown.

Her stomach felt strangely empty, and she didn't like the dead, hollow feeling of her body. She wanted her child in her arms. Her mother was keeping the baby from her. Ilsa thought he should have been pinker in color. The girl was scared and angry. She thought Mutti was denying her the child, and that her mother wanted to steal him for herself. He was a boy. She knew she had borne a boy and her mother envied her.

But, her mother's face changed to a scowl that made Ilsa quiver. All her mother said was, "A boy." She said it so heavily Ilsa thought her baby was dead. She knew when the labor went on so long as hers had, babies and mothers often died. Tears began to run down her face. In spite of hours of pain becoming days and nights beyond endurance, she had held to the belief that her child would live if she could not give in to pain and fatigue.

"Is he alive?" she cried.

From her pillow she stared at the tiny child her mother held. Dawn had brightened the window behind them. Light was beginning to stream into the room. Ilsa prayed, hoping that God could hear prayers said in her mind. Words would not come from her mouth. *Please, God, give me my baby living. Please make him live. Please God...*And then she saw one tiny leg move.

He was alive. God had answered her prayer.

"Give him to me!" she cried to her mother. "He is alive! Give him to me."

"*Ya.*" Her mother's voice was bitter. "Alive, but *schwachsinnige.* A boy, but not a good child." Her mother held him up to the window again. "*Nine.* Not good," she said. Instead of giving Ilsa her newborn, Mutti walked with the baby past the girls down to the foot of the bed. Ilsa tried to sit up, but she was too weak. Hetti reached to help lift her up, leaning in from the side of the bed. Ilsa didn't know what her mother was doing, but Hetti had her back turned as she tried to help Ilsa.

"Hetti!" Ilsa cried.

The girl looked back over her shoulder where Ilsa was looking. The girls' mother turned her back more to try and block Hetti's view of the corner where she was. But Ilsa leaned to the far side of the bed and saw what her mother had done. She saw her mother place the baby down on the bed. The woman pulled up a corner at the bottom of the birthing sheet and drew it across the baby's small face.

Her mother put her hand down on top of the fabric across the baby's mouth and compressed its tiny nose with her thumb and forefinger. She held it there. The baby lay very still. Ilsa again tried to lift herself up to reach her child, but she fell back. She screamed out, frantic, but too weak to get up and take her child. Hetti was slow to move but quick to think. She understood what their mother was doing, and she understood the plea in Ilsa's wailing scream.

Hetti was large and strong, built like Papa Mueller. She pulled the girls' mother's fingers away from the baby's face. Shoving her mother back away from the bed with her elbow and swinging her back to block the woman's access to the baby, Hetti grasped the fabric away from the newborn's face.

From behind the wide back of her second daughter, Mutti said, "No! Leave it. You girls know nothing. I know what needs to be done here." She hit at Hetti's back and tried to go around the girl. She tried to reach the baby from the foot-rail of the bed. But Hetti turned her body and thrust out her elbows to keep her mother from the baby.

Ilsa, exhausted from over two days and nights of an exhausting labor, was weeping. "Help him, Hetti. Oh, please help him."

Hetti ran her hands over the baby. She lifted his head and opened his mouth to blow into it. The baby didn't respond. Mutti was calling curses at them and hitting at Hetti's back and arms, but with one hand Hetti reached for a flannel from the stack prepared for the newborn. She was stroking the infant's chest, never once taking her eyes from the baby to look at either Ilsa or the girls' mother. Hetti swiftly swaddled the child and lifted him up into the air. It was the first human birth the girl had witnessed, but she had seen other animals in the barns during birthing.

She swung the baby up and down, her own energy urging him to breathe. He made a small sucking, gasping sound. Ilsa saw his small chest inflate. Hetti watched him for a few moments as he took quick deep breaths. She cuddled him to her chest and smiled at her sister. "He breathes."

Mrs. Mueller moved back from the bed. Her voice grew gutteral and low.

She was disgusted with the sisters' intervention in what she had been trying to do. "Foolish girls. Suit yourselves. You bring yourself only trouble, Ilsa. So much trouble you are bringing down on yourself. Hetti, you did your sister no favor, but this trouble is on you, Ilsa. You are the older. You should have more sense." She turned to the door. "I'm done with you both, but blame yourself, Ilsa. This brings trouble to you." She left the room.

With her first child alive and in her arms, Ilsa had an explosion of feeling such as she had never known. Not when she was a child and Papa held her in his arms, not when Franz first entered her, not on any birthday celebration, not at her wedding party. She knew her mother was wrong. Her son was perfect. His cheeks were fat and soft. His little arm jerked once and she noticed how pretty his tiny hands were. She named him for her father, as she and Franz had planned. He was Emil Mueller Rohe.

Before she moved baby Emil to her breast, Ilsa determined that the first baby girl Franz gave her would be named for her sister. She knew Hetti to be her best and most trusted friend. She never thought Hetti would have had the courage to defy their mother. Ilsa clung to her child and kept him in the bed with her. She wouldn't let him go to the cradle where her mother might come in while she slept and steal him away. How could her mother think that there was anything wrong with this beautiful baby?

Franz seemed so proud that his first child was a boy when he came in the room, after Hetti had taken the bloody rags and the afterbirth basin away and straightened the room. She worried what her mother may have said to him, but only saw love in her young husband's eyes. The days of Ilsa's confinement went by. Her sisters and the housemaids took care of her.

Her mother never entered the room again. Mutti would not even come back to help her get the baby Emil to nurse properly. Hetti had to run and ask the midwife to come to help Ilsa teach him to suck and not choke. Her sisters clustered about to admire him, the first boy in the family. Hetti came in to sit with Ilsa and help her bathe. Lena said he was the prettiest baby she had ever seen. Franz slept on the floor for the first few days. When he saw that Ilsa never put the baby to sleep in his cradle but kept Emil in their bed, he built a rope pallet and put in a straw mattress for himself. It fit between the bed and their wardrobe. Franz was kind with her but he was quiet. Ilsa kept waiting for her father to come to the room she and Franz shared in the Mueller farmhouse. Papa hadn't come to see Emil at all. Emil, named for him, was the first boy to be born in his house. At first she didn't understand why he hadn't come to see little Emil.

She was sure that her mother had poisoned her father against her baby. Mutti was hateful and wrong and trying to hurt her. Her sisters weren't jealous, but her mother was. Mutti had never borne a son for Papa.

Slowly, as the weeks passed and became months, baby Emil grew. But he never responded to Ilsa. He didn't babble. He didn't even cry in the same way other children cried. She would not admit it, not even to Franz or Hetti. Something was very wrong with her tiny Emil. But he was alive.

O<<>>O

168

28 ~ Prayers Against Evil

After he was born, Ilsa's baby choked so often at the breast she'd have to stop and turn him over and pat his back forcing little bubbles to come out of his mouth. She had seen her little sisters choke at her mother's breast during their infant feedings but it happened rarely. She had to help her baby clear his lungs many times during his feedings. Then, he didn't reach out his hands as she remembered other babies having done so. He didn't smile. His little arms and legs would either jerk or lie limp. His cry was a bird noise, not like other babies' cries. Sometimes he'd look at her but often his eyes roamed lazily, not appearing to see anything and no matter what she did to cuddle and coax him, he didn't smile.

When she carried him downstairs, or out into the yard for sunshine, her mother took no interest in the baby. If she had to say something to Ilsa or Hetti, Mutti spoke curtly. The children, her sisters would hold Emil so she could help with the baking and cheese making. She soon learned that she was expected to take the baby upstairs when her father and his men came in to dinner or guests were in the house.

Her Papa made it clear that he hated the sight of her child. And it was her father's guttural reference, nearly under his breath, to "Ilsa's *schwachsinnige,*" that made her continually remember how her mother had voiced that word as she held Emil to the window's light at his birth.

Little Emil's life meant no more to Papa and Mutti than the animals her father culled in the farmyard. Ilsa, Hetti and their younger sisters had learned from Papa to judge a new litter of piglets and pick the frail ones out for him to kill. She'd been just six when her father took an axe and struck down a sleet new red colt with a white forehead blaze. It was trying to get to its feet and balance on only three legs. Its fourth leg was curved and too

169

deformed to hold its body's weight. She and Hetti had been watching from between the slats in the barn. By the time she was ten and Hetti nine, they were busy in the house learning how to run an admirable family Their little sisters took their turn helping Papa ferret out new litters of kittens to drown. As much as they loved playing with the kits, the girls understood that a proper barn and yard needed three or four cats to keep the rodents down, but not more. Papa would sometimes let them pick one or two to save.

Ilsa came to realize that Papa expected that her mother or the midwife would cull any imperfect child just as he did runty piglets. It was Papa who was behind Mutti's action. But Ilsa's child was not a farm animal, nor was she a sow, or cow, or cat. *Gott in Himmel* had raised people above the animals of the earth. She had dutifully loved her parents for sixteen years, and truly loved her father. But hatred grew in her with each sunrise and sunset. She took her child in her arms to church with the family after the first month, but there, the pastor's face told her that he didn't want her child there. No woman in the congregation asked after her child or asked to see him. She knew Mutti had told them that something was wrong with Ilsa and Franz's baby. Ilsa never went back to church after Emil was shunned, but she felt herself made one of God's archangels, ferocious in her determination to protect her son.

Ilsa had once been the favored child in the Mueller household. Now, even squinty-eyed Lena, the youngest of her sisters, was given preference over her. Her parents favored her husband for his amiability and hard work on Papa's dairy farm. They had strongly encouraged her marriage to him. He now had taken her place in the family, a first son to replace their first daughter who had disappointed them. Instead of Franz being their daughter's husband, she was only their foreman's wife.

Before her eighteenth birthday, Ilsa Rohe was again pregnant. She hoped the child would be a girl, but she bore a healthy boy. Papa Mueller came to carry him downstairs. On Jacob Mueller Rohe's christening day, Franz was made manager of the Mueller Dairy. It was a position far better than being the dairy's foreman. But Jacob, the perfect son she bore, did not redeem her in her parents' eyes. She was still held to account for bearing Emil Mueller Rohe, a child with beautiful features— who at over a year could not sit up, or grasp, or follow voices with his eyes.

The drifting of her mind back to Papa's house ended, and she heard the clock. Tansie would not come to intrude upon her thoughts today. Ilsa need not spend her day in pretending to be a good woman for the housemaid's eyes. She looked down at her son, fed and comfortable, then glanced over at Ainslie's little Johnnie playing on the rug with Andrew.

170

The three children made no demands other than she remain calm and be their mother.

She had an idea that she might pray. She would give God another chance to help her. If Almighty God had so often shown her that he had turned her from Heaven, He should have fairness enough to drive Ainslie Elias Buchanan from earth. She knelt down beside Emil's cart and turned her mind to God.

Her memory had no power. The only prayer she could remember was for children, so she said it three times slowly, and she listened to its words.

> Ich bin klein, mein Herz ist rein.
> Soll niemand drin wohnen als Jesus allein.
> Amen
>
> Ich bin klein, mein Herz ist rein.
> Soll niemand drin wohnen als Jesus allein.
> Amen
>
> Ich bin klein, mein Herz ist rein.
> Soll niemand drin wohnen als Jesus allein.
> Amen

If she filled her heart with Jesus, there would be no room for monsters like *Rübezahl*, like Ainslie Buchanan.

But she needed better words to reach God. Her own were useless. The commandments ran through her mind. "Ich bin der Herr, dein Gott. Du sollst keine anderren Götter, haben neben mir...Du sollst den Namen des Herrn, deines Gottes, nicht missbrauchen.....Du sollst den Feiertag heiligen......Du sollst deinen Vater und deine Mutter ehren........Du sollst nicht töten.........Du sollst nicht ehebrechen............Du sollst nicht stehlen...

She stopped at seven, Ainslie's sin. *Du sollst nicht stehlen.* Thou shalt not steal.

The words of a prayer came whispering from her lips.

"Please dear God burn the vile bastard thief Ainslie Buchanan in Hell fire forever. Send him to the deepest part of the pit for the theft of this farm, which is mine, for taking the children, who are mine. If you have any justice, you will help me strike evil down."

Ilsa felt better. A great peace came over her. She arranged her skirts and got to her feet.

She bent to Emil and stroked her sweet boy's face and chest. She could feel his heart beating faster than was normal for him. She stroked his head, and as she did, her touch soothed him from whatever anxiety had come to him.

She picked up Johnnie and carried him into the kitchen with her. Andrew followed. She gave the little boys biscuits. Baby Johnnie was a sweet child too.

O<<>>O

IV

ILSA ROHE
~~~1845~~~

Josiah Buchanan's Home

29 ~ Another Move

21 March 1845, Friday afternoon

I've been thinking about what you might want me to tell you. You probably most need to hear what I most don't want to say.

I've told you about so much of our life, but little about last November. I promise I will. It is just that I want to tell it all correctly and in order, as it happened. The summer after Mr. Rohe died, my gran befriended Mrs. Rohe. She worried that Mrs. Rohe didn't seem to have friends. She had heard the French girl had left. I think Gran would have been friendly earlier if she'd known the Rohes weren't papists. Vallerie who worked for them was a papist. And so Gran thought that the Rohe's were too.

There are only two churches in Cossette, the Christian Church where we, and all our kind of people, belong, and Sacred Heart where the French families and the other kind of Irish go. Gran strongly disapproves of the Catlick religion. Excuse me, Mr. Laughton if you are a Catlick, but what

I'm saying is what was.

You're not. I'm glad because then I didn't offend you. It isn't my intent. And Gran wouldn't be happy for me to tell all this to a papist.

Mariette Bernier goes to Dry Creek School and she is a nice girl. I've known her for more than two years now, and she is as good as anyone for all that she goes to the wrong church. Mr. Herbert thinks highly of her and her work although that he goes to the Christian Church and not to Sacred Heart. But I must get back to what I ought be telling you.

When Mr. Rohe died, Gran found out that the Rohe's were members of the German Christian Church in Taylorsville. Many German families live in Taylorville's Township, but here in Anderson Township most of us aren't German. But what that meant was on weekends Jacob and Hetti would sometimes come down the road. Hetti would come in the house with me and Libby, Andrew, and Johnnie. We'd play or talk Libby and Mrs. Walker into making cookies or scones while Josiah and Jacob ran and played like boys do. Da was extra kind to Jacob over our boy cousins or any other friends Josie had because his father had just died. Josie went to the Rohe house often on a Saturday afternoon after his chores.

Hetti is much younger than I am, but she is good at math and quick at games. She often beat me at checkers. She liked to play with my sisters' and my old dolls. She said she had a beautiful doll at home but her mother wouldn't let her bring it down the road for fear it would get dirty.

Hetti wanted me to go to her house, but Libby and Gran wouldn't let me. Libby said I needed to stay at home in case she needed me to help her with the house, and Gran said that Mrs. Rohe had enough on her hands without having to watch out for extra children. She said boys played outside but extra girls, who were not family or servants, were a nuisance in a house. So I didn't see the inside of the Rohe house until Da took all of us there for dinner one Sunday before Christmas last year. It was right after that that he told us that he and Mrs. Rohe were getting married and she would be our new mother. Libby hadn't wanted to go. She had told me that she thought Da and Mrs. Rohe were going to get married, and she would have no part of it. And when Da told us we were going to dinner there, Libby looked at me. She put her chin up to say, "See, I was right."

Libby spoke up to Da and refused to go. Da took her into the parlor and talked to her with the door closed. And Libby behaved and went with us to pay our visit to Mrs. Rohe in her home. My sister made much of taking care of Johnnie so she didn't have to take part in conversation. But Josiah and I were excited. Andrew was too, because he hadn't been anywhere but church and Gran's in a long time since he didn't go to school yet.

Josiah had already told me that Jacob and Hetti's house seemed to have no walls inside, but that it was a nice place. But he hadn't described it further than that. It was just as he said. I thought it was a place out of a storybook. There were paintings on the cupboard doors, and embroideries hanging from the walls like paintings. Mrs. Rohe had an amazing big clock, like ours, but with carvings on it. It rang out so nicely, it would scare a person if they didn't know what it was, but its tick was soft. Ours has a loud tick and its chimes are rude sounding, not so like music. You have seen ours. It is in Gran's kitchen now. We didn't take it with us when we moved to Rohe Farm and Da didn't want to leave it to the care of his tenants in our farmhouse.

Mrs. Rohe and her maid, Mrs. Wilson, served us a fine dinner that Sunday. As we rode home in the wagon afterwards, Da told us that he and Mrs. Rohe would be married at Christmas. Johnnie was sleeping on my lap, and Libby had her arm around Andrew. It was late afternoon. Josiah whooped, and said, "Hooray, Jacob will be my brother!" He startled Johnnie awake.

Libby just looked at me to say, "See, I was right again."

I think it would have been all right with Libby if the Rohe's had moved in with us as we thought they would. But that evening, Da told us that that the Rohe's were not going to come live with us, but we would be going to live with them. We'd be moving to Rohe Farm right after the wedding and we needed to tag that which we wanted to take with us. Libby was so angry she raised her voice to him. She said that she would not live in that German place, and it wasn't as our mother Fiona would have had us live. Libby said she wasn't going to become Mrs. Rohe's housemaid. She swore that she'd never take care of "that feeble child of Mrs. Rohe's that was bigger than our Josiah and needed to be carried to the pot and fed by hand."

Libby wept bitterly and argued more. She said Da was unfair to her, and that he was unfair to Gran who had worked so hard for us. Da listened to her and did not scold her. He led her to a chair and sent the rest of us upstairs.

175

But, of course, by then my da loved Mrs. Rohe. He wouldn't give her up for what Libby wanted.

My sister Libby ran away from us and got married. She made a fine adventure of it, but we children came apart without her. Gran had to move back in to help us. Tillie, our maid, didn't seem to know what to do without Libby. Johnnie cried so much, and Andrew spilt ink all over Da's desk ruining some of his papers when Josiah and I were in school. Gran Da wasn't very happy either.

When Christmas Eve came, and Reverend Johnson came with all the Buchanan family and Adam Mueller, Esquire to Rohe Farm and we had a wedding. Libby and Billy came too. I could tell how happy my da was to see her there. He had taken her a fine dress and new cape and bonnet to wear, but I thought that he dressed her because then she'd have to come to the wedding. Da had been afraid that Libby wouldn't come and be with us that evening.

When Gran Da made a toast for Da and our new mother, I whispered to Libby that she disappointed me in that she didn't have a proper wedding to Billy. She gave me a scorching look and told me her wedding was very proper. She truly put me in my place and I felt ashamed of what I'd said.

That night our Da stayed at Rohe Farm with his new wife. Gran stayed with us. It was the first Christmas night Da was away from us ever. But the next morning it was a clear day and my uncles all arrived early with their wagons and some of my big cousins and they moved us from our house to our new mother's. We spent that day putting our beds in place and our own little cupboards and chests near them, and Da showed where he had made a little miniature room for Hetti and me so we'd have privacy. We were all that busy, that we didn't even think of presents. Mrs. Rohe asked us if we would like to call her Mutti, as her children did. I told her I'd call her Mutti Ilsa, and she laughed and said she liked that name.

She fixed a grand dinner for us with the foods left from the wedding the evening before. Mutti Ilsa had a tree from the woods in her house that her worker Benjamin brought into the house for her. We always brought greenery into the house but Josiah and I had never known anyone to bring a whole tall tree inside. It was standing upright with its trunk in a bucket and surrounded by an embroidered rug.

After the table was cleared and scrubbed, Hetti and Jacob brought out papers and ribbons and scissors and a pot of paste and we set about making little folded birds to put on the tree. They did this every year and said that the tree was the *Christbaum.* They decorated one every year on Christmas and tried to keep it green as long as they could into January. It was a fine custom. We taught Andrew how to fold the birds. It took him all afternoon to learn and he was proud, though his still weren't folded perfectly and Josiah and Jacob had to help him. Josiah's were better than mine although I am older, and it made Andrew feel better about his.

Mutti Ilsa took care of Johnnie all that day while we made decorations and explored the house. Da had wondrous presents for all of us hidden away, and around the fire that evening he had Josiah and Jacob help him bring them out of their hiding places in the barn. Even without Libby, we had a fine Christmas. It took away the sadness I'd been feeling from remembering the year before, and gave me hope for more good Christmases to come. We sang Christmas carols together, and though I think Da missed Libby and was a little sad that she wasn't with us, everyone else felt cheerful.

Andrew was happy sitting on Da's lap by the fire. When I looked at Mutti Ilsa cuddling our little Johnnie so happily in her chair, I cried just a little to think that our mother Fiona wasn't here to cuddle him herself. I knew Josie and Da were thinking of Harriet and our mother Fiona too. Christmas is that kind of a time when you miss who isn't there. But I thought our people in Heaven would be happy that we were becoming a good family again. It would be a better family than we were with just Libby and Gran patching us together.

I'll go now. Please don't worry, Mr. Laughton. Gran Da used to say that some tears only wash the heart clean again. I will be all right.

O<<>>O

~~~0<<>>0~~~

30 ~ A Valentine

24 March 1845, Monday afternoon

And a good day to you too, Mr. Laughton. I have to tell you that I am going back to school. Mr. Herbert has set April 7th as the day he will expect me. I'm a little frightened, but I made a promise to him when he came for my lessons on Saturday, and I will keep it.

I have something to show you, and something to give to you. My friends from school came to see me yesterday. First I'll show you the gifts Lucy Brown and her mother made for me. There are three, each a little different.

Yes. They are a fine and soft lace, stitched to flannel. They tie in the back. Aren't they pretty? Mrs. Brown thought I'd like something fancier than my gran's scarves for wearing at school. Jane and Suzanna begged Mrs. Brown to make them lace collars like mine. Mrs. Brown said she would. She will make one for Lucy also, so that the four of us can start a new fashion.

I have been out walking too. I have walked all around Gran Da's farm and been out to see the lambs and chickens with my brothers. Johnnie and Andrew grow so fast. Johnnie ran ahead of Andrew and me and wasn't shy of the animals at all. I wish that the boys were here all the time. They live with our uncle and aunt. Aunt Mattie is good for them, and though Gran wants my brothers, she is already overburdened. Gran and I are going back to church next Sunday. My Uncle Cameron will stay here and watch out for Gran Da and Uncle Johnnie, and my aunt Matilda and cousin Suzanna will drive Gran and me on to church in one of uncle Cameron's new carriages. It will be Gran's first time back since Gran Da had his stroke.

179

She has had to nurse both of us and watch out for Johnnie Reid that he didn't go wandering. Gran and I have planned to hold our heads high and walk into the church together.

My Uncles James and Andrew were here yesterday too with their families. They and Uncle Cameron put their heads together and made this plan for Gran and me. I was outside with my brothers and some of our cousins. Aunt Mattie said that my uncles worry that Gran is not getting enough chance to get out of the house and visit with her old friends.

My Aunt Mattie has asked me if I'd like to go and live with her and Suzanna and Uncle Cameron. I don't want to leave my gran, especially now that Gran Da takes care. I think if I stay here I can be a help to her. Libby comes often to help out, but I think Gran needs me.

This isn't helping you write for your magazine. I must get back to what happened in November, so you know it as it was then. And not bother you with what is now.

On Friday, I was telling you about our move to Rohe Farm. What happened was our lives became better. Our housemaids here at Gran's, Mary and Tillie, think that it must have been terrible for us to live there, but it wasn't. Mutti Ilsa had the cleanest house I'd ever seen. There was much work to do to keep it that way, but I liked working with her and Tansie. She was never shrill as Libby had been, and although she wasn't the great fun that our mother Fiona had been, she was very much a good mother to all of us. If I want to tell you the truth of all that happened, I have to say that.

My brothers and I began living at Rohe Farm on Christmas, and it was an adventure for us. It was almost like a dream or a storybook tale after we had struggled so when our mother Fiona died. There was something bright and happy there with Mutti Ilsa, Hetti and Jacob. For all of us. It seemed we went from holiday to holiday. The first was Valentine's Day. On the Saturday before it came, Mutti Ilsa had Jacob and Josiah go up into the attic with her and they brought down a long, flat box. In it was a beautiful embroidered tablecloth with chains of red hearts and yellow, blue, pink and purple flowers and a trellis. Along with it were twelve napkins to service the table. Mutti Ilsa laid an old quilt on the table and heated the iron and pressed out all the folds in the tablecloth. It was big enough to cover the whole huge table and drop to the floor.

Our da had a grand idea. He took Mutti Ilsa into the storage room where they always went to talk away from our ears. When they came back, Mutti Ilsa looked around the room and said, "Yes. It will work."

Da took Josiah, Jacob and Andrew outside with him, and then they came back in with a ladder and Da's toolbox. The boys held the tools and ladder while Da put big barn hooks up high into the pillars in the big room. Then they went out and got a long pole. While they were doing that, Mutti Ilsa was busy stitching red ribbons from her sewing chest to one long edge of the cloth so that they made loops. She let Hetti and me make some of the stitches. We held the edges so they wouldn't wrinkle as she ironed the cloth again. Then when the loops were done and the cloth pressed, Da and Mutti Ilsa ran the pole through the loops and then Da climbed the ladder again to set the pole across the hooks. It was something wonderful!

The cloth hung down across the room from the fireplace and made a Valentine wall between the kitchen part and the parlor part. Mutti and Da were so pleased with it that they said that next year and forever after, they would hang Mutti's grandmother's tablecloth up for the whole month of February. Truly, Mr. Laughton, I never saw a room change so much or look so beautiful.

That week had been so jolly. On Wednesday, which was Valentine's Day, Mr. Herbert gave us each a card he'd had printed with a pretty rhyme. It was from a book he read to us often. He wanted us to illuminate the card, each as we liked, and said we'd have a Valentine to take home to our families. Jacob gave his to Mutti Ilsa and Hetti gave hers to our Da. I still have mine from last year. I wasn't in school this past Valentine's Day. It is for you Mr. Laughton. It is over a year old, but it has never been given to anyone before.

When we made the Valentines I thought I'd give it to Gran. Then, I remembered that Gran didn't approve of Valentine's Day, or of saints and thought it all was papist foolishness, though everyone else in my family likes the holiday. All my uncles and aunts do. My da thought it the best of holidays, better than Christmas.

The year our mother Fiona died, we had been moving into Uncle Francis's house and were too busy to bother with Valentines. Da was so sorrowful that although Libby and I remembered the day, we didn't mention it.

To
Mr. Laughton

The Valentine

The rose is red, the violet's blue,
The honey's sweet, and so are you.
Thou art my love, and I am thine;
I drew thee to my Valentine:
The lot was cast, and then I drew,
And fortune said it should be you.

from:
Gammer Gurton's Garland
or The Nursery Parnassus
London, 1810, p. 21

from

Anna ,

your friend

Gran is dead against rosaries or icons or other things our church doesn't hold with and she says that the Bible is the word of God and enough for anyone.

Everyone else in my family likes the holiday, though. All my uncles and aunts do. My da thought it was one of the finest of all holidays. I don't think even Reverend Johnson is as strict about religion as my gran.

Please take the Valentine in your pocket to remember me when you go back to Boston. But please don't put what I said about Gran in your journal. She will read it. She has been chiding me for talking so much about my family and school. She says you are only interested in what happened last November and I am taking your time without telling you what you came to hear.

You don't mind?

Your magazine says you can stay in Ohio as long as you need?

Well, Mr. Laughton, that is very nice for me.

I didn't want to talk to you, but it has been very enjoyable. I promised Gran that I would tell you the whole of it. Then you can go back to Boston. And I will go back to school. I promised that too.

I'm glad you like it.

Mr. Herbert said that he thought my illumination on the Valentine card was very imaginative. It really wasn't. I think he was being very kind, but not very honest.

He had shown us some pictures of the paintings in books that monks in Ireland did hundreds of years ago when books were written by hand. We were supposed to do an illumination down the left hand side of the card like the monks would have done. I couldn't. I'm the worst at artwork of any of the older girls, and my paints always ran away from where I thought I was putting the brush to paper when we had a painting lesson.

So I had to pick something less complicated. I tried to copy a bit of Mutti Ilsa's tablecloth. So you see, it wasn't imaginative at all.

I don't know what kind of church you belong to, Mr. Laughton. Mr. Herbert comes to our church often. But he visits other churches. He says he likes to survey the practices of all Christians and he is sure God approves.

I've thought about that. The monks' illuminations that are in Mr. Herbert's book are much about Jesus. They have crosses and other symbols woven into them. But those old monks were Catlicks, as it was so long ago before even John Calvin. So wouldn't it seem that they must have been Christians too?

Oh, you think that they were. I won't tell Gran you disagree with her. She thinks that they are not.

I'll stop here. Is that all right? I have been dallying this week and have schoolwork to complete. My Uncle Cameron is coming this evening to help me with the arithmetic I don't understand. Gran and my Aunt Mattie say it is too advanced for them.

I will see you again on Wednesday.

Don't forget to take the Valentine with you. If you take it to Boston with you, that will be the farthest away that anything of mine has ever gone.

O<<>>O

31 ~ In Mutti Ilsa's house

26 March 1845, Wednesday afternoon

It seems very odd, but I've talked more to you than I've talked to anyone since November, and yet you were a stranger to me. Gran reads what you are putting down in the journal you keep. She doesn't talk to me about what she has read, but she asked me if it was easier for me to talk to strangers than to my family. I've been thinking about that, and I think it is. Strangers cannot love me so I cannot disappoint them. Nor will I embarrass them in what I say.

I can't talk to Gran Da or to Uncle Johnnie, though I help Gran care for them. Gran Da can't talk and Uncle Johnnie only argues. It bothers Gran very much that I have had so little to say to her. But I talk to her more than to anyone else. I've spoken to Libby, but only about small things. I can't talk with my school friends yet. They come to see me, but I can barely greet them. But they know I'm happy to see them. I think that they understand, because they are willing to talk so much about everything themselves. Perhaps they think it still hurts me to talk, that my injury is preventing me. I have resolved that the next time they come here to see me, I am going to talk, and I'll talk about you.

Yes. I will. Don't shake your head at me.

I'll tell them that you are Mr. Herbert's friend from his school days. I will tell them what you look like, and how quickly you can write, and what fine penmanship you have. Gran will bring little cakes in for me to serve with a pot of tea. She will creep in and out making no sounds and pretending she is invisible. She likes that they visit me, and she wants to encourage their visits.

I know, sir, that you want to know about Ilsa Rohe. But it has been hard for me to talk about her. You might not believe that she was ever kind to me, but she was. She was never sharp or rude with us. Only sometimes, now and again, Hetti would try her patience. I said I would say what was true, and you must know that we were happy living at Rohe Farm.

We were crowded somewhat there, and there was little privacy. But Da built a little half-wall around the cots where Hetti and I slept, and when we were tired of the boys we could go there and read or play checkers. Mutti Ilsa wouldn't allow the boys to come around the little wall to tease or bother us.

If we were doing our schoolwork and Johnnie was being a nuisance, Mutti Ilsa took him into the sleeping room and made him lie in his crib. He soon settled down and knew not to be a pest when we had work to do.

Johnnie was just beginning to walk when we all moved to Rohe Farm. Mutti Ilsa doted on him. She said she loved babies, and it was true. She seemed fonder of Andrew and Johnnie than her own children, but I think it was just that they were younger and needed her more. But she was most fond of Emil. He always had her heart. But it was necessary, because he was an invalid child and took so much care. He was helpless, you see. He couldn't even feed himself. Mutti Ilsa taught me to be a good nurse as she taught me to help her care for him. In the beginning, when we were first there, it frightened me to touch him. Not because I was afraid of the way he looked, or of his fits, but because I didn't want to *cause* him to have one of the fits.

Emil liked us. Not Johnnie so much in the beginning. I don't think he knew what to do about babies in his mind. He couldn't see Johnnie unless we lifted him up, until my brother could walk around freely, for Emil's cart had him raised up above the floor. Johnnie didn't seem to have figured out about Emil being a regular person either, in the beginning. One other thing, I don't think Emil liked seeing his mother holding Johnnie. His wobbly eyes would turn away and he wouldn't look at her.

Once I told Mutti Ilsa that Emil felt envious when she favored Johnnie, and that I'd take care of my brother so as she would not make Emil jealous. She said that a very fine, world-renowned doctor had once explained to her that Emil's brain could not understand anything more than comfort and discomfort. She said that I shouldn't worry, since she spent every day of her life making sure Emil never felt discomfort.

I didn't say anything, and I know a girl can't contradict what a famous doctor had said about Emil, but I think he does understand many more things than comfort and discomfort.

He liked to watch us, though I don't think he heard what we said. And if Mutti Ilsa went outdoors or to the storage room, or even in to gather the laundry and take our covers out to air, and was gone too long he would begin to move his eyes about frantically. I know he grew scared and I went to calm him. He is a sweet boy for all that he can't make a real smile, and it's hard for him to hold one's eyes for more than a second. I know he felt reassured when I rubbed his cheek gently or patted him. I hope he is well wherever he is now. I hope someone is taking good care of him.

I would have helped more if I could have lifted him. If I had been fifteen, like one newspaper said I was, I could have helped Mutti turn him and prop him up, and even get him to the commode. I thought it was a wonder that he, poor boy, didn't mess his paddings. But Mutti said he did once but that she had found that if she kept his feeding regular and with the clock, she knew when it was time to take him to the commode. But he wet himself frequently. It wasn't so easy to train that part of his body.

I felt great pride when Mutti Ilsa told my da that I was a good enough nurse to grow to learn midwifing. He didn't look disagreeable, but he said his daughters could do better than that. He said that he had in mind that I'd "grow to *marry* a tradesman, not be one." I think he meant to make her laugh, but she scowled at him.

I don't think my da understood how we rely on women like Mrs. Cochran who attended my mother Fiona. One would never call a doctor a tradesman. Women and babies live and die through good care from a midwife. They are much more important that someone who just sells goods. And I knew Mutti Ilsa to be giving me great praise in what she had said. But Da had not meant any harm. With all due respect to you, Mr. Laughton, men do think differently than we do.

But I am meandering on now, and not saying what I meant to say.

Emil had to be turned many times a day so the muscles in his limbs wouldn't get tense. And he had to be kept very clean so his skin wouldn't get sores. I wasn't quite strong enough to turn him, yet. But by next year I would be. I could feed him. It took a long time to feed him, just like a baby. But five times I'd fed him at suppertime. He choked more in the mornings

---

187

so Mutti Ilsa didn't let me try then. But he was usually calm and swallowed cleanly by evening. Josiah helped as much as he could with Emil. He and Jacob moved the cart for Mutti Ilsa. It was heavy and it took both of them.

Our sister Libby had been shrill with us so often, but Mutti Ilsa was always patient and kind with us children. Even though Hetti could be cranky and impertinent, Mutti Ilsa never hit her once. If I had talked like Hetti did, my mother Fiona would have taken her hand to my cheek and made it burn.

Oh, no, never. Our mother Fiona didn't ever hit me, but I knew she would have if I'd been impudent. Libby got slapped more than once.

Mr. Laughton, I think I have to tell you truly that we were happier once our Da married Mutti Ilsa, than we had been since our mother Fiona died. Hetti and Jacob were happy too, though they missed their father as we still missed our mother Fiona and our sister. We had finally come back to a happy life living at Rohe Farm. Mutti Ilsa was a good and kind mother to us. I know you don't want me to say that, but it is true. The constable and doctor, and my aunts and uncles want me to say that it was terrible living with Ilsa Rohe. But it wasn't. It was good.

Often my da would go to bed soon after the children were asleep, so tired from his hard work outdoors. A farm is hard work, and his horses doubled his work from other farmers. When all was quiet in the evenings, I liked to stay up late with Mutti Ilsa. She had a red rocking chair that she and Mr. Rohe brought from Pennsylvania. She would sit in it, and I would compose myself on a stool or in my da's chair. We would put the sewing basket on a small table between us and share its threads and needles. We didn't talk very much. Though Mutti taught Hetti and me German songs when we worked together in the daytime, at night when we were alone, we were very quiet so not to wake the family. It was good sitting in the firelight, the two of us together, stitching, hemming or darning.

I must go now. Excuse me.

O<<>>O

32 ~ That Last Day

28 March 1845, Friday afternoon

I've thought about everything that happened, and I will tell you what you are interested to hear. I only saw my father's wife whom I called Mutti Ilsa get cross once. That was when school started last September. She was not cross with us, but cross with my da. I know everyone who has read the newspapers must think it would have been terrible for us to live in that house almost a year, but it wasn't. This is how it was.

The Valentine's Day's tablecloth hanging in the big room gave our parents the idea to use tablecloths that Mutti Ilsa had stored and change then with the season, so when April came in, Da and Mutti Ilsa sewed ribbons on a tablecloth of spring flowers. Then for summer, she had one that had vines and green leaves and for fall, a tablecloth of autumn leaves. Fall was still hanging up, but the trees were going bare then for winter.

That last night in November, after everyone went to bed, I'd asked Mutti Ilsa if she had a tablecloth we could put up for the Christmas season and she said she did. I went to bed that night thinking that we'd need to sew ribbons on it so that it could be hung. I remembered that then we'd have to wash the autumn tablecloth with soda when we took it down, because the fire would have put soot on it. Soot was as hard to clean from a hanging cloth as food stains were from one used flat on a table. If a tablecloth is put away dirty, the dirt will get so deep in the weave that it will never come out. It took work to keep the house so pretty as we all liked. Mutti Ilsa worked hard and I liked to learn what she taught me.

Oh, Mr. Laughton, I wish you could have seen Rohe Farm as it was.

It would have cheered you just to walk into the big room there. I can't imagine any house so pretty inside. Gran came to visit on a Sunday afternoons often, when she had no other thing she needed to do. She would marvel at how bright and clean it was. She told Mutti Ilsa that she had never known a homemaker so clever, or a home so colorful. I remember I told Gran that had been Da's idea to hang a tablecloth from a pole to make a beautiful wall where none was before. Mutti Ilsa agreed and said it was.

No, sir. Our parents did never fight at Rohe Farm. I can only remember one time when Mutti Ilsa grew cross with Da.

Yes, I'll tell you about it. It was about school, and it was about Hetti and me so I remember it well. The kitchen was full of garden produce that had to be made ready for winter. Everything was ripe, and the outside men had picked baskets and baskets full and brought them to the house and we were working every day of late summer from very early until late. We had no time to sit and sew in the evenings. We worked in the kitchen. We had jugs of pickled foods put up and barrels filled, and still every day the men working in our garden brought more. We still had boxes of late apples that needed coring and stringing to dry in the attic stacked up in the shade.

You can't imagine if you are a city man, how much work can happen in the late summer for farmhouses. Josiah, Jacob and Andrew tried to help, although Mutti Ilsa didn't think men or boys belonged in the kitchen for any purpose but to eat. Tansie, our maid, shooed them out the door and told them to go to the barn and learn how to milk the cows and shoe the horses.

There was so much to keep us busy from mid-summer on that Hetti and I put our aprons on before breakfast. Tansie was coming to the house an hour earlier. We were doing all right. Summer had been a busy time in the kitchen for all the life I could remember. The work had been the same with my first family. It is a very busy time for us, washing, paring, peeling, slicing, and toting the cores and peelings and tops trimmed out to the chickens and pigs.

But then September came and school was beginning. Mutti wanted Hetti and me to keep from school to help her. It would be just until the work was all finished. Hetti didn't want to miss a day of school, but I didn't mind. I knew I could catch up at school once the work was caught up at home, and the harvest comes in but once a year. But, my da wouldn't let us.

Mutti Ilsa was very cross with him. But he was steadfast that we were to go to school. That morning, Mutti Ilsa looked as though she wanted to run down the road after the school wagon and pull Hetti and me out of it to haul us back home by our braids. But she wasn't cross with us, only with Da.

And soon all was back as it should be — and even better. No one could be cross with Da for very long. Da engaged my sister Libby to come and help in our place so Mutti Ilsa would have the help we needed. Libby is a wonder. She works fast and furiously, and she never gets tired. My sister Libby had been a tyrant when we lived across the street in Uncle Francis' house, and I knew she would see that short work was made of the harvest. Once the farmhouse was clean and the work was getting done, and Emil had fresh clothes every time he needed them, Mutti was happy again. We girls were in school so Da was happy. It was nice for me that Libby had come, because she worked on Saturdays too and I was home from school to help. I liked having my sister back for those harvest weeks.

Mutti Ilsa was sometimes sharp with Hetti, but only because Hetti was often contrary. I thought she missed Mr. Rohe, her real father and though Mutti Ilsa was her mother, she wasn't enough for Hetti. She liked Da, but of course he wasn't the same either. No more than Mutti Ilsa was the same as our first mother. Mr. Herbert wouldn't believe you if you told him I said Hetti could be contrary. She was very good at school. She was wondrous good at her studies. She was only a bother now and again to her mother, not very often and not to anyone else.

Mr. Laughton, in all our everyday ways we were happy. And not long after Libby came, all that food was dried and in the attic. Long ropes of beans and bundles of German peppers and dried tomatoes, enough to last a year more, hung from the rafters. Barrels were in the cellar with carrots, potatoes both white and yellow, onions and leeks well packed in straw so that they wouldn't touch each other and spoil, or see light and want to grow out of season. The storage room was full of our winter needs. Mutti Ilsa had Da take the excess out to share with the workers on both her farm and Da's. She told us it was expected of a farmer, that gifts of abundance be given to those who worked for him.

Our Libby had to bring a wagon to take home what was her share for her work. And Mutti surprised Da with a sweet cordial she had made from cherries. She had put up twelve bottles, enough that he could have a sip every evening if he wished not to have tea before bed.

She kept back two bottles for Uncle Adam, and two to save to dribble on the dark cake she made on our birthdays and served with beaten cream.

Mutti Ilsa was so proud of her work. And Da was too, of his. He had to run two farms and I think he wished that Libby had been a boy so he'd have a son to help him. He'd be riding back and forth from one to the other to make sure all was done that needed being done. The corn harvest on the two farms was very good. Gran Da said it was because Anderson Township had the most fertile land in all of Oho.

Truly, Mutti Ilsa was never upset with Josiah, Jacob, Andrew or me. Sometimes she had to remind the boys to be tidy in the house and that if they left a vest outdoors the rain would soak it. Or sometimes she would send them back outdoors to finish a task not done to her satisfaction. As sometimes she had to tell me to do something that I'd forgotten. But she was as pleasant to be around as our gran. She was never harsh in speech nor did she hit or pinch us, as Libby was prone to do when we were careless. Mutti Ilsa didn't ever in my hearing get cross with *things*. Our Mother Fiona didn't treat us impatiently or harshly either, but I will tell you that she sometimes would get cross two or three times in a day and speak loudly and rudely at the crockery for breaking, as though it went to dropping out of her hands on its own accord, and she'd curse the fire for going down when she needed it up.

Her words would sound like prayers, but Gran says that words said crossly to God are curses nonetheless, no matter that they are spoken "loud or soft." Mama would whisper, "Oh, Lord Jesus, give me patience, patience, patience." She could speak out loud if a tool broke while she was using to whip batter, or weave yarn. She would send us to find our Da and bring him to fix whatever was wrong while she cursed it.

He would come quickly, leaving his work to the grooms or farm workers, and if he could not fix what was wrong, he gave comfort and promises of a correction as he did with us when our playthings broke. Truly, Mutti Ilsa was more quiet and patient than I remember my mother Fiona being.

Gran says I must tell you about the last day, so I will. But it was a normal day. There is nothing special to tell. We had breakfast and went to school. We came home in the afternoon and I stayed inside to read my history book and help Mutti Ilsa in the kitchen if she needed me to help.

I remember the day before better than the last day. On the day before, Hetti and the boys were outdoors with a kite Da had helped them make. It was a windy day. I remember because of the kite. On that day, Mutti Ilsa's uncle Adam came to visit, and he had candies for us as he usually did. Then Mutti Ilsa went outside to talk to him. I went to the kitchen and see what I could do there, for it was getting late in the afternoon.

We all stayed in the house but my brother and Jacob wished that they could go out and see Uncle Adam's new small carriage.

After that, Mutti Ilsa came in and we made rolls for supper, and had a soup started. Mutti Ilsa didn't talk very much, but the boys did. They usually chattered about all the things that they were planning to do on the next Saturday after their chores. I've thought about the day it happened and the day before, and I think Emil choked at supper. But I'm not sure which day it was. But I remember Mutti Ilsa was upset that she might have fed him too fast, and it was the first time I'd seen her cry. It might have been that night, or the night after her uncle came to visit.

I know the last day was a normal day. Da went to work and we went to school. Jacob and Josiah were always making plans. Perhaps Jacob would ride with Josiah to visit our Gran Da on Saturday. I don't remember exactly what they were going to do, just that something good was expected. I'm sorry. I only remember that they were excited and happy.

I do remember that Da read to us that evening, but he usually did after Emil and Johnnie were abed and our schoolwork was done. I remember because he was reading from Robert Burn's book and all the time I was sick I kept remembering one poem he read that evening. When I was well enough to write notes, I asked Gran for the book and she brought it to me.

Yes, I know its title. It was "On the Banks of Nith." It has beautiful lines, Mr. Laughton. "Ambition is a meteor gleam, Fame, a restless idle dream..." No, I haven't memorized it. I have read it over since many times. I don't know why I remember that one, of all he read to us that night, but I do.

The book's title? It is *Poems, chiefly in the Scottish Dialect, by Robert Burns, printed for the Author, and sold by William Creech, 1787*. It is in the second parlor if you'd like me to fetch it for you.

Of course you have libraries in a city like Boston. But if you ever read it, you will find that poem in the book.

No. Nothing else was out of the ordinary. Mutti Ilsa and I did our mending before I went to bed every evening. It was our custom, and we did it that last night too. I usually stayed up sewing with her for a while after the boys, Hetti and Da went to bed, and I had that evening. Da came to kiss me goodnight and then he kissed Mutti Ilsa and said something to her, but I couldn't hear what he said. They said a few words quietly before he went to bed every night and it is rude to pay attention to private conversations. At the strike of nine, Da poked at the fire and then went to bed, just like every night. I only remember the evening so well because I've thought about it so much.

No, Mr. Laughton. I know it must disappoint you, and I don't want to. But it was just a normal sort of day. Not memorable in any way.

I know Monday will be our last visit. I'll try hard to remember anything that might be important. I'm sorry that I had so little to tell you.

O<<>>O

VII

ILSA ROHE

Rohe Farm, Anderson Township, Ohio
1844

33 ~ Without Hope

After Emil was born Ilsa poured out prayers to God. And God hadn't healed Emil, but her second child, Jacob, was born truly perfect. She saw that as an answer of kind, but it didn't meet the pleas she had given God. It was a perverse answering, not what she wanted from Him.

When his sound and robust child Jacob was born, Franz seemed to care for Emil more. In the new infant's responses, his gurgles and smiles, his arms reaching up to Franz, Ilsa imagined that her husband only then realized what Emil might have been, and how sad it was that he was not like Jacob. He became tender with Emil, less inclined to look away from their first son, more inclined to go to his aid, if the child was choking or distressed. Emil lay on his cot and grew. Jacob grew too but soon took cooing interest in all about him. He knew his parents, and showed his happiness when his father lifted him up. Emil only grew. He made no responses.

Franz learned of a doctor who was a specialist in unsound children. Her husband hired a nurse to stay in Ilsa's parents' house and care for Jacob. Against his father-in-law's counsel, and using all the money he had saved toward the future purchase of his own dairy, Franz took Ilsa and Emil to Frederick, Maryland. His intent was that the famed Dr. Adolf Bentzinger should examine Emil.

The doctor had private infirmaries in Austria, and in Virginia and Maryland, for afflicted children. The renowned Doctor Bentzinger insisted that the parents stay at his establishment for a week, that he could evaluate their child's disorder— and the sisters there would teach them better ways of caring for their child.

Since Franz insisted on making the trip to Maryland, Emil Mueller commissioned his son-in-law to make use of the opportunity to also go to the stock market in Baltimore. He trusted Franz's judgment and wanted him to scout for additions to the Mueller farm's line.

After the doctor's initial interview with the young couple, he was agreeable that Ilsa alone learn his system of care for brain-injured children, as his interview had proved her to be intelligent and motivated to learn. Though Franz did not want to leave her, he traveled to Baltimore as his father-in-law and employer requested. Under his father-in-law's authority, Franz purchased a new, prize-winning bull and three promising heifers to be freighted to the Mueller farm in Waynesboro.

Ilsa stayed with Emil, under the care of the good nursing sisters at the Bentzinger Infirmary. She spent hours learning from the sisters how to care for Emil during his spasms and choking spells. She spent more hours on her knees in the chapel in the Frederick infirmary praying for her child, because as the days passed she lost hope. Few of the children in the infirmary were as limp and hopeless as her child. Most could smile and move an arm or a leg purposefully. As the nursing sisters gave her son tests and worked with him, Dr. Bentzinger spent much time with Ilsa. While at the end of the week he hadn't been able to give Ilsa even false hope, he had given her honesty, kind comfort, and consolation.

Ilsa returned from Maryland knowing there would be no help from anywhere but God for her beloved firstborn. Franz returned knowing that he had done everything that he could for Emil.

On Franz's arrival back in Waynesboro, he seemed to feel on their return to the Mueller farm that he could now give his love to his healthy son without guilt over the state of his first son. He finally began paying attention to his son Jacob.

Hetti was born, after an easy and quick labor, on an afternoon just a week less than nine months later. She was a petite, delicate little thing, but as perfect a girl as Jacob was a boy. Ilsa named her daughter after her sister, keeping her promise. Then the new mother turned away from her child and began to weep quietly. The midwife, worried with Ilsa's reaction, called Franz to look at his daughter and comfort his wife. Though Ilsa and Franz and their children lived in Papa Mueller's home, her mother had never come into her room after Emil's birth. Frau Koehler knew not to call Frau Mueller. If Ilsa had been dying, the frau wouldn't have come.

Ilsa could see in her husband's eyes during his slow scrutiny of their new baby girl, that he understood very well why she was weeping. He instructed the midwife to take the baby and show her to the family. The woman looked at him questioningly and nodded. She bundled the baby and took her out to Ilsa's sisters.

As the door closed and they were alone, Ilsa waited for Franz to shout at her, perhaps to hit her. She cringed back on the pillows in fear of him. But to her great surprise, and then to her gratitude, Franz came to the bed and knelt beside her. "I did this to you, my Ilsa," he said softly. There were tears in his eyes also. "I left you alone in Frederick at the infirmary. I should not have done that."

Ilsa saw true grief in his eyes. She couldn't bring herself to speak.

"I knew then," he said, "I should not have left you. It was not your fault that this happened. You are only a woman. What could you have done?" He took her hand. "You must forgive me. I had no choice. I had to do as your father ordered. I work for him."

She looked at her husband and saw his regrets were heartfelt and true. Ilsa had prayed all during the months of her pregnancy that the child in her belly would be a blond Rohe child. He or she would look like Emil and Jacob. But God denied her prayers. She knew the child might be the doctor's. If it were, she didn't know what would happen to her. She never expected that Franz would be so good to her.

Before Mrs. Koehler came back into the room with the baby, Franz' husky voice whispered, "We will love this child as we do our others, Ilsa. We will treat her well. I hope you will someday forgive me for leaving you alone. I am only a man who must work for his family's bread. I could not disobey."

She thought about this. The man loved her so that he would take the blame of her transgression and apply it to himself. When the midwife brought *winzig, zarte* and delicately beautiful Hetti back into the room, she could put her to her breast and love her as a daughter ought to be loved.

But what was obvious to Ilsa and Franz was obvious to her parents as well. Ilsa's sister Liesl came into the room that evening to tell Ilsa that Mutti paid the midwife in gold coin not to talk of her new baby. "Mutti doesn't want all of Waynesboro to know that your baby has dark hair and cunning eyes. Frau Koehler won't tell anyone. Mutti trusts Frau Koehler to keep her word because Mutti keeps some secrets the midwife doesn't want told. But, Ilsa, Papa is so angry that he threw a tankard at Franz and cursed him."

Ilsa suckled her petite new daughter and listened to her sister chatter. She knew that the midwife saw that the baby wasn't like the Rohes or Muellers and wanted to ask her about the baby's father. She knew the woman wouldn't dare ask directly. Ilsa also knew that it was valuable to a midwife's business to be able to keep secrets and that Frau Koehler knew secrets from many families.

Ilsa could see that her sister wanted the titillating story of Ilsa's unknown lover as much as the midwife had, but Ilsa was too wise. She would talk to no one but Franz. If she told her family nothing, they might suspect, but they could never *know*.

That night, when she and Franz and their three babies were sleeping, her daughter not yet more than half a day old, Papa Mueller came crashing into the room. He always smelled of beer and his pipe, but Ilsa could smell the stink of whiskey on him. Papa Mueller roughly pulled Franz up from the cot where he lay near Ilsa and dragged him out into the hallway. Through the doorway she heard her Papa cursing. He demanded that Franz put Emil into the state infirmary and throw Ilsa out into the street. Her father wanted her cast her aside like a Biblical whore. Foul language came from his mouth. She heard a crash and knew her father had knocked Franz down.

The uproar and noise disturbed Emil. The child went stiff and was choking beside her. Ilsa cried out. Ilsa was still bleeding from the birth and hadn't strength yet to lift the four-year-old child. Franz lifted Emil up and took him to the chair by the window to help the boy as Ilsa taught him. Jacob woke frightened and began crying.

Papa did not stop his shouting. *"Einmal, aber nicht zweimal! Einmal, aber nicht zweimal sie Stech mich im Herzen!"* Her father's bellow rang through the house cursing her for what she had done to him not once but twice.

Then it seemed that he was finally worn down, and fallen to the floor. From her bed she could hear her sisters crying out from the doors to their rooms. Mutti came into Ilsa's room for the first time since the morning Emil was born. In the dim room, she found her way to Jacob's cot and scooped him up to comfort him. When the small boy quieted, Mutti took him to Ilsa's bed and put him in her arms.

"Verführerische," she mumbled. "You have done this to us. You." In the room, lit only by a faint lantern glow from the hallway and a night candle on the dresser, Mutti's eyes caught the light and showed pain as she stared at her daughter. She spoke coldly. "I protect you no longer. You have destroyed my family. You will hurt us no longer. Papa wants you thrown out in the street, out with the dogs, and that is where someone like you belongs." Ilsa's mother reached down to stroke Jacob's fair hair. "You ignore this perfect child Jacob, and you give all your love to an idiot. And now you dare to bear a bastard child in my house. I disown you."

Sneering at Ilsa, Mutti walked to the cradle where Hetti lay and spit on the baby, then she left the room.

Ilsa could hear Papa Mueller, broken down and weeping, in the hallway. Mutti called out to Maria and Liesl to help her take the man back to his bed. Franz brought Emil back to Ilsa's bed and put him down gently beside her. He took Jacob back to the boy's cot and kissed him.

"I'm sorry," Ilsa whispered after the house quieted and Franz had gone back to his own cot. That night, Ilsa slipped down from her bed to kneel and pray for her children. She prayed and prayed, promising God her life, if he would make Papa love her again and not throw her away.

The next morning, Franz defied her father and refused to divorce Ilsa. Mutti sent Ilsa's sisters to her room to tell her what had happened. Liesl began. "When Franz said he would not send you away, Papa hit him and knocked him down. Franz tore his scalp on the edge of the breakfast table. Papa picked up Jacob and was holding him while Mutti helped us get Franz up and stanch the bleeding from his head.

"Papa wept over what he had done to Franz. He begged Franz to forgive him. But then Papa insisted again through his tears that Franz cast you aside and send you away."

With great drama, Liesl's eyes grew big. "Franz refused! Ilsa, Franz refused to give you up."

"So Papa is sending you all away," sister Lena said, bubbling over with the excitement of the morning's happenings. Maria and Liesl began to cry. Ilsa thought that Lena could at least show care, but the girl was young enough to be thrilled by any kind of novelty. "Papa wanted to keep Jacob and send the rest of you away.

"He begged and begged, Ilsa. But Franz only repeated that Jacob was *his* son, not Papa's, and that the Rohe family would not be broken. Oh, Ilsa. Would you have thought? Franz is as stubborn as Papa is."

Somberly, Maria spoke through her tears. "Mutti told us Papa already has sent a letter this morning to Uncle Adam in Ohio, asking him to find a place for Franz and you there. He is sending you away, Ilsa."

Lena spoke up. "Franz went out to tell the farm men that he will be leaving, and giving them instructions. Papa is sitting in the house. He won't let go of Jacob."

"He doesn't want to give him up," Maria said. "But Franz said he'd call the constable if Papa tried to keep him. And he knows Franz would do it."

Emil Mueller filled Franz Rohe's pockets with money to hire a team of oxen and a traveler's wagon. He told his son-in-law he had sent a letter to his brother with authority to purchase a good piece of property in the name of Franz Rohe. Franz was to carry a letter from him, to Adam Mueller, Esquire, to identify him. Franz promised his father-in-law that he would raise Jacob to be the man Herr Emil Mueller would have wanted his grandson to be.

As soon as the wagon was ready, Franz and Ilsa and their children were banished to the western wilderness. Ilsa couldn't say goodbye to Hetti or her other sisters who were married. Their husbands, once aware of the trouble, would not allow them to visit the Mueller house until Ilsa was gone. At least she could hold each of the two youngest girls a last time and kiss them goodbye. Mutti wept over Jacob as the wagon was readied, but she had nothing but disgust for Ilsa.

In parting Lotti Mueller said, "Now Papa must lose his valuable Franz to get rid of you. Franz was like a son to your father. You brought us nothing but shame. You are not my daughter! I'm happy that you won't be here to shame me again.

"The only thing that saves you from the street is your husband."

Ilsa prayed through all the weeks it took to get from Waynesboro to Cossette that her father, in his love for Jacob, would call them back. But no horseman came riding up from behind them bringing a message from Emil Mueller asking that they return.

By the time that they arrived in Ohio, and Adam drove them from the Cossette Inn by a hired carriage to see the property on Clark Road that he had purchased for them, she had no more words of prayer. God had abandoned her as surely as her father had.

O<<>>O

~~~O<<>>O~~~

34 ~ Resolution

Ilsa looked around the big room. God hadn't abandoned her. He was not so kind. He gave her over to the trickster as a toy for his amusement.

Now, in the first full day of her grief, Ilsa listened to the clock and time to move on. She had made her resolution. She knew what she was about. She only had to wait. She had held to a delusion for too long. She held it from that day Ainslie first came to call at her door. She had been so sure that her beauty drew the man to her door once he knew she was widowed and free, and she was as sure that the power of her womanhood compelled him to return again and again until he was hers, committed by the love he felt for her.

The reality was that he had come only because his mother sent him. He stood in her doorway and saw her standing in her house and surrounded by the acres and wealth of Rohe Farm, the man in him decided that she, Ilsa Rohe, and her farm might suit his devouring greed.

The man in him was greedy. It didn't matter what he said, what Ains did proved he had been greedy for her land. Avarice gave the trickster full entrance to his body. And Ainslie's body was the only tool *Rübezahl* needed to trap her. If Ainslie, the man, was gone, the trickster would have no power over her.

Ilsa once asked Ainslie when he had first noticed her. "When, dear husband was the very first time you looked at me and saw who I could be to you? When did you first love me?"

He had answered, "That first day when my mother sent me to talk to you about Tansie Wilson."

"But you met me before!" she exclaimed in disappointment.

She expected him to say that he had loved her from the first day he had seen her in the yard as he'd ridden by when Hetti was still a baby, or that he'd loved her when Franz Rohe first introduced them in the yard when Hetti was three. She needed to know he had coveted her when she belonged to another. She needed the assurance that he had loved her as long as she loved him.

Ainslie saw the hurt on her face but had not the sense to say what she wanted. He said, "Ah, yes, my love, I had seen you. But I didn't *notice* you as other than Franz's wife, until that day my mother sent me to your door."

Oh, how cleverly he lied. The man had seen her. The trickster in him had chosen her all those years ago. He noticed her from his horse as he rode down Clark Road years before she first lived as neighbor to his parents. When she turned her innocent gaze at the road he took her as a woman to taunt and beguile. He teased her by turning himself into her fantasy of a husband. And then as years passed, he made her languish for him.

She made a pledge firmer than any she had made to God. She made it to her own self. Ilsa called the Devil and demons of hell to be her witnesses. She pledged she would save herself from *Rübezahl*.

Emil was still asleep. She fed Johnnie and Andrew milk and a biscuit each and put him to play. There was wash to be done and she went to carry the basket out to the yard and set the fire under the wash pot. But she found that she had done that early. The clean garments and quilts were on the line. She found it odd that she didn't remember.

It was hard to reconstruct her morning, but she slowly remembered each step she had done. She went to the woodshed and gathered kindling to take in. Benjamin's man had cut more stove-sized pieces that morning. Things must stay as they ought. She would send Jacob to fetch what the house needed when he came home from school. She would send Josiah too.

When she thought of Ainslie's children, she thought how like him they were. *Rübezahl* was the father. *Rübezahl* was the child.

Ilsa went to the cellar to get oil and made sure the lanterns throughout the house were full. It was good she checked. The small lantern in the washroom was low in fuel. She shook out all the rugs and put them on the rail of the work porch while she swept out the house. Then she pinned up her skirts and got on her knees to wash the slates, beginning at the front door. The kitchen corner was finished before Emil's impatient sounds alarmed the other boys.

She had to get up from the floor, dump the scrub bucket, and care for the children. After she turned Emil over, and changed his padding, she left Andrew to watch him while she took Johnnie to the commode, and then cleaned him and gave him a new dress for the day. She played the tender mother, listened to Andrew read, then coaxed Johnnie's numbers from him as she counted his toes when she put thick socks on his small feet. "Un, two, free, four..." the little trickster said with her in his guise of a child not yet able to pronounce all his words correctly.

Ah, but she was not fooled. *Rübezahl* was the fool today.

It was time to exercise Emil, as she did every day before she began kitchen work for the day's big meals. She spread a large colorful rag rug out on the clean floor. Johnnie watched and Andrew helped her as she placed a quilt down on it. She put her arms around Emil and pulled him to her chest to carry him to the quilt on the floor. There she began to exercise his legs and arms the way she had learned at Dr. Bentzinger's infirmary. One of the sisters had told her. "Keep him turning, and keep him moving, and he will have no ulcers on his limbs." Ilsa was proud that her child's skin was as smooth and pink as it was when he had been at the breast.

Emil made a short noise and turned his eyes toward Johnnie. He quivered so slightly she hardly noticed, but Ilsa thought he seemed to want to turn himself toward the little boy, and she pulled him in that direction until he was lying on his side. Emil gurgled and seemed happy lying on his side. Emil seemed happy, as much as he was able. Andrew should start school after Christmas. She would miss the boy's help with Emil and Johnnie. She seldom left her invalid son on the floor, lest he take cold or some bug crawl on him, but he was happy on the rug with the boys.

She thought perhaps he had an understanding of who he was, and he liked being a boy with the others. Maybe Anna was right and Dr. Bentzinger was wrong.

Maybe Emil had senses like other children and knew who and where he was. If he did, perhaps he knew she was his mother.

She bunched the quilt up behind the child that he not fall back. Ilsa wanted her unsound child to have these moments to watch Ainslie's sound children play if he could gain any kind of pleasurable sensation from the watching. The woman got up from the floor, and saw that the heavy fire screen was well fixed. Johnnie could not accidentally burn himself in his stumbling childish movement.

She went to get potted beef, made fresh that week, from the cooler. She put the potatoes and beets on the back of the Franklin in their pots to simmer down for Ainslie's dinner. All would be in readiness when he came in at noon. She could play the perfect wife, as she played the perfect mother. Ilse knew so well how to mime a *gute Deutsche weibe*. She just needed to be today the same person who she had been for the past eleven years.

Afterward she went to the washroom to groom herself. The perfect wife was clean, efficient and attractive, and if she felt none of those things, she could still mock them. She scrubbed her self twice over, pumping more water and finding a jar of lavender water to add to her rinse. From *Grossmutti* Mueller's *gegenstande,* she took out her combs and mirror. If the man of greed loved her hair, then she would make him notice it today. She would twine ribbons in her braid and make a crown of it in the Pennsylvania way.

As *Rübezahl* taunted her, she would taunt him when he came for his meal. He could not best her now. She knew as surely as she knew she was Ilsa Rohe, that she was the Devil's favorite. She wanted to see herself. She wanted to see how beautiful she was. Dr. Bentzinger said he had never seen such a loving mother or a woman so beautiful in all of his time in America. But the mirror in the washroom was metal and reflected poorly. Only *Grossmutti's* mirror of silvered glass set into a frame with African elephant ivory inlaid into its handle, would show her beauty back to her. The mirror came from the old country and had been her grandmother's pride. Her sisters resented that Papa gave it to her when *Grossmutti* died. They wanted him to have them draw lots, and thought him unfair.

Papa had always loved her more than anyone else. It was only that her mother drove him away from her. Of all the objects one could possess, this mirror and the treasure chest where she kept it were second only to Rohe Farm itself. These had been gifts from her Papa. Ainslie would take neither from her. She braced the silvered mirror on the shelf above the basin so her hands would be free to groom herself, and looked into it. She was surprised to see Elizabeth Buchanan's rabid and fierce-faced, wild-haired screaming banshee looking back at her.

O<<<>>O

---

35 ~ The Banshee

Ilsa wondered that the children hadn't been frightened of her face. In her silvered mirror, she saw herself as she had imagined that creature from Elizabeth Buchanan's ancient stories would look.

What had happened to her to turn her face so dark and her eyes so glittery? There was natural light in the washroom. It was almost noon. She had washed carefully, and began to comb out her hair. The banshee woman could scream. Ilsa had wanted so much to scream. She never had. Now she didn't need to.

If she held the silvered mirror and stood aligned with the washroom mirror, she could see the back of her head. She twisted her hair up in green and red ribbons, and held the mirror so she could see that they were centered and would hold. She wanted to look nice today. When the hair was done she went to her wardrobe and put on a red vest. Her skirt was pieced in green and red.

Johnnie came to the door and called her. She didn't have her shoes on yet but she followed him back through the sleeping room to the big room. Emil had fallen forward. Andrew was struggling to hold him up and keep Emil's face from the floor. Her son was not hurt. He could still breathe, but he couldn't see anything but the rug and was twitching in the struggle to raise his head.

She smiled at Andrew and Johnnie and told them they were good boys to come and get her. The children looked up at her. "We helped Emil," Andrew said. "But I couldn't lift him all the way, Mutti. I tried but he is heavy."

She took her handkerchief and wiped Emil's drooling before she lifted him up. Then she hugged him to her and dragged him to the cart. With a great effort, she lifted him into it. The cart made a shuddering move as his weight settled down into it. He was getting too big for the conveyance. He would soon need a larger one built for his daytime comfort.

Franz had built this cart. He had an anvil in the barn, but he asked the blacksmith in Cossette to make the axles so they would be sturdy for years of use. The wooden wheels were thick and rolled smoothly. They were secured with metal cotters, as was the back piece that let Emil's head and shoulders be raised to different slopes so that she could adjust it. Franz' design had been good. Franz built Emil's chair as need demanded.

Knowing that the woman in the mirror could hear her, Ilsa softly called to the banshee in the far room, "Your needs *must* wait until night, then you can scream out, *Meine Schwester, mein Zwilling.*"

The banshee woman didn't answer. It was Johnnie who she heard answering, reminding her it was time to feed the children, "Mutti, I'm sirsty. It is time for dinner."

It did not take her long to prepare their food. She spread the same potted meat on Johnnie and Andrew's bread that she was going to serve Ainslie for his dinner. While the boys ate at the table, she softened the same food for Emil, adding boiling water to turn it to a beefy porridge, and spooned her son's mid-day nourishment to him. And after they were fed and washed, she set them into the routine for their mid-day rest in the sleeping room putting Johnnie to his crib and pushing Emil's narrow cart through the wide doorway. Andrew climbed into his cot.

"When I go to school, I won't need naps, Mutti Ilsa."

Ainslie came in for his dinner. He greeted her, but she didn't respond. He washed while she ladled out a broth and set out the bread and meat.

"Are you still so angry, lassie?" he asked her, recognizing her silence.

She trusted herself to look directly at him, knowing he would see nothing had changed between them.

"It will be all right," he said. "It is only business. You will see that nothing changes in our lives but that Adam is done with Benjamin and the dairy accounts. You and I can do them easily ourselves. I can use your practical mind to help me."

He gave her a grin as though his words had meaning to her. She thought of the banshee, astounded that not even *Rübezahl* saw the woman who was looking out of her eyes. He got up and came toward her. She backed away.

"It is all right, my girl. Tomorrow you will love me again. You know you will. I did nothing that wasn't for the good of our children. You must know that is true." He wiped his face and hands and blew her a kiss as he went back out to his work.

The worst of her day was over. She could feel easy. The trickster had been tricked. He never saw who was looking out through her eyes judging him, and waiting for time to scream.

Ilsa spent the boys' rest time going through cupboards and pantry, making sure all was tidy, everything in its place, all tools hung on their hooks, all cloths folded neatly. She wanted her house to be perfect.

She saved the kitchen for last, then polished the pump handle and scoured out the sink, though it was never let go gritty. She got a stool and washed the glass on the window over the sink. She polished the spoons and forks and then took a whet stone to the knives. One knife was her favorite for cutting meats, in its weight and length. Ilsa gave it more draws across the stone, finding pleasure in the grating sound of blade. "Cut, cut, cut," she sang under her breath. "*Scharf sein wenn sie schneiden.*"

She put the children to their schoolwork when they came home and insisted that it was too windy for kite flying. Anna and Hetti folded all the clean laundry and put it away, and she put them all to cracking the nuts from a bag that Benjamin had brought that morning. They were too old. Hetti shrieked at the mealy worms, fat and yellow. Ilsa told them to discard the nuts and take them to the burn pit, but Jacob and Josiah thought to crack the nuts and put the worms into a bowl to take out to the chickens for a treat, then give the webbed and damaged meats to the pigs. Ilsa agreed. Andrew and the girls were given different tasks to do at the sink in readiness for supper.

Ilsa kept to her resolution all that day and evening. After Emil and Johnnie were abed, Ainslie chose to read from the Bible only a short time. Then he had a surprise for the children. He told them that a piper and a drummer were coming to Cossette on Saturday with a puppet show and he had paid for a pocket full of tickets. The show would be in the afternoon at the hotel.

He was going to take them to town for the entertainment.

———

"I knew about it," piped up quiet Andrew. "Robbie Hunter told me at school today."

"Ah, yes. Robbie's da runs the hotel. It is a sudden thing. I only heard this afternoon when I went to town. The piper and puppeteers were scheduled to play in Richland Saturday, but the man who engaged them did not have a secure place for them to perform. Rob Hunter was in Richland last evening and thought that town's loss could be Cossette's gain."

He looked up at Ilsa, and then finished what he was saying. "Rob gave them cash to come to Cossette. Richland's loss is our gain. He knows we need to encourage entertainments that find their way to our town."

Anna asked, "Might Libby come with us, Papa? Do you have enough tickets for Libby?"

Ainslie answered, "I have tickets enough for Billy too, if McKee will let him off work. I purchased enough to give away and to thank Robbie's Da for having the grand idea. Yours is a grand idea too, daughter. I'll ride to McKee's tomorrow morning and invite our girl and her Billy."

Ilsa had forgotten Libby. She was a problem to be dealt with too, but Ilsa had no time to think of her. She must keep to her plan without the distraction of that girl. She was not part of Rohe Farm's household. She was something other. Ilsa's mouth curled up in a smirk, thinking of how easily this day had gone.

Ainslie spoke out. "My love, would you like to go with us. I know I can find a way to take Emil to town. He might like the ride even if the show were beyond his ken. Would that suit you?"

The children clamored their approval of the idea, but Ilsa shook her head.

"Why not Mutti?" Jacob said.

"I will help. I can help," Anna said.

Only Hetti seemed reluctant to support Ainslie's idea. "It is too cold," the little girl said. Emil can't go out in the wind or cold. You should know that," the child corrected Anna and Jacob.

"In the spring, then," Ainslie said. "We will make a plan to take Emil out in the spring when the weather warms." He glanced at Ilsa meaningfully.

"You children know he likes to go on picnics with us. There is no reason he cannot go to Cossette with us."

Ilsa's body tried to make her respond to his lead. He was playing with her again, pulling at her memory with his voice and words. Cruel memory wanted to carry her skin and eyes and breasts, her hair and cunny and her mouth to the sensations of that first picnic in their courtship. She could see the trees and sunlight and water trickling. She remembered how they made love in the spinney woods while Emil lay in the small goat cart.

It was the trickster who spoke to her over the children's understanding. But she felt nothing. She had won. Her body was subject to her now, not to him. She had bested *Rübezahl* before she killed him, and she felt great satisfaction.

O<<>>O

~~~O<<>>O~~~

36 ~ By Lantern Light

As the children readied for bed, Ilsa set things right in the washroom. Towels hung neatly, clothes on each child's hook along the back wall. The basin emptied and a fresh pitcher of water had been pumped. The family's sleep would not be disturbed by the pump's crank in the dead of night, if someone needed to quench his thirst or wash his hands. When they were all in their cots but Anna and Ainslie, as she did every night Ilsa turned the lantern down to glow softly through the doorway to the sleeping room. She returned to the big room and took up her sewing. Anna was already busily mending one of Hetti's apron ties, roughly torn at school during some game.

Ainslie had returned to his Bible. She hoped he would not need to read aloud, now that the children were in bed, and he did not. There was no noise but the crackle of the fire, the clip of Anna's scissors and the soft sound of his pages turning.

"I'll take no tea tonight, my dear love," he said, lying that he loved her, and reminding her that she hadn't offered him any tea this evening. Ilsa sat rigidly, giving him no satisfaction.

Anna put the work on the footstool near her and got up. "I can make some, if either of you would like. Mutti Ilsa? Would you like me to make tea for you and Da?"

Ilsa shook her head.

"No, my sweet daughter," Ainslie said. "I'll be abed before nine tonight. There is much to do here tomorrow, and I must see Thomas to insure that the other house is readied for winter."

———

213

Ilsa wondered if he would ever stop talking and just go to his bed.

"I've promised you that I'll also fit in a visit with your sister." He leaned back on the chair and closed his eyes.

"I'm going for a drink of milk," Anna said. "Would either of you like me to bring you some?"

Neither responded. The girl put down her sewing and got up. She went over and kissed her father's head and then went into the shadows of the big room toward the kitchen. Ilsa heard the cooler cabinet beneath the sink open, then close.

By the time the girl came back, Ainslie had stood up, put his book on the shelf, and was stretching before the fire. He turned to kiss Anna and say goodnight to her, then came to Ilsa's chair. He bent down and whispered to her.

He didn't want Anna to hear, but was speaking so softly Ilsa could not be sure what he was saying to her.

She thought he asked if she'd like to meet him later this night. The corners of her mouth turned upward, and she tucked her head down so he wouldn't see. His play at awakening her body tonight must have worked on his own. She knew that in the language they had built together, if she did not respond, she gave him no encouragement.

She wouldn't respond. She wouldn't even look up from her sewing. She hoped his body gave him torments of wanting what she would never give him again.

Anna stayed up until after ten. The industrious girl had completed the mend on five garments. "They need pressing, Mutti Ilsa," the child said. "I'll do them after school tomorrow."

The girl went to bed. Ilsa sat and listened to the clock. She was purposeful this night. Last night she was in anguish and paced like a mad woman. Tonight she just waited.

It wasn't until the clock struck eleven, that Ilsa went to the door of the sleeping room. All was quiet. The children and her husband were deep asleep. Ilsa went to the kitchen and took her apron from the thin wardrobe by the storage room door. She put it on, and put a kerchief over her hair. She put her favorite knife into the deep pocket of her apron, went to the wood box by the fireplace and looked down into it. It was dark enough that she had to go and carry the lantern from her sewing table to see into the wood box. What she needed wasn't there.

She put the lantern back in its place and went into the sleeping room and picked up her outdoor shoes from the low shelf by the bed she shared with Emil, came back and sat in her chair to put them on in place of the soft slippers she wore in the house. She went out the back door holding a lantern, managing with one free hand to open the heavy door softly, and close it behind her quickly. She didn't want the cold night air to rush through the house.

By the lantern's light, she walked with the cold west wind in her face to the woodshed. She found the hatchet she wanted. The axe was there too. Its blade gleamed in the light from the lantern. The axe would do what she wanted with one blow, but she knew she wasn't tall enough to swing it properly. It could throw her off balance, or it might not come down just where she wanted. It was not that it was too heavy. Years of lifting Emil had made her muscles strong. But she was too small for a tool so long. The hatchet was just right. It would stun Ainslie. She would bring it down on him so quickly that he couldn't wrest it away from her. Then she would slit his throat, just like Papa did the beasts when he butchered them.

The hatchet was often in the wood box inside by the fireplace for splintering kindle sticks for the fire, but it hadn't been there tonight. The wind was still blowing, and the moon was up. She was happy to think it was a banshee night, and it was time to let the banshee woman scream and scream. She looked down and saw how her white apron shone out. She could have found the hatchet without the lantern by moonlight alone. Ilsa put down the lantern long enough to tuck the handle of the hatchet down in her apron's waistband at her right side where there was no blocking bib. Then she went back to the house.

The knife was in her right apron pocket, she felt for it with her left hand as she went into the sleeping room. She crossed the room and went to the big carved bed taking care to walk slowly and quietly. Her outdoor shoes weren't as silent as her slippers. She looked down at Ainslie and smiled.

She struck him hard, lifting the hatchet high before bringing it down. The sound it made wasn't loud.

"Papa is dead," she soundlessly mouthed as the hatchet thwunked down into his hair." That was strange. Papa wasn't the trickster. It was Ains that she was killing. That puzzled her for a moment, but she had work to do. She looked down at his body. He might have been dead after the first blow, but she didn't trust what looked like death. She wanted to know that the *Rübezahl* in Ainslie was dead.

A low sound came up from him. She lifted the hatchet again and brought it down harder and straighter. The third time the blade sank down into him, and she left it there. She didn't need it for the children. She could manage even if they woke, but she hoped that they wouldn't.

By the dim light coming from the big room and the low lantern light from the washroom, she could see that she had cleaved her husband's head, and she had smashed it nearly to soup. Blood had splattered all over her apron and his pillow. She bent down to see him better and smelled an ugly butchering smell, and she knew he was dead. One of his eyes was gone, sucked down into a cleft. She had the knife. She didn't need to slice his throat. She had other work for the knife.

He and his children were guilty of theft. She needed to cull the trickster's litter.

Ilsa looked around the room. The dull thwack of the hatchet coming down on *Rübezahl's* head hadn't woken any of the children. They all lay quietly in their places, breathing in and out. She watched closely. Johnnie turned over in the crib making its mattress creak. Jacob passed gas.

She listened a little longer. One of the girls made a shifting sound as she turned on the straw mattress.

Outside the wind was blowing branches against the shutters. She heard a cat and was reminded of the banshee, but it was only a cat. Where was the banshee? She should be screaming now. Ilsa wanted her to scream. Ilsa carefully pulled the hatchet out of Ainslie's head and placed it on the bed by his still body. She turned toward Josiah, sleeping on the trundle cot beside his father's bed. She reached into her apron pocket and withdrew the knife. The boy was sleeping on his back, arms spread out one leg bent, the other leg straight.

She noticed the quilt that was over him as she leaned forward. She had pieced the quilt top when she was waiting for Hetti to be born. It had faded more than she expected it would. She had washed it too many times.

Scharf sein wenn sie schneiden," she so softly whispered. She took the knife and set it near the little boy's ear and slit his throat all the way from his pillow on one side of his head to the other.

She knew to press firmly. She knew to be quick. There was a gurgling sound, and blood spurted up. It fountained up in pulses. It splashed her. She was glad she put her kerchief on and the blood wouldn't get in her hair. She watched Josiah's body twist up in a bunch, his throat still pulsing. Then, just as Emil did after a spasm passed, the boy relaxed. She knew he was dead, and she need not cut him again.

She went around the half wall to Anna's bed. This seemed wrong, and she stared at the girls in the faintly lit part of the room until she figured it out. The beds were in the wrong order. Anna was the older. Josie's bed should be here not Anna's. She should have killed Anna first after Ainslie, before Josiah. Ainslie set the beds out of order. It should be Ainslie, Anna, Josiah, Andrew... No matter, she told herself as she looked down on the girls. She smiled. No matter, Mutti wasn't here to scold her, and the devil wouldn't care.

Ilsa stepped farther into the partition and stood between the two little girls' beds. It was darker here because of the half-wall. The washroom lantern scarcely reached this far. She had to peer to see if the girl was in a good position for the knife. Anna was curled on her side and facing Ilsa. Her face and neck picked up light against her dark hair on the pillow. The knife still had Josiah's blood all over it, as did her hand. She wiped it on the quilt hanging down from Anna's bed. With her left hand she wiped a tag of quilt over her hand too so it wouldn't be so slick.

Then she placed the blade at the girl's right ear. But as she twisted to press it to the girl's neck, she had flashing pictures of the girl feeding Emil and her sister breathing into newborn Emil's mouth. Anna was too like her sister Hetti. Blood was flowing from the girl's neck. It wasn't spurting high in the air like Josiah's and *Rübezahl's* had, but it was flowing. Ilsa didn't stop her downward stroke, but the skittery memories pulled her wrist back.

She straightened up and looked around the dark room, making out shapes of the children in their beds. She could smell the blood in the room. Her hands were covered with blood, sticky and dark. The knife still gripped in her right hand, Ilsa ran from the bloody room. She lifted the latch on the front door with her free left hand and ran across the porch and down the steps into the night. She ran down the drive to Clark Road and when she reached it she turned onto it. She turned toward Pennsylvania. She had never been out on the road on foot past the post box before. It was exhilarating being out in the night.

217

She ran and ran and heard night sounds but she couldn't hear the banshee. She ran away from Anna's blood, but it was on her right hand and on the knife she held. It was on her clothes and on her face. She was wet with the *Rübezahls'* blood.

Ilsa knew it would take a long time to get to Pennsylvania. She kept running past farm fences, past stubble fields that used to be rows of her corn, past the edge of her property, past farmhouses dark to the night. Her chest hurt and her hand hurt where she gripped the knife. It was freezing cold. Still she kept running. The moon led the way. It kept the road bright before her. The wind made her eyes tear and stung her face. But she kept running. She came to a bridge. The sound of her shoes changed to a harder sound as she crossed the bridge. She could hear water rushing below her. She had an urge to go down to the water, but it was too dark away from the road so she kept on running. Finally she couldn't run anymore. There was a ditch beside the road. She fell at the side of the road and pulled herself to the mound between the road and the ditch. She was near trees. She twisted her wrist and ankle when she fell but she had held onto her knife. She couldn't let the knife go. When Ilsa began to breathe steadily again, she tried to think where she was. An owl hooted and the wind had died down. She didn't know where she was. She thought if she just sat and waited near the trees, her Papa would come and get her and take her home.

After a long time she woke up. She was lying in the dirt. Her kerchief had come off. It was dark and cold. She had been dreaming about her Papa. He ought to be here. She knew he was sorry and he was coming after her. He forgave her for taking Franz away from him. She knew he did. But she couldn't go to Ohio alone. She needed Franz.

She didn't know why she killed him. It was just an impulse. She didn't plan to kill him. He was high at the peak of the roof and she called him down for his dinner. The ground was uneven along the edge of the house, and he had stacked stones under the long pruning ladder's lower leg to balance it. As he stepped down from the roof onto the first rung, she thought she could easily unbalance the ladder. She thought just how she could do it, and then so quickly she *was* doing it.

When both of his feet were on the top rung of the ladder, and he began to drop one foot to the next rung lower, she kicked the side of the ladder that was so precariously balanced on his foolish pile of stones. Franz was such a fool to do that. The ladder came crashing down. Franz was broken. His head and neck were twisted between two rungs of the ladder. His face was looking at the sky. Sometimes she missed Franz. Her Papa had liked him and made him foreman when he was only twenty.

She mustn't tell Papa what she had done. He wouldn't understand that it was an accident. He was so fond of Franz. She was cold. The sticky blood had frozen on her clothes and she didn't know why there was a knife in her hand.

She could hear Papa coming and tried to get to her feet. It was hard to do because she couldn't let go of the knife. She staggered. Her legs and hips were stiff from the cold and from sitting on the ground. Finally, she was upright, her apron was twisted and her skirt and petticoats heavy. They wanted to pull her back to the ground. The moon was behind clouds, but she could hear her papa's horse. She knew it was the big piebald gelding he liked best. It was coming fast and making a lot of noise. There was so much noise it sounded like all Papa Mueller's cows had gotten loose and were running down Clark Road behind him. He'd be here, and he would take her home to Pennsylvania.

There were lanterns and horses. There were so many men. She couldn't find her papa among them. She was screaming "Papa! Papa!" The men were grabbing at her. She didn't know their faces and they didn't smell like her papa's pipe. They didn't belong to her papa's farm. She slashed back at them with the knife. One of the men took the knife from her, and other men pushed her down on the ground. They were rough with her and didn't touch her nicely like men were supposed to touch women. She wanted her Papa.

The men were hurting her. There was noise all around. Lanterns cast light that hurt her eyes, and she couldn't breathe.

O<<>>O

~~~O<<>>O~~~

VIII

ILSA ROHE
~~~1845~~~

Josiah Buchanan's Home

37~ Anna Says Goodbye

31 March, 1845, Monday afternoon

Dear Mr. Laughton, it makes me quite sad that this is the very last time we'll meet.

Yes. Perhaps someday I will go to Boston. But, I cannot imagine that I'd ever go traveling far from here. First I have to summon courage to go back to school.

I know you do, and I think it will be easier for me that I've met you. I will be brave and courageous. Not just for you and Gran, but for my parents too. My grandmother told me that I must remove my scarf and show you what was done to me. I'm badly scarred and it is inflamed still. You might not want to look at it.

Yes. It goes around my neck from my right ear to just past my chin. No, I won't mind. I know you well now, like my uncles or Mr. Herbert.

The doctor says my injury would have been worse if the knife had been sharper. Both doctors who have been here have complimented my grandmother that she was such a fine nurse.

No, but it is hard for me to turn my head to the right. Doctor Gainey says it always will be, and I should be grateful that I am alive. There are still some festering spots, but I am healing. Gran says that only thing that liquor is good for is keeping wounds from going putrid, and she makes me clean the scar with it twice a day. It stings and makes my eyes water.

Gran has told me that I must tell you about the night my da and brother were killed, or your long stay here will have no value. So I will try. When I told you I didn't want to answer your questions the day we first met, it was because Constable Davies had been so hard on me that night in November. He wanted me to tell him what I didn't know. I was still bleeding and faint. Gran was holding compresses against my throat and trying to make me drink water to thin any blood I might have swallowed. She was sure I might have done that and my own raw blood might poison me. Gran Da and my uncles grew so angry with the constable and his men that they drove them all from this house. They could have been arrested for doing it. I think it was morning by then.

This is what I remember of that night. I had gone to bed. I told you it had been a normal day and it was a normal evening. Sometime after I was in bed, but not yet full asleep, Ilsa came into the room. I thought it sounded like she was getting her shoes, and I wondered if she were going out to the privy, though usually at night Mutti Ilsa, Hetti and I used the commode. But I didn't hear the outside door open or close.

I curled up and must have gone to sleep. Sometime in the night I woke up. I didn't know why I woke up, or what time it was. My pillow was wet. And there was a strong smell that frightened me and made me come full awake.

I was bleeding and the wet was blood and the smell was blood. It was in my hair and on my shift and on my bed. I got up and ran to my da to shake him awake, but there my feet slipped in blood on the floor between his bed and Josiah's cot. My da was dead. His head was broken and crushed. Blood was dripping on the two beds and between them there was a river of blood around my feet.

The blood looked black on the wall and on Da and Josie. I'd bumped backwards into Josie's bed and I knew he was dead too. Their blood had mixed on the floor and my feet were in it. I kept thinking of the blood and how I could get out of it. I'm ashamed that that is all I thought of. I ran from the house. I don't think I screamed. I think I was too scared to scream. The front door was wide open and I just ran through it. I could only think to go to my grandparents' house. I didn't think to go to the McFarland's farm although it is nearer. I only thought to get to my grandparents.

I feel so guilty now that I didn't think of the other children. I just ran away.

I ran to the road and then to my grandparent's house. I remember I was holding my throat so I wouldn't bleed any more. I ran until I was here. I never felt my feet though they were bare and there are stones on the road that cut them. I ran so fast. When I got here I screamed and screamed. I didn't know that I'd hurt my feet until much later when Gran and Mrs. McFarland were washing me because I'd gone to sleep.

When I woke up, my throat was packed tightly and my feet were wrapped in towels. Some of the blood was washed off, but I could still smell it on me.

The bells were ringing. Oh, you are from a city and wouldn't know. The bells are for fires. Every farm has a big bell, usually in the barn. When there is a fire on someone's farm, he rings the bell for help. Gran Da must have started them to ring. Libby told me that the bells were ringing all the way to town that night, going from one farm to another. They woke her and Billy up.

Sometime later, Gran fed me tea, with liquor and honey in it. I tried to nod my head when she said that my da was dead and Josiah was dead, but it hurt to move my head. I didn't know about the children, and tried to ask her with my look because I couldn't speak.

She understood and told me that all the children but Josiah and me were unharmed. Gran said that it was not a man's hand that held the hatchet or the knife. Then she asked, "Ilsa Rohe did this, didn't she?" I squeezed Gran's hand because I couldn't talk, and it hurt to try and nod a yes. So I couldn't even do that.

I know Mutti Ilsa did it to us, though I was asleep. I didn't see her do it, but I know she did it to us.

Gran spooned me some of the tea, though it was hard to swallow. Moving my face hurt, and moving my head or swallowing was very painful. But I was not cut through to the inside of my throat as Libby said our brother was. I didn't die.

After that, it was hard. I only wanted to sleep and I remember that Constable Davies came bursting into the room with other men. They questioned me and were so angry when I couldn't answer. They scared me. I tried to turn away so not to look at them but I couldn't move my head for the pain. So, I closed my eyes.

Constable Davies grew sharp with me. Finally when he put his hand on me, Gran Da and my uncles began shouting and drove him and his men out. I went back to sleep.

A long time later I woke up again. I was upstairs and a doctor was with me. He had come all the way from Dayton while I was sleeping. He said Gran had done as well as any big city doctor could have done, but he made me drink more of the tea and corn liquor. Then he scraped roughly at my neck and it hurt so my gran had to hold my arms up above my head. The doctor sewed me up so I would heal better. From that day until just before I met you, I couldn't talk. I didn't go to school. I just stayed here with my grandparents.

The doctor said I could speak once I could move my jaw without pain. My voice was all right. But my words wouldn't come out. When the worst of the wound healed, I still couldn't talk.

Constable Davies kept coming to bother me and try to get me to answer when it hurt to talk, but Reverend Johnson was my defender. Mr. Herbert was too. Finally Constable Davies stopped coming here. But Mr. Herbert insisted that I do my schoolwork no matter that I couldn't talk, and Gran agreed. That is all I can tell you. It is all I know.

No, sir. I don't know why Ilsa Rohe did it. I thought she loved us all. She was never unkind. Not once. We had no troubles that I saw.

One of the newspapers said she was found the next morning hanged by her own hand from a tree. Did you know that? It can't be true. The paper said that she was hanged with a bridle. Mr. Laughton, my mother Fiona knew how to saddle and bridle a horse, but Mutti Ilsa couldn't even ride one. She only knew to ride in a carriage or wagon. She knew nothing of the outdoors or handling stock.

Where would she have found a bridle? She might have had yarn or string, or a piece of clothesline rope. But she'd have had to go to the tack barn to get a bridle. I don't think she had ever been in that place, and it was dark. I know she didn't kill herself.

The bells brought Constable Davies and men from all around. I think about them.

Yes, sir. I think the men rode her down and killed her. I understand why they might have wanted to do it. But I hope my family didn't kill her.

Gran reassures me that my grandfather was too brokenhearted, and my uncles had nothing to do with it. She says that they were too busy bringing Andrew, Johnnie, Hetti and Jacob out from "hellish mayhem" and getting them to comfort.

She says my family was never party to killing Ilsa Rohe. Gran swears that Gran Da brought Josie's body into the house in his arms, and then Gran Da crumbled down on the floor and cried the whole nightlong. She swears that my uncles went back to Rohe Farm to tend to the body of my father, and bring it here to her. After that they spent the rest of the night finding caretakers for Emil, Jacob and Hetti.

I hope my gran isn't spinning stories to lull me like a child. I don't want to think my gran da or uncles killed Ilsa Rohe, but they may have done. I know Constable Davies is rough and brash. I want to think he and his men did it.

Thank you for the handkerchief. I'm sorry I wept. We don't have that much time to talk and I wasted it. You must go back to Boston, and I must go back to school.

I'm all right now.

I want to tell you some good things before you leave. Libby visited me yesterday. She said she and Billy Frazier are saving money to move to California. The two of them have taken jobs at the hotel in Cossette. Billy will work in the hotel's livery and Libby has already begun keeping the hotel's books and serving at the dinner meal. She says it is far easier work work than she had to do when she was taking care of all of us, the months we lived in the brick house across Clark Road.

Billy didn't want to leave working for Mr. McKee, but he will make twice as much at the hotel, and they will be able to save, since their board is part of their hire. She says that they have been given a nice room in the attic. It has two gable windows that overlook Cossette to the north, and they will have Wednesday afternoon and Sunday morning free. Billy will continue helping Mr. McKee then on his time off from the hotel.

Libby says that the hotel doesn't care about Billy but it wants her because what happened in November gives her notoriety. That makes people want to come and take meals in the hotel dining room just to see her. But whatever the cause she is hired, she doesn't mind because she and Billy have a nicer place to live at the hotel than they did in the cabin at McKee's.

She has read of opportunities in the Golden West and wants to be a pioneer woman. Libby said that I could come west with them.

No, I won't leave my brothers to go with Libby. Gran needs my help. My grandmother has the same griefs I do.

Gran Da wouldn't have had a stroke if that terrible thing hadn't happened. His brain struck him down the day after my da and Josiah were killed. I know Gran sorely misses the man my gran da used to be. He has lost his fine manner of speech and can scarce walk without help. Old Johnnie Reid is no relation to her, but he is to me. I could not leave her as long as she needs me.

My Uncles Cameron, Andrew, and James are working with Mr. Mueller and Judge Warwick to do the best for all of us. Yesterday Libby told me that before Da died, he bought Rohe Farm from Adam Mueller. So, it is part of my da's estate. I told Libby that Rohe Farm should go to Mr. Rohe's children and not to our family. They are Rohes. We aren't.

Libby laughed at me. She said I didn't understand, that since Da had paid money to Mr. Mueller for Rohe Farm, what it was worth went to Emil, Jacob and Hetti Rohe. She said that it was a goodly amount that would support them well and was probably more than Rohe Farm was worth. Our uncles Jimmie and Andrew are taking care of it for us. I wish that they would sell it. Our uncle Cameron is taking care of Da's horses.

When Gran told me Emil had gone to the state infirmary in Columbus, her look told me it was a bad place, and her words were that as long as she had strength in her body, Gran Da would *never* be sent to the infirmary, nor would she allow poor Johnnie Reid to be taken there. I wonder that Emil's relations couldn't have a place better for him. It is horrible to think of him being sent to that kind of place. I asked Gran if we could go and retrieve him. I told her I would care for him. But Gran just looked at me. If I had persisted in pleading for him, her look might have gone angry. Emil gave no fault. He carries no blame for his mother. I don't like to think of him so abandoned.

Yes, I do understand. I understand that each time Gran looks at me, she can't help but see my scar, no matter how many scarves and laces I cover over it. She can't endure more reminders of what she has lost. She blames herself. She says over and over that if she hadn't felt so much sentiment over Mr. Rohe's death, she would never have sent my da to his death. She says if she hadn't sent him to help Ilsa Rohe, our tragedy would never have happened.

Sir, *if* is a terrible word. It sets us to wondering uselessly. You shouldn't write this down, sir. I am only telling you our feelings and not giving you facts for your magazine. But Gran was not at fault, no matter that she blames herself.

Goodbye, Mr. Laughton. It is time for you to go back to Boston. I will miss you. I trust you won't write anything unkind, or that isn't true. I have enjoyed talking to you. I didn't think I would, but I have.

Good luck in your work and travels. I'll keep you in my prayers. I'll keep Ilsa Rohe in my prayers too. She stayed her hand. She didn't hurt Andrew or Johnnie, or her own children. I think that at the last, she remembered she loved us.

<< The End >>

John Weller Stephenson   from 1864 photo

A Very Personal Afterword

The photo on the preceding page is of my grandfather John Weller Stephenson, born in 1842. His mother died shortly after his birth. When he was two years old, his stepmother killed his father, his nine-year-old brother, and gravely wounded his thirteen-year-old sister. John and four other young children were asleep in the murder room.

It is rare for a person living today to have a grandparent of such antiquity, but my father was the child of his father's old age, as I was the child of my father's old age. We have but three generations of separation between us where most people would have four. When I began school, my classmates' fathers were fighting in World War II. My father fought in World War I, a generation earlier.

This book about a family's tragedy is based on fact, but it is a fiction. A book based on fact is not fact. The characters and their motivations are imaginings; the dialogues are inventions.

I didn't know my great grandfather's role in the tragedy when I began to create the character of Ainslie Buchanan. But I could comfortably develop it for this novel by applying an old maxim: *The apple does not fall far from the tree.* The many men who have descended from my true, historical Ainslie have been literate men, tall and lean, kind, and though sometimes vain and faulted by pride, they have never been faulted by greed or grand ambition. My fictional 'Ainslie' follows this familial model.

However, I found scant research to help me build the character of Ilsa from an authentic model, or to provide her with sufficient psychological motivation to commit such an unspeakable crime. There is little data in public record on the actual murderess, and almost no genealogical trace of her. No family tree on Ancestry.com to this day is willing to claim her. The documented facts are these: She and her first husband were of German descent and came from Pennsylvania. She was young. She had three children. The oldest child was severely handicapped. She remarried soon after her first husband's death.

Eleven months later she committed the 1844 murders that made quiet, rural Ohio notorious for a few days of criminal fame. It wouldn't be until fifty years later, in 1892, when New England's Lizzie Borden became infamous for a similar act.

229

A newspaper article, written at the time of the earlier crime in Ohio that involved my great grandfather and grandfather, gives a speculative motivation to its perpetrator. But it is hardly strong enough motivation to justify a vicious murder. The Dayton Transcript, in its Dec. 7, 1844 issue, on p.2, describes, in lurid prose, an obsession the woman may have had that her second husband was stealing her former husband's estate:

"...The only reason assigned, why Mrs. S. committed the bloody deed, is, that she was afraid, from some circumstances that her husband would so manage matters as to defraud her children, by her former husband out of their property. This idea, it is supposed preyed so much upon her feelings, as to destroy the equanimity of her mind, and drive her in a fit of insanity, to the commission of the awful deed...."

The "manage matters" in this fragment cues directly to an inference an author might justifiably draw from history. Times were not good for women when their *matters were managed*. Research documentation shows that the actual property was not managed by the second husband at all, but by a lawyer cum justice of the peace thought to have been her relative, either brother or uncle.

In the mid-nineteenth century, any monies that came to a child belonged to his father or male guardian whether it came from wages, gift, or bequest. Once that child became a man, it was his own. This financial coming-of-age did not happen for women. A woman's father or guardian kept control until she married. With marriage, her husband became her de facto guardian.

Most women had no financial rights. For example in the case of entailed property if a woman's grandfather left a trust income to her, her father, guardian, or husband could not access or squander its principal, however he did have total control of what came by *distribution* to her, any monthly or yearly payments given to her from the interest on the principal.

The average woman went from living under her father's financial management, to her husband's, and then — if she outlived her husband — she came under the financial control of his primary male heir. This might be her son, but it might as well be her stepson, or one of her husband's brothers, nephews or cousins, or his father.

A man's signed and witnessed legal testament *could* give a woman control of his property upon his death, although that wasn't usually the custom and was fairly rare. If her husband died intestate, his estate bypassed her and went to his children, or if there were none, to his next of kin. No part of its ownership came to his widow.

There was some cultural justification for these practices, though they seem irrational from a twenty-first century point of view. The death in childbirth of wives was common, and unless a wife was wealthy and well cared for, she was usually overworked to the point of an early death. The average man could easily, and often did, bury three wives in his lifetime. What could happen was that if his most recent wife were to outlive him and *allowed* to inherit his property, his estate might pass into the hands of her children by a subsequent husband. It could potentially skip away from the man's own bloodlines. It is a stretch to think that this might happen often, but it was a valid threat that I'm sure that the legislators and judges of the day, all male, would see as a serious concern.

Dower rights gave a surviving widow only the guarantee that she could live in her deceased husband's house until she died or remarried. It gave her no ownership of the property. The man who owned it could send other people to live in it with her. He could allow it to fall into ruin. The only right she had was that she couldn't be evicted. But a beneficiary could surely find ways to force a widow to leave.

Looking through old census records, one finds many widows living in in the household of a brother or a sister's husband. Were they the victims of clever property management? Starved out? Squeezed out?

I can't help but wonder about the women who were sent to madhouses in those olden days. Were they really insane? Or was it a property owner's expedience, simply a 'trash removal,' an action to circumvent a woman's dower possession.

A woman not only had no rights to assets, she had no rights to authority over her own children. They, in law, belonged to their father, not to her. If a widow's children were minors, the court appointed a guardian to manage her husband's assets and provide for the children until they were of age. Though they were often left in their mother's care, she would need to rely on what their guardian doled out for the children's support. It is a testament to great love and trust when one finds a historic will wherein a man's wife is named his beneficiary.

No stack of reasons behind an evil act, no matter how toweringly high, will serve as its excuse. But still, I feel a great retrospective sympathy for the problems faced by women in earlier times in the English speaking and culturally patterned world, even sympathy for women like the fictitious Ilsa Rohe, even sympathy for the real-life woman who killed my great-grandfather. I don't know how I would have fared trying to walk in the small, very tight shoes women wore in that not-so-distant century.

Not only did women not have economic freedom, but also educational opportunity was considered of little importance to females. During those times, there was no system of intervention for children who were physically or sexually abused. Nor was psychological counseling available for the children of abuse — or for the compromised adults they often became. Mentally handicapped children and adults were shunned. The phrase "locked in the attic" was more true than not. There was no respite care for caretakers of the invalid or the handicapped. An inequitable standard of social and sexual behavior was demanded of women, who were judged harshly for the same offenses that were overlooked and often applauded in men.

One of the values of understanding our cultural history is that we can look back and examine the abuses of the past, proudly count those that have been corrected, and find incentive to identify and correct the abuses of our own times.

Stephenson Ross
September 2014

"Novels arise out of the shortcomings of history"
Georg Philipp Friedrich Freiheer von Hardenberg,
aka Novalis
1772-1801

Acknowledgements

There are often odd and pleasing moments that come during the writing of a book. I thank R. E. Ross, who came to my desk one day to tell me that he had just begun reading a non-fiction historical text that opens with the American nation's craze for Valentines in the 1840s, (*A Wicked War*, Amy S. Greenberg, 2012). He wanted to let me know that my impulse to add a Valentine to one chapter of this fictional book was historically 'right on target.' Thank you, R.E., for never dropping your loving connection to all I do.

I wish to especially thank Velda Stephenson who gave me the keys to this story and D. M. Mahnke for her careful reading and quality editorial feedback. D.M. has been never failed anyone who needed her help, and I'm lucky to have been the recipient of her largess during more than one career.

N. P. Ross and T. N. Ross volunteered thoughtful advice on cover design. Roger Boling shared his knowledge of colloquial German, and the author of the 'Lunch Break Books', Tamworth Grice, deserves thanks for her excellent handbook to electronic publishing, (*Basic Formatting & How To Create A Hyperlinked Table of Contents, 2014)*. The Old Vandalia Book Group unfailingly encouraged my work, as did the members of the Exeter Writer's Guild. Two long-time friends, Helen Lindstrom and Sandra Arnold, served as the novel's necessary beta readers. Thank you, all.

I am very grateful to all these good people for their help. And, as I review the production of this novel and help I have received, I sincerely acknowledge and thank the reading public. It is your interest in reading stories that justifies the work of those of us who like to write them.

SR

German Language Glossary by Chapter

(Note: This book follows English custom in capitalization usage and does not capitalize nouns. The definitions given are only colloquial approximations. They may or may not be useful to a reader.)

Chapter 1
1. *hausfrau* : housewife, married woman who doesn't work out of the home.
2. *kräftig und schlank:* strong and lean

Chapter 2
3. *Pfarrer : pastor, reverend (also; Herr, Frau : Mr., Mrs.)*
4. *bettler haben keine wahl:* beggars have no choice
5. *kleiner schreibtisch:* small desk

Chapter 3
6. Es ist gute für mann frau zu finden.: *It is good for a man to have a   woman.*
7. Gott zufrieden ist: *God approves.*

Chapter 4
8. *meine liebst*: my love

Chapter 5
9. *Deutsche:* German
10. *quarkkuchen:* a type of cheesecake made with 'quark' cheese
11. *Prince Streifen*: Prince Stripes

Chapter 6
12. *Dummkopf:* stupid

Chapter 7
13. *un kleine gegenstande:* a small, decorated chest
14. *grossmutti:* grandmother

Chapter 11
15. *apfelstrudel, stollen:* pastry and Christmas bread
16. *verführerische:* seductress

Chapter 13
17. Flecken, Flöhchen: dog's names - Spots, Flea
18. *das kinder:* the children
19. *un vertrag:* a robe or coverlet
20. *sie verraten wurde:* she was betrayed
21. *tränen zeigen schwäche:* tears show weakness
22. *das manner*: the men
23. *leibchen:* beloved, an endearment for a woman
24. *armen naiven frau:* poor naïve woman
25. *genug von euch:* finished with you

Chapter 15
26. *geh zur Hölle:* be gone to Hell

Chapter 18
27. *mutti:* a familiar term for mother (*mutter)*

Chapter 20
28. *ein narr:* a fool
29. *ein, zwei, drei, vier, funf:* one, two, three, four, five

Chapter 21
30. Rübezahl: a folk figure who tricks and makes fools of others
31. lächerlich: ridiculous, foolish
32. *guten arbeit und gewissens*: good work and conscience

Chapter 22
33. *Gott in Himmel:* God in Heaven
34. *winzig, zarte:* delicate, tiny
35. *einmal* aber nicht zweimal : once but not twice
      sie stech mich im herzen: you stab me in the heart
36. ficken: coitus, sexual intercourse
37. kuh scheisse: cow shit, dairy manure
38. *eine mutter die liebe*: a mother's love

Chapter 23
39. *Muschi:* *(vulgar)* pussy, twat, fanny

Chapter 24
40. schwachsinnige: an imbecile, severely mentally disabled
41.   *Ich bin klein, mein Herz ist rein.*
            Soll niemand drin wohnen als Jesus allein.
            Amen:
                        I am small, my heart is pure
                        Nobody may dwell in here but Jesus.
                        Amen
42. *gute Deutsche weibe:* good German wife

Chapter 31
43. *mein schwester , mein zwilling:* my sister, my twin
44. *Scharf sein wenn sie schneiden:* be sharp when you cut

incidentals~
text font: Ilsa chapters: Georgia 11
text font: Anna chapters: Book Antiqua 12
total word count: 85,405
cover and interior design: SR 2014

A Guide to Significant Characters and Relationship to Ilsa or Ainslie and Page of First Appearance

Jacob Rohe, b. 1835, Pennsylvania, Ilsa's younger son p.7

James Buchanan, b. 1798, Kentucky, Ainslie's oldest brother p.47

John (Johnnie) Buchanan, b. 1841, Ainslie's youngest child, a son p.25

Johnnie Reid, b. 1771, Ulster, Ireland, uncle of Fiona Reid Buchanan p.32

Josiah Buchanan, b. 1775, Kentucky Dist. Virginia, Ainslie's father p.17

Josiah (Josie) Buchanan b. 1835, Ainslie's fourth child, first son p.14

Lotti Koch Mueller, b. 1795, Pennsylvania, Ilsa's mother p.200

Mr. Laughton, writer for The North American Review in Boston p.57

Mr. Herbert, schoolteacher for the Rohe and Buchanan children p.15

Mr. Higgins, benefactor for the township's school children p.73

Pfarrer Gruber, the pastor of German Christian Church in Ohio p. 6

Reverend Johnson, the pastor of the Cossette Christian Church p. 19

Tansie Wilson, servant at Rohe Farm and mother of Benjamin p.10

Vallerie Bernier, a servant employed by Ilsa Rohe p. 5

~~~O<<>>O~~~

www.ingramcontent.com/pod-product-compliance
Lightning Source LLC
Chambersburg PA
CBHW060152180626
46813CB00007B/2722